ENGLISH JACK

or

BRITISH FLAG

TOUCH IT WHO DARE!

"Boys of England" Office 173 Fleet St. E.C.

ENGLISH JACK AMONGST THE AFGHANS;

OR,

THE BRITISH FLAG—TOUCH IT WHO DARE.

BEAUTIFULLY ILLUSTRATED.

VOLUME I.

LONDON:
"BOYS OF ENGLAND" OFFICE, 173, FLEET STREET, E.C.,
AND ALL BOOKSELLERS.

ENGLISH JACK AMONGST THE AFGHANS ;

OR,

THE BRITISH FLAG—TOUCH IT WHO DARE!

"JACK CLUTCHED THE AFGHAN'S WRIST AND SMOTE HARD."

ENGLISH JACK AMONGST THE AFGHANS;

OR,

THE BRITISH FLAG—TOUCH IT WHO DARE!

CHAPTER I.

COMING EVENTS CAST THEIR SHADOWS BEFORE.

IT is night in Cabul, the proud capital of Afghanistan, but it is by no means dark, for the great white moon of India, shining like a silver shield from out a dark blue sky, that glitters with a myriad stars, illumines the flat roofs of the houses that line the narrow streets, the rounded domes of the many mosques, the parapets of the old feudal fortresses of the ameers, the vast roof of the bazaar, the huge palace and fortress of the Bala Hissar, and far away in the distance the mighty peaks of the Kohistan and Hindoo Koosh mountain ranges, capped by eternal snows. Night and silence.

The windows of the Zenana, or that portion of the Bala Hissar devoted to the five hundred young wives of Shah Soojah, the king, whose dynasty for good or for ill Great Britain had engaged herself to uphold, was brilliantly lighted up, and the luxurious Eastern potentate was therein paying homage to Venus.

His very home is guarded by British troops because the warriors of his own country cannot be relied on, and there on the broad terrace-walk that girds the palace fifty feet below the aforesaid windows, march to and fro the scarlet-coated sentries of old England.

The gallant Kentish Buffs, or Light Bobs, as they are more commonly called, and whose valour and discipline is second to none in our glorious service, garrison the Bala Hissar with two hundred men, and at this very moment little Bobby Rogers and Evan ap Morgan, the youngest of the regimental drummers and sworn chums, though hailing respectively from Yorkshire and Wales (for they are by no means all men of Kent in the Kentish Buffs, though the great majority do hail from the land of hops), have just found out the quietest part of the ramparts, it being against the rules that they are out of bed at such an hour, have a talk and a confabulation.

Bobby Rogers was about fourteen, and his fair hair and fair freckled face betrayed his Anglo-Saxon birth and parentage, but Evan ap Morgan on the other hand was a little swarthy black-eyed lad with close, curling, raven-hued hair, and with an excitability of manner and gesture that were almost French in their vivacity.

He was a year younger than his companion, mischievous as a monkey, garrulous as a parrot, and brave as a little bantam cock.

No two boys could have had more different dispositions, yet no two boys could have loved each other more ; and how often do we find completely opposite temperaments thus mysteriously drawn together?

But having thus introduced the young rascals, let us see what they are talking about.

Talking? They are doing something

more than talking, for from the swallow-shaped tails of their little scarlet coats they have drawn forth a couple of short black stumps of pipes, primed them with villainous shag tobacco, and are now coolly puffing away at them.

"Won't they be jolly sick presently?" surmises the reader.

No, not they, for they have been jolly sick so many times, the little fools, that they have at last conquered the feeling, and now the two cock sparrows consider themselves to be men, and gallant soldiers as well, every inch of them, which to be sure would be no great compliment regarding the inches literally.

They ain't very happy here in Cabul, for Afghanistan has too many horrors and terrors for little folks, even those of the cock sparrow order.

And even since their arrival with a reinforcement from the English depot a few weeks ago, not a day has passed but what they have heard the hoots, hisses, and execrations of the Afghanistan rabble hurled at such handfuls of the occupying British force as dare to parade the public streets of the city.

Not a day has passed in which they have not seen the wild horsemen of the rebel chief Ackbar Khan, from their eyries nest on the summit of the Bala Hissar, gallop up in wanton bravado almost to within pistol range of the British cantonments, brandish their spears, and then dash off again with shouts of laughter to their temporary home in the mountains.

Hardly a day passed either in which some foully assassinated British officer has not been borne past them into the palace weltering in his gore.

"This is an awful land!" suddenly says Bobby Rogers. "I almost wish I'd took to making swords at Sheffield, instead of wanting to use them on savages."

And as he spoke, he drew forth his little brass hilted weapon, and gazed with a sigh on the justly celebrated name of the maker.

"Ay," continued he, "feyther worked 'i that foundry for years, and, perhaps he had a hand in forging o' that very blade; an' it was seeing all these things turned out spick an' new as made me first long to be a sodger. Well, I won't disgrace what I

am, an' I won't disgrace our true Sheffield steel neither; no, nor the good old county of York that gave me birth, yet I don't like this sodgering half so well as I thought I should."

"And I like it much better. It is so nice to be frightened out of one's life twice or thrice in every twenty-four hours," retorted Evan ap Morgan, with that grammatical fluency of speech with which every Welsh boy speaks the English tongue. "I intend to be a hero, I do. And why shouldn't I? I've begun early enough, and as it seems to me in an uncommonly good field."

"You'll never have the strength to be an hero, my boy, if you nip it in the bud, and dwarf your stature by sucking away at that dirty pipe," said an unexpected voice at this instant at the young drummer's elbow, and then a light cane unceremoniously struck the black dhudeen out of his mouth, and the same voice continued—"I don't know that it wouldn't be true kindness to report you to the quarter-guard, but I won't this time if you'll promise me on your honour that you won't smoke any more both of you."

"Oh Mister Jack, is that you?" came from both the drummer-boys at once.

"Rather, and it's lucky for you that it's not somebody else, or that other somebody would assuredly have got you into hot water. You thought you were hidden away, did you? Well, and so you were pretty well, but I smelt you out. Do you fancy officers' noses are not to be relied on?"

"Oh Mr. Vere, look over it this time, will you, sir, and we won't smoke any more," quoth Bob Rogers, stamping his pipe into bits under his feet.

"Look over it, of course I will," said the newcomer, genially. "I don't forget, youngsters, when I was a boy myself," and the speaker drew himself up to his full height and stroked an incipient mustache, that it was somewhat difficult to believe in the existence of unaided by a powerful microscope, for Jack Vere, albeit bearing her majesty's commission and a pair of epaulettes, had only left Sandhurst a matter of nine or ten months and was barely seventeen.

He was a Kentish lad, and a noble specimen of England's fairest county too.

He had obtained his commission in the Kentish Buffs, not by purchase, but in the good old fashioned way, abolished for ever in 1845, of bringing into the regiment with him twelve strapping recruits, all young fellows belonging to his father's broad estate, and clothed, kilted, and armed at his private expense.

Each one of these would have laid down his life for his young master, as they still loved to designate him, at any date or hour ; but Jack Vere was loved besides by the whole regiment, for in addition to being handsome, he was gay, light-hearted, chivalrous, and brave, and had as kindly a word for the private soldier as for his brother officer.

"Here," said he, when he perceived that the two drummer-boys had not only smashed their pipes, but had also scattered their small stock of tobacco to the winds, " is something that should at all events be a great deal more in your line, it is in mine, and I'm not ashamed to own it. I thought I might come across some of you youngsters in my rounds, and so when we rose from mess, I just cleared the dessert plates."

And Jack Vere proceeded to haul out of his swallow tail pockets some oranges, bananas, and nuts, which he distributed pretty equally between the two lads.

"Oh, thank'ee, Master Jack ; and have you any good news for us as well?" asked Bobby Rogers, with his mouth chock full of flowery banana.

"Yes, Mr. Vere, do tell us, if you can, when we are to be let loose at these rascally Afghans ?" added Evan ap Morgan, firing up.

"Ah, well," answered Jack, a cloud coming over his sunny face, " that will be in Heaven's good time, no doubt ; but we despatch a mail-bag to England to-morrow, and do you write home to your parents, my lads, good, hopeful letters, if you can, for, perhaps, one day they will value them more than any you have ever yet written them, and we are not sure of being able to keep the passes open for another week."

Having spoken this in a perturbed tone, strangely unlike his usual manner of speech, Jack Vere turned on his heel and walked hurriedly away, muttering to himself as he went along—

"Yes, I'm glad I bade the lads do that, and I must write to my dear old dad as well, for if I don't the opportunity may never occur again. The next he, and the next England hears of us will be that we have all died at our posts like men, or I'm indeed greatly mistaken."

And the young officer continued his rounds in gloomy silence.

CHAPTER II.

THIRTEEN MEN IN THEIR SHROUDS.

WHAT did he mean by saying that we were not sure of being able to keep the passes open for another week ?" asked the Yorkshire boy of the Welsh one, in an awesome kind of a whisper, when Jack Vere had passed on.

" I think he meant that the Afghans might have occupied them," replied Evan.

" Well, if so, we must drive the Afghans out again."

" Do you know what I heard an old sergeant of ours say to one of the rank and file as we were coming through them on our road up, lad ?"

" No ; what did the old sergeant say ?" demanded Evan, jeeringly.

" Why, that if the Afghans once succeeded in possessing themselves of them, and then got the better of us at Cabul, not one of us would ever live to see our homes again. What think you of that, lad?"

"I think that your sergeant was an old fogey who should have stayed at home instead of coming out and talking of never getting back. But—oh Lor'! what was that?"

"What was what, Evan?" asked Bobby.

"There—there, Bobby!—that line of spectres creeping along under the shadow of the wall and going in through that tall, narrow door that I never saw open before now. One, two, three, four, five, six, seven, eight, nine, ten eleven, twelve—thirteen! there are just a baker's dozen of them. See how they glide along. They must be spectres."

"They are not spectres, Evan; they are men, and they would not sneak along like that unless they were going to do what they ought not to do. We must follow them and see what they are up to. It is our duty, no matter how frightened we may be; so come along, and let us be cautious."

"Oh, all right, old man; but don't think that I'm one little bit frightened."

"I am, very, Evan, but I'll do my duty nevertheless, if I can."

"If we'd had more sentries here those fellows could not have passed unperceived."

"Ah, Evan, we haven't a quarter enough men for anything here. Let us take off our boots, and carry our drawn swords in our hands, and hold the scabbards so that they don't rattle, and steal after them like dormice, for we must learn everything, Evan, everything, although I am so frightened."

"If you are so frightened let me go first, Bobby," quoth the Welsh boy.

"Not I, Evan. It's my duty to go first because I'm the eldest, and I mustn't shrink from duty, no matter how terrified I am. It wouldn't be English—and, above all, it wouldn't be Yorkshire. Hang it! this blade of Sheffield steel that I hold in my hand would turn round of its own accord and pierce me to the heart were I to disgrace old England."

And off went Bobby's shoes, and the next instant the two boys had crossed the broad terrace walk, entered the mysterious doorway, and proceeded down a dark passage within, that led they knew not whither.

It seemed to be endless, and not until Bobby had paused a dozen times to tell his companion how frightened he was did they perceive a pale blue light at some distance before them, and guess they were coming upon something.

And so they did, for a minute later the end of the passage was gained, and they looked in through an aperture let into a thick wall, and shaped like the mouth of a baker's oven, upon a scene as weird and wild as it is possible to conceive.

They beheld some kind of a temple of worship, for in the middle of it was a rough stone altar, on which burned a pale blue fire, whilst beside it lay a huge and open book—the Al Koran.

This blue fire, pale and ghastly, and giving but a dim, uncertain, light, just served to show that the temple was circular in shape, with a domed roof, having many holes or recesses in its walls.

Each of these recesses seemed to contain a coffin.

Floor, pillars, arches, and roof were all of black marble, and on thirteen stone seats that surrounded the central altar sat the thirteen shadows that Bobby and Evan had seen enter the mysterious door, with faces painted of a ghastly whiteness, and wrapped in the flannel cerements of the dead.*

They were speaking to each other in low, muttering tones, that sufficiently declared them to be in solemn conclave.

But not a word that they said could Bobby or Evan understand, which was no wonder, considering that they were unacquainted with the Afghan tongue.

"I wish Mr. Vere was here, old boy." whispered the Yorkshire lad to the Welsh one.

"Shall I go and try and find him?" retorted the latter, quickly.

"Do, if you will; but don't be long gone; I'm so frightened."

Away sped Evan ap Morgan as fast

---

* A fact as may be seen by reference to the illustrated papers of that period.

"THE BRUTE WAS ON THE POINT OF DASHING EVAN AGAINST THE WALL."

and as noiselessly as his little legs would carry him, whilst Bobby immediately concentrated his gaze with extra fervency upon the diabolical-looking fraternity, as though fearing that did he not do so they would suddenly utterly vanish down into the ground or up through the domed roof.

Evan was fortunate enough to encounter Jack Vere almost the first instant that he debouched out of the subterranean passage into the bright moonlight that deluged the broad terrace walk of the ramparts.

The young officer was just returning from visiting the outposts, few and far indeed between, owing to our insufficiency of men.

He was much struck by what Evan ap Morgan told him, in a voice almost breathless with excitement.

"Lead on, my boy, and I will follow close at your heels," said he ; and then he kicked off his shoes in turn.

Five minutes later they stood beside or rather behind Bobby Rogers.

"Oh, I'm so glad you've come !" said he. "I was getting so frightened."

Jack Vere held up his finger to impose the most rigid silence, and then he bent his gaze on the queer conclave seated within the temple.

But as he did so the thirteen, until this moment almost motionless figures, sprang to their feet as with one accord, threw aside the cerements of the tomb, and appeared as warriors clad in ringed mail, spur on heel, and basnet on head.

Each was armed to the teeth, and with one accord they approached the rocky altar, and bringing the flats of their hands down on the great open book, shouted aloud—

"Death to the accursed British—death to the accursed ghiour !

"Death—death to old and young, to wives and mothers, to daughters and young children—ay, even to the babe that is unborn !"

And as they concluded the hands of the conspirators leapt from the great book to their sword hilts.

The bright blades came flashing forth, and as they were brandished on high, the thirteen men shouted, as with one voice—

"We swear it ! Death to the British !"

"Come away," whispered Jack Vere ; "murder is around ! We haven't an instant to lose."

And he pushed Bobby and Evan before him down the passage.

CHAPTER III.

ONE SWORD TO THIRTEEN—THE SEVERED HAND.

TO them it seemed that Jack Vere was continually stepping on their heels ; and very probably he might have been, for it wasn't a pleasant thought, that of being overtaken and assassinated in the dark by the fierce and revengeful Asiatics, whose awful vow of British extermination they had just been the concealed witnesses of.

Directly they had all three got out into the moonlight, Jack Vere exclaimed, excitedly—

"Run to your drums boys, and beat an alarm at once. We must arrest these traitors as they come forth. God of Heaven ! to think that there should be such within the very palace walls of Shah Soojah ! Our lives and those of the English ladies and children hang indeed upon a hair now."

Half of this was uttered as a mental soliloquy after Bobby and Evan had taken their departure, and as he concluded the young English officer shrank into the shadow of the open doorway, and drew his sword, resolved that if the conspirators sought to pass out ere others came to his assistance, they should only do so across his dead body.

It was an anxious moment or two, for ae felt that their business was over in the temple with the awful oath he had heard them give utterance to, and that at any instant now they might come forth ; and while he stood there, still as a statue of iron, he could hear the metal ghurries or gongs sounding midnight in the distant British cantonments.

Hark !

Scarcely have the gongs ceased when he hears steps coming down the passage.

Creeping, cautious steps, that he knows must be the steps of the conspirators.

Then his heart seemed to beat louder still, for he is but seventeen, and has never yet been engaged in deadly fray.

Yet in less than a minute his single blade may have to be pitted against thirteen Afghan scimitars.

He does not flinch, however, and when a dusky hand and arm pass outstretched close to his face, Jack clutched his wrist, and smote hard.

The hand falls severed at the wrist.

A gasp of pain, a subdued Afghan malediction, and the dark passage seems to be full of white, rolling eyeballs, flashing jewels, and gleaming steel.

But English Jack Vere bars the way as determinedly and doggedly as ever did " Horatius on the Tiber's bridge in the brave days of old," as sang by Lord Macaulay, and the thirteen are for a moment held at bay by one.

Then they are about to rush forward and slay him, strong and confident in their superior numbers.

Jack does not flinch—not he.

He is every inch an Englishman

He is ready to die at his post, if Heaven wills it so—die in the performance of his duty, which is the highest privilege and the most glorious fate that can befall a British officer.

But at that moment " rub-a-dub-dub, rub-a-dub-dub!" sound the little brass side-drums of Billy Rogers and Evan ap Morgan beating fiercely the alarm.

Then comes the thrill scream of the fifes, the rush of many feet as the main guard turns out, and the white, rolling eyeballs and the gleaming blades of the long Afghan swords and knives seem to shrink back into the deeper gloom and in a twinkling disappear.

Jack Vere's first impulse is to spring after them.

But a second thought tells him that it would be madness to do so alone.

So he waits like a fiery charger controlled by the curb until he sees a dozen of the Kentish Light Bobs approaching at a run, with their muskets at the trail, and the two drummer-boys marching gallantly at their head.

He waves them impatiently with his blood-reeking sword, and as he does so the very fact of its blood-reeking recalls to his mind the hand he has so recently lopped off, and by a sudden impulse he stoops, picks it up, and regards it intently.

It is a little hand, no bigger than a woman's—but then the Afghan chiefs of high rank are renowned for the smallness and beauty of their hands and feet.

The nails are painted a bright crimson, and on one of the fingers gleams a ring set with a magnificent opal, which seems to flash and gleam with a baleful and malignant fire.

Jack shudders, wraps the hand up in his handkerchief, and transfers it to his pocket, for it is evidently the hand of one who is strong and mighty in the land, and it may have to be brought forward in proof against him.

Then he calls upon the soldiers, who by this time have reached the black and forbidding-looking passage, to follow him, and, sword in hand, he penetrates it for a second time.

Bobby Rogers and Evan ap Morgan persist in coming next, plucky little Bobby declaring all the while that he is awfully afraid.

But there proves to be nothing to be afraid of, for the passage is discovered to be empty, and the temple likewise.

The expiring fire still flickers on the stone altar, and the Light Bobs manage with their bayonets to stir it up into a brief blaze.

But it reveals nothing.

The great book is gone and the temple is deserted save by themselves, though they search every hole and corner, even to banging about the coffins in their pigeon hole recesses.

Nothing comes of it all, and at last Jack Vere leads his little party out on the broad terrace wall again, and there dismisses them, urging them to keep on the alert.

"And do you go to bed, my boys," he says, kindly, to Bobby and Evan. "You have done enough for one night—and what is more, you have done it nobly. Go to bed now, and if you can, dream of your mothers and your sisters in far away, beautiful Britain."

And so he left them.

CHAPTER IV.

"BETRAY AUGHT AND YOU DIE!"

JACK VERE knew that his first duty was to go and report what had occurred to the officer commanding the detachment, Major Tomlinson.

He did so, and found the major, in company with Captains Freeman and Falkner, in a plain, whitewashed room, that formed their quarters, smoking like the funnels of so many Greenwich steamboats, and rather overcome by the juice of the grape in addition; for the wine manufactured of the amber Cabul grape was potent as it was luscious.

Jack Vere doffed his foraging cap and tersely explained what he had seen and done, winding up by inquiring whether the king, Shah Soojah, should not be promptly informed of what had happened.

"Of course he should," grunted Major Tomlinson, in a rich vinous voice. "But the devil of it is—who's to inform him? Now (hiccough), I don't feel very well."

"I—I'll tell the old boy myself," said Captain Freeman, staggering to his feet, and endeavouring to adjust his swordbelt, but getting the scabbard between his legs he went somehow mysteriously under the table.

"You go, and go quickly," then said Captain Falkner, who, though the most sober of the trio, knew, perhaps on that very account, that he was not sufficiently so to explain things as they should be explained.

"Confound it, man! who can relate a thing so well as he who took part in it?"

Jack Vere happened to be of exactly the same opinion on this point, and considering that the importance of the disclosures he had to make would be sufficient excuse for his undress uniform, he sallied forth at once.

But just outside the major's quarters, who should he meet but a brother ensign, called Dunbar, and his very particular chum.

"What's all this I hear about mysterious conspirators, men sitting in their shrouds, a severed hand, and all the rest of it?" quoth he.

"Accompany me to the king's presence, and I will tell you all about it on the way," said Jack, taking his arm. "To begin with, there are traitors in the palace."

"I've not the least doubt of it," replied Willie Dunbar. "A monarch who has an amiable *penchant* for having kinsmen's eyes gouged out with red-hot dagger points and who will sentence a courtier to be cut into kabobs for the slighest breach of etiquette is not likely to have many friends. But when added to this, he is a voluptuary, a wine-bibber, and almost a drivelling dotard as well, maintained on his throne against the will of the entire nation by foreign bayonets who can wonder at conspiracies? Hang it! I'd be a conspirator were I an Afghan."

"Great Britain must have some good reason for putting him on the Afghan throne and maintaining him there," rejoined Jack. "They say that his predecessor, Dost Mohammed, whom we deposed, was too thick with Russia by half, and you know we must secure our northwestern frontier against even the prowlings of the Northern bear."

"We have gone about it in a most clumsy way in the present instance. We should have thirty thousand men in that plain below there," pointing towards the British cantonments, "instead of four thousand three hundred. Why, Jack Vere, there are five millions one hundred and twenty thousand hostile natives between us and British India, which they have all resolved that we shall never regain or see."

"Oh, nonsense, Dunbar! There is no such word as fail to British troops."

"British troops may be brave as lions, but they can't perform miracles, Jack; but to make our destruction more certain, we are waiting for the approaching winter to block up the passes eighteen or twenty feet deep with snow. We are already far into November, yet Elphinstone still delays his retreat, still hopes to make terms. Fool! as if Ackbar Khan was not temporising in order to lead us the more surely to our doom," said Dunbar, bitterly.

Jack Vere frowned, then rejoined—

"It is our duty as British officers, Willie, to obey the commands of our chiefs. General Elphinstone must know better than we do."

"He does not Jack; he is in his dotage. I saw him planting asters and chrysanthemums in his garden but a few weeks ago, as if there was even then a chance of our staying here and being let live to see them flower. They were in bud to-day as I passed the compound fence. Take my word for it, Jack, before those buds change to blossoms, the knives of these bloodthirsty and murderous Afghans will be at all our throats,"

"For Heaven's sake, don't be such a croaking prophet of evil," said Jack, im-

petuously; and then his voice suddenly faltered and his face turned of an ashen whiteness, as he almost wailed forth—

"Oh, would that we were all men here, for if these awful things that you predict do come to pass, the fate of the women, the girls, and the children will be most terrible. Fancy a hideous Afghan's hand wreathed in May Vivian's golden curls, and his fierce eyes fixed upon hers like a beast of prey while he draws a knife across her throat, or buries it in her snowy bosom."

Jack Vere staggered as he walked, so overcome was he by this thought, May Vivian, the only child of Colonel Vivian, of the 37th Madras Native Infantry, being more dear to him than life itself.

"Come, come, Jack, it is you who are the croaker now," said his fellow-ensign to console him. "Rouse up, man, for here we are."

They had, indeed, by now reached the head of the grand flight of marble stairs that led from the broad terrace-walk bastions of the Bala Hissar to the entrance of the palace proper, a building worthy of its founder, Baber.

Many windows of the huge building were still lighted up, and the great gates of gleaming silver leading into the outer court were wide open.

Jack Vere and Willie Dunbar walked quietly in, and the next instant found themselves amongst the Afghan king's gaily-trapped Gholandazees or outer guard, fellows whose loose Asiatic garb was of all the hues of the rainbow, and who carried a perfect armoury of knives, daggers, and pistols stuck in the cashmere shawls that girt their waists.

An officer, came forward to receive the two Englishmen, but he frowned and shook his head when Jack intimated that they must see the king.

"His majesty, the light of the world, has deigned to visit his Zenana," said he, "and it would be death to disturb him there."

"It may very likely be death if he is not disturbed," retorted Jack, impatiently; "so just announce us, and on our heads be it."

"But, excellencies, how will the king forgive your attire? It is of the morning."

"He who is the bearer of most important tidings generally escapes having his clothes scanned," persisted Jack. "We must and will see the king."

The swarthy Gholandazee officer shrugged his shoulders, looked doubtful for a moment, and then saying—

"Remember, on your heads be it; suffer not the rod to fall on my shoulders," turned round and led the way.

The court of the fountain left behind, rich Persian and Turkey carpets usurped the place of the cold marble, costly hangings rustled on the walls, and in lieu of the opening of doors, there was every now and then the lifting of massive and heavy velvet curtains, all corded and fringed with gold.

Here and there were stands of ivory, mother-of-pearl, and gold and gem inlaid weapons and implements of the chase, whilst birds sang within golden cages, and courtiers, warriors, guards, and servants seemed incessantly passing up and down, though generally with empty hands.

Many of these dusky courtiers and wild barbaric warriors regarded Jack and Dunbar with curious and searching glances; and presently one of them, wearing a suit of gleaming chain mail, and a cap of steel with a lofty heron plume rising from its very centre, strode up to their Gholandazee conductor and said, curtly—

"I will conduct these Franks to the presence of his most serene majesty."

Thereat their former conductor looked cowed and walked away, and their new guide, in whom Jack Vere recognised the king's shazadah, or master of the horse, signed to them to follow him, and strode on haughtily in front, taking no further notice of them.

Then through corridors, far less thickly peopled now, until in traversing one that seemed perfectly empty, a sullen murmur suddenly broke on Jack's ear of—

"Betray aught and you die!"

He glanced around, but no one could he see.

He looked at Dunbar, but from the calm composure of his face, 'twas plain that the hideous warning had not reached his ears.

Jack Vere tried to convince himself, therefore, that his own had played him false, that he had imagined the words and so on.

But it was impossible to do this.

Now, however, the sounds of silvery laughter reached them, and a minute later they came to a vast hall, at the further end of which two heavy drooped curtains were guarded on either side by two hideous black giants leaning on their swords.

Their guide made a sign to Jack Vere and his companion to come no further and he advanced alone towards the curtains, and passed between them.

Again came that warning murmur as he disappeared—

"Betray aught and you die!"

And from the start that he gave, Ensign Dunbar heard it, too, this time.

The young men had no time to interchange a word, however, ere the curtains were dashed aside by two arms suddenly thrown out T fashion, and as they fell again by their owner's sides, they formed a background to a tall, lean old man, clad in flowing robes of white and crimson, and whose green turban, the colour of the Prophet's, was surmounted by a heron plume rising from an aigrette of diamonds.

Jack Vere and Willie Dunbar dropped each on a knee, for it was the puppet king, Shah Soojah, who stood before them; but hardly had he cast his eyes on them and then raised them, as was his wont, towards the ceiling, than an expression of horror and dismay crossed his haggard countenance, and he exclaimed, pointing upwards—

"Allah, what dreadful meaning hath this?—a cross of blood—of still dripping blood, slashed across the very ceiling of our palace?"

And Jack and Dunbar, looking upwards, the cross of blood met their sight also.

CHAPTER V.

THE THREE CROSSES OF BLOOD.

A MINUTE'S breathless silence ensued, and both Shah Soojah and his two visitors, as well as the shazadah gazed upwards at the great cross of blood that had been splashed, by some mysterious hand, upon the white enamelled ceiling.

Who had done it? How had anyone got up there to do it? and when had it been done? were the questions that everyone mentally asked himself.

That it had recently been perpetrated there could exist no doubt, for the blood was wet, and great drops were even now falling on to the rich carpet.

The shazadah sternly interrogated the two black African giants, but they declared that they knew nothing of the matter, and had never noticed it until the moment previously.

"Do you, Franks, know aught of this?" demanded the Afghan king, then bending a lowering brow upon Jack Vere and Willie Dunbar.

"We, your majesty; how could we know aught about it?" replied Jack, with little show of courtesy; "we have sought the presence of your majesty to warn you of something more serious than signs and omens—to assure you that there are traitors and conspirators of flesh and blood within the very walls of the palace, who have sworn a general slaughter of Europeans."

"Well," demanded Shah Soojah; "and how does that concern me?"

"It should concern your majesty mightily," said Jack, more brusquely still, "since those same Europeans form the sole prop of your throne."

"And what a throne it is that I have to thank them for," replied the lean and slippered monarch, petulantly; "Allah il Allah! it is one whose cushions are stuffed with thorns, or rather with vipers' teeth, and tigers' claws. Do I not live in hourly dread of assassination, either by the knife or the poisoned bowl? Better had they left me in the happy retirement in which they found me than stick me on so high a pinnacle merely to be toppled down again."

"It was in your power to refuse the position, oh king; yet having accepted it, we have a right to expect that you will attempt to hold it with some royal dignity," said Willie Dunbar, speaking just as boldly as Jack had done.

"And do I not uphold it with dignity?" yelled the old Afghan, furiously; "Bismillah! this is too much, and from beardless boys, too. I am a king but in name if I permit it to pass unpunished. Soo Tal," this to his master of the horse "lead them to instant execution!"

Soo Tal seemed nothing loth to obey the order. A gleam of joy flashed in his dusky eyes, a devilish smile curled his thin lips, and hastily whispering to the two gigantic blacks to help him, he laid his hand on his sword hilt.

But the irascible old monarch had by now changed his mind.

"Stop," said he, "if we kill them they will be able to tell us nothing about this conspiracy that they prate of. We will at all events hear them first."

"Your majesty, be assured that no conspiracy could be hatched in your palace without my knowledge. Their words will be empty wind, that is all," replied the shazadah, evidently not very well pleased with this arrangement.

"I say I will hear them, and my will is law. Soo Tal, look to thine own head, for it may not be so secure on thy shoulders as thou thinkest," said the king, angry with his courtier in turn. "Now, young Englishman, speak out."

Jack accepted the invitation at once, and narrated in as few words as possible, everything that had taken place in the old temple.

"AS THE AFGHAN CLUBBED HIS MUSKET, EVAN SHEATHED HIS SWORD IN HIS BODY."

"And did you recognise none of their faces?" asked Shah Soojah.

"How could I, your majesty, when they were all as white as a whitewashed wall? I could not even make a reasonable guess," replied Jack.

A close observer might have noticed Soo Tal grin at this.

"And their dresses, did you notice them?" asked the king again.

"No, your majesty, for there was nothing very particular in them save that they were evidently those of warriors and Ameers of some rank. But I have brought away a memento that may give your majesty a clue to the identity of one of the party, a hand, bearing on one finger a magnificent opal ring. I had the good fortune to lop it off at the wrist with my good sword. Here it is."

But there it wasn't, for on Jack searching the tail pocket of his coat, where he thought he had so securely placed it, lo! it was not to be found.

The other pocket on being fumbled in proved to be empty.

"Your majesty, it has gone," exclaimed Jack, in mute amazement.

"If it ever was there," muttered the shazadah, under his mustache.

"Yes, I believe that it was there, slave," said Shah Soojah, turning on him sharply, "I believe that my palace is full of knaves and cut-throats, of which you may be one for all I know to the contrary. Curses on these British meddlers, say I, who sought to checkmate Russia and destroy the dynasty of Russia's ally Dost Mohammed by placing me on the tottering Cabul throne. Think you that the Afghans would love me better were I to throw myself entirely into their arms? Eh, Soo Tal?"

"In that case there's not a man in Afghanistan but would lay down his life for your majesty," replied the shazadah, with a low salaam, whilst the cruel twinkle came again in his almond-shaped eyes.

"Your majesty must not deceive yourself," quickly retorted Jack, perceiving how serious matters were getting. "But for the British protection, your reign and your life would be equally short—of that be assured."

"Allah il Allah! which side am I to believe?" moaned the old monarch. "I've a great mind to retire to my zenana, poison my five hundred young wives and die in their company. I should, at all events, thus win peace."

Jack and Willie Dunbar were both so shocked and horrified by this barbarous proposition, for the beauty of the young girls constituting Shah Soojah's harem was a matter of fame, that they actually, for a minute or two, lost the power of speech.

But then Jack, resolved to prevent so horrible and cruel a catastrophe by some means or other, said wildly—

"Your majesty may by no means despair, for your friends are many and your foes are few. Fresh British regiments are on their march hither; so that a reign of peace, security, and prosperity will be established long before the year is out."

"Do your chiefs say so?" demanded the old king, brightening up.

"Yes, your majesty; intelligence came in to that effect this very night."

"Then why have not Burnes or McNaghten come up to tell me the good news? Seek the cantonments immediately on leaving me, and bid them do so at once. Go, for I thirst for their assurances. They may be able to advise with me as to the discovery of these conspirators whom you talk of also; for it is evidently more their affair than mine. Away, young men. Soo Tal, conduct them."

He would not hear another word, so impatient was he to be in communication with higher authorities, and so Jack and Willie had nothing to do but to retire; the former feeling that he had put his foot into it pretty deeply, and that in his attempt to save the girls of the old Bluebeard's zenana from wholesale slaughter, he had, in all probability, brought upon himself a trial by court-martial, if nothing worse.

His mind was full of painful and embarrassing thoughts, therefore, as he and his companion re-trod the sumptuous corridors on their way out of the palace, following closely in the steps of Soo Tal.

He conducted them all the way to the Court of the Fountain, and then bowing, suffered them to pass him by; but hardly had they done so when the way in which the guards who still lingered about in groups, stared and pointed at them, caused them to survey each other care-fully in order to guess at the cause, and suddenly each perceived that on his companions's back was slashed a great cross of blood.

CHAPTER VI.

THE OUTBREAK IN THE CITY.

THE two ensigns felt that those crosses of blood made them in some way marked men, but they were too wise to betray any emotion before so many witnesses, so they walked calmly on, though with their hands ever ready to lay an their sword hilts in case of any sudden and unexpected attack.

"Betray aught and you die!" seemed to be ringing in their ears, and these twice-repeated threats, the crosses of blood on the palace ceiling and their own backs, together with the loss of the black, opal be-ringed hand from Jack's pocket, gave unmistakable proof of the existence of a very numerous body of the traitors within the royal walls.

"By George!" exclaimed Dunbar, "I believe the Bala Hissar the only place for a hundred miles round wherein we could secure ourselves and keep the enemy at bay if matters came to the worst."

"I should not wonder if there were enough rogues there to seize it out of the hands of the few honest men when the right moment came," retorted our hero, in the same guarded whisper. "Even the half imbecile old king hates us, and if such is the feeling of our friends towards us, Heaven save the mark, what treatment are we to expect from our foes when they get the upper hand?"

"Death to the accursed English! Death for man, youth, and boy; for woman, girl and child! Death—death—death!" hissed a voice from out of the darkness, close to Jack's ear.

Then there were half-a-dozen pistol shots, and the next instant they descried three Afghans hurriedly making away round an abutting angle of the black rock, the weapons flashing in the moonlight.

English Jack Vere drew his sword and was for following them, but Willie Dunbar grasped him by the arm and held him back, saying—

"Perhaps they are running from us, purposely in order to entice us into some deadly ambuscade. There are deep pits in the hillside round that way, the work of earthquakes, down which our dead, ay, or even our breathing bodies could be hurled without a chance of their ever turning up again until the mountains are rent asunder at the last great day. We'll be after them, Jack, but we'll take a file of soldiers with us, for precaution is still the better part of valour."

"But they will be gone then," quoth Jack, hotly.

"Perhaps so, perhaps not; but better that they should disappear than us, old fellow. Halloa! what the deuce is that I wonder?"

"Where?" asked Jack, looking round very anxiously.

"Why that sullen murmur in the streets of the city?—that lurid glow advancing from the north to the west? Look, old fellow, that light is the flare and glare of torches, and the murmur is that of an angry and blood-lustful multitude. Jack, there is a wholesale rising in Cabul."

"God forbid! for many of our officers and their families still reside within the city walls," retorted Jack. "Hark! are those shots that I hear?"

"Yes, yes, Jack, they are shots, as I

live—the sharp crack of Afghan jezails, too! Why, there are not a dozen fighting Englishmen in the entire city ; only a few civil servants with their wives and families. God of Heaven! I hope our bulldogs will be let loose at the black devils' throats."

At this moment the British bugles sounded their shrill notes, and as Jack Vere and Willie Dunbar rushed towards the main guardhouse as hard as they could tear, they saw brave little Billy Rogers and Evan ap Morgan running out with their drums braced on, and in another minute they were sounding the assembly like mad, the sticks falling as quickly as a shower of hail.

Out turned the English guard, all spick and span as a box of toy soldiers, and in another minute out poured their comrades, their shakos perched on their heads anyhow ; some in the act of pulling on their jackets, and even the more advanced carrying their crossbelts and their muskets in their hands.

Less than five minutes served to get them into shape, however, the officers and sergeants shouting all the while—

"Fall in, thirty-seventh! Fall in, lads!"

"Stand to your arms!"

Major Tomlinson and Captains Freeman and Faulkner were sober enough now, and every man of the gallant Kentish Light Bobs was just as cool and collected as though he were going to be reviewed instead of to fight.

Scarcely were they ready when a young English boy, with his clothing all torn and his face bleeding, clambered over the parapet of the bastion, and fell forward on the paved terrace walk.

Then quickly recovering his feet, reeled forward till he clutched hold of Major Tomlinson's skirt tails, when he gasped feebly—

"Sir Alexander Burns — my father! They have beset the house—they are trying to murder poor father! Oh, hurry, hurry, or you will be too late!"

And having said thus much, the little English lad fell at the major's feet in a dead swoon.

The major picked him up, and bearing him into his quarters, laid him on his bed, and then, hurrying out again, locked the door behind him.

"He'll be safe there," he muttered. "Plucky young fellow—hardly in his teens either. By Jove! to save time he scaled the almost precipitous face of the cliff. Didn't think a cat could have done it, blest if I did! The worst of it is, if a boy can do it, an Afghan can. It must be seen to at once!"

By the time that he had ceased his self-communing, he was at the head of his slender column, where, drawing his sword, he gave the signal—

"March!"

Down the zig-zag pathway, with the bright musket-barrels and fixed bayonets glittering in the sunshine, go the gallant Kentish Buffs, not a man out of step, or who is not earnestly longing for a brush with the enemy.

"Well, Bobby," says Jack Vere, to the little drummer, who is vigorously rub-a-dub-dubbing by his side, with a face as white as marble ; "you aren't frightened, I hope? We shall get safely out of this, depend on it, my lad."

"Oh Mr. Jack," replies Bobby, piteously, "I do hope I won't run away ; I want to be brave, I do indeed. Just promise that you'll run me through if you see me funk, or look like a coward. Perhaps that'll keep me straight."

"I'll run you through all right enough if I do see you running away. But I haven't much fear that I shall. How do you feel, Evan ap Morgan?"

"Oh, fine, Mr. Vere, and mean to have a good slice at the rascally Afghans. You just come and look at my sword-blade when it is all over, and you shall see it dyed pretty red, I promise you," was the bold reply of the little Welsh boy.

"Don't brag quite so much, Evan. I've more faith in Bobby," said Jack.

"Ah, that's because he's a countryman ; but I'm a fiery son of Wales."

Jack could hardly help smiling at the little bantam, but he remarked to both in as kindly tones as he could—

"Don't go thrusting yourselves into needless danger, youngsters, for it isn't needed, and some of us would be very sorry to lose you, believe me."

By this time they had reached the strongly-guarded outer-gate of the fortress, or rather double gate with a portcullis between, and a formidable 32-pounder in the rear of the treble defence, all of which were now thrown open or drawn up to admit of the Kentish Buffs passing out.

"God grant that you come back again," said Lieutenant Ward of the Royal Artillery to Major Tomlinson, as he marched past him at the head of his men ; "you are but two hundred to sixty thousand."

"But the two hundred are men of Kent, and the sixty thousand are black sheep, whom, like wolves, we will worry to the death," was the reply.

They were in the streets now, and as they turned the corner, they heard the great iron gates of the fortress crash home in their rear, and Lieutenant Ward, shouting to his gunners to load the ponderous 32-pounder to the very muzzle with grape and canister.

"He thinks that we shall be driven back," muttered Major Tomlinson to himself. "Well, we shall see."

And the detachment marched on and on, till they at last caught sight of a blazing house, and yelling thousands around it.

CHAPTER VII.

THE KENTISH BUFFS IN ACTION.

NOW an Afghan mob is not like an English one, for in that lawless country everyone carries arms and knows how to use them as well. Even boys of eight or nine are handy with knife and pistol, and their mothers and sisters can handle them at a pinch.

Thus it will be seen that the Kentish Buffs had their work cut out for them.

But they were not one whit afraid, not they ; for they had confidence in their officers and in themselves as well ; being just a hundred and fifty bayonets in strength—for it had not been thought prudent to rob the palace-fortress of all its European defenders.

On went the Kentish men against some three thousand rebels.

"Rub-a-dub-dub, rub-a-dub-dub, rub-a-dub, rub-a-dub-dub !" still went Bobby Rogers's drumsticks with mathematical precision, although his face was very pale and his upper teeth were gnawing into his under lip with a nervous energy that made the tears start to his eyes.

Evan ap Morgan, on the other hand, had ceased playing, stuck his sticks into their proper receptacles in his crossbelt and drawn his little brass-hilted sword, though it must be owned that he did not look half so thorough-bred a bantam cock as he had done five minutes previously.

"You don't seem to hunger for the fight so much as Evan," said Jack to Bobby, for the two drummers were marching beside him.

"I'd feel safer like, sir, with a sword in my hand than a drumstick ; but it's my duty to drum, and so drum I will to the last, if I can only keep myself from fainting or running, for I didn't think 'twas possible to be in such a funk."

"Bob, my lad, you'll do, for even the great Napoleon owns to having been frightened the first time he was under fire, as we are now, by Jove !"

Hardly had Jack Vere uttered the exclamation than an Afghan mob, suddenly perceiving their approach, began to yell and fire their jezails at them, happily with more eagerness than accuracy of aim.

"Oh !" screamed Evan ap Morgan, "they have got a white man's head stuck on a spear! Look, Bobby! look, Mr. Vere! Isn't it awful?"

Jack saw the bloody trophy plainly enough, and recognised the face of Captain Johnson, the British paymaster of Shah Soojah's Sikh and Hindoo contingents; but he had no time to make reply to the little Welsh drummer's remark, for the next moment Major Tomlinson shouted out—

"Halt! Present! Steady, men, steady! Aim low and aim true."

"Fire!"

Then there was a rattling discharge, followed by shrieks, groans, and imprecations coming from the ranks of the mutinous Afghans, several of whom were observed to fall, whilst the rest wavered to and fro like a field of barley in a heavy gale, and not wishing to give them time to recover from their momentary confusion, the major yelled out—

"Now, my lads, at 'em; give 'em the bayonet. Don't be too tender with them, for they've butchered our countrymen in cold blood."

"Charge!"

With a genuine British cheer, the Kentish Buffs went at them, and the Afghans saw with what grim determination they were bent on slaughtering them.

Their rear ranks were still brave, however, and would not hear of those in front, alone exposed to danger, giving way before the British charge.

They had to fight, therefore, and as Afghans fight well, ofttimes from choice, they struggled like very devils now, of necessity.

They hacked, they hewed, they stabbed at the British infantry, hurling anathemas at them, and spitting in their faces the while, and even when bayoneted through the body, they would grasp the weapon that had transfixed them, and holding it with the clutch of death and hate, strike or thrust at the soldier handling it, with the last remnant of their departing strength.

Children, like venomous little wasps, crawled in between the soldiers, and stabbed at them, or tried to hamstring them with sharp knives.

Women rushed bare-bosomed, and with flashing eyes and streaming hair, into the thickest of the fight, and struggled as desperately as the men.

It was five millions one hundred and twenty thousand people of this breed that our little force of less than four thousand five hundred men were expected by an imbecile civilian government to conquer and keep in subjugation. Fools, idiots, to deem such a thing long possible.

The bayonets of the gallant Kentish Buffs were soon bent and bloody, but there seemed just as many Afghans left to kill as there had been at first. Added to this they were exposed to a deadly fire from the flat roofs of the houses, a fire they could not return, their hands being too full of other work. Yet it was precise and deadly, and they were dropping fast before it as well as from the deadly struggle that was being waged hand to hand in the street.

It soon became evident that they would not be able to achieve the object for which they had come—the rescue of the two English families of Burnes and Johnson, whose houses had been beset by the furious rabble.

Doubtless all had been murdered, just as Johnson had been, ere they had put in an appearance upon the scene. The light of the still burning stables and outhouses, showed no white faces at the windows, or on the balconies, and Major Tomlinson began to fear he had come on a bootless errand.

But the difficulty was to get away, for another great crowd of dusky Afghans had come up in their rear, cutting off their retreat.

Jack Vere and Willie Dunbar, though on different flanks of the little detachment, and therefore unable to hold any communication with each other, had fought like lions, but the two boys, Bobby Rogers and Evan ap Morgan, had been naturally terrified at the wholesale carnage, and though they had each worsted two or three Afghan boys of their own age, who had measured steel with them, neither had gone in quest of mightier game.

The soldiers and officers alike had protected the little rascals as much as possible, thinking it was a pity that they had been suffered to come, for all the good they were, though that state of things wasn't to last, for long since they only wanted some extra strong motive to set their valour aflame.

To Evan ap Morgan it came in the shape of a huge Afghan, who sprang at Jack Vere whilst he was engaged with another opponent, and slung round a clumsy matchlock, intending to brain him with the but-end thereof.

Before he could do so, however, the little Welsh drummer, with a cry of mingled rage and terror, sprang upward rather than forward, and sheathed his sword in his heart.

Down went the black monster without a groan, and Evan, with a shudder, drew his little sword out of the body and gazed at it half wonderingly.

"Thank you, General Tom Thumb. You saved my life then, and I won't forget it, if I live to be as old as Methusaleh," said Jack Vere, on striking down his antagonist, and then he looked out for a fresh one.

There were plenty to choose from, and he was at it, hammer and tongs again, in another minute, whilst Evan shrank back to Bobby's side, saying—

"I settled him bravely, didn't I? I wasn't afraid of the monster."

His teeth were chattering in his head, however, whilst he spoke.

"Oh," said Bobby, dolorously, "I'd never have had the pluck. I'm an awful coward, Evan. I'm a disgrace to the regiment, I am. I believe I'd run away if there was any way to run, but they're all around us, and we'll all be murdered, Evan."

"Bobby, Bobby, don't say that, or you'll make me as frightened as yourself," cried Evan, in tremulous tones.

"Oh Lor', that was a bullet through my shako, that was. An inch lower and it would have been through my head. Isn't it awful? Why look, Evan, there's a little girl up at that window. A little white-haired girl, with her head bleeding. Oh, what lovely curls she has. My! if it isn't Captain Crolly's little girl; and the place is swarming with Afghans."

And as he concluded, the gallant little Bobby slung his drum behind his back.

"Why, what are you going to do?" asked Evan ap Morgan, breathlessly.

"Why, I'm going to have her out of there, or be killed in trying to do it, anyway."

"But—but I thought you were such a coward, Bobby. You said so."

"And so I am. I'm shaking in my shoes, my teeth are chattering in my head, and my hair is on end. I know it is, but I'll save that little girl for all that, for I'm a British soldier and she's a girl—so here goes."

And away rushed Bobby towards the house, sword in hand.

It was one of those from the roof of which the Afghans were firing down upon the gallant Buffs, so Bobby thought that in all probability it was full of them in every part, yet nevertheless sword in hand he rushed forward.

CHAPTER VIII.

SOME DEADLY PERILS AND HAIRBREADTH ESCAPES.

A BOY can get where a man cannot, and thus, though there were many struggling groups of combatants between Bobby and the house in question, yet he dodged around some, and dived between the legs or under the upraised arms of others, and at the cost of a knife-thrust through his clothing and a knife-cut on the shoulder, he gained the house.

"Oh Lor'! aren't I frightened," he groaned to himself, as he entered the hall where three Afghans lay stone dead across each other's bodies.

But he didn't stop for all that, but marched resolutely up the stairs sword in hand.

At the top lay a British officer, hacked and hewed out of almost all resemblance to humanity though either hand grasped a double-barrelled pistol, the weapons doubtless that had settled the three Afghans lying across each other in the hall below.

Bob tried to recognise him, but couldn't, his face was so disfigured, so he stepped over him and sought out the room in which he had seen the little girl standing at the window.

He went into several first, and in one lay a lady murdered in her bed, and in another three young children and a black nurse also weltering in their gore.

The woman's head lay in quite a different part of the room to her body, but the children, who ranged from between two and six years of age, looked as though they had been held up in the air by the feet and then cleft in twain with a heavy sword.

It was a truly hideous spectacle.

Poor Bobby could have screamed in the excess of his horror and terror, but he was true to his mission and never for an instant forgot the little girl, whom he had seen crying at the window, with the blood dappling her glossy curls.

He found her at last still in the same position, aud she never turned when he entered.

A hasty glance round the room showed another girl child of nine or so, lying dead on the floor, evidently killed by a blow on the head from some blunt instrument, for there was no blood about, and the whiteness of the wounded limbs, as she lay stretched on the polished floor, was as that of snow.

The noble boy, by the exercise of all his strength, raised her up, put her back in her bed, and covered her over, so that the sight should not unnecessarily distress the one who lived, should she turn round.

Having accomplished this, Bobby went straight up to the window, and laying a hand gently on a soft bare shoulder of the frightened little creature who stood there, said softly and quickly—

"Don't be afraid—I am a friend!"

She turned quickly round, looked him in the face with a strange and vacant expression, and then burst out into a very loud peal of mocking laughter.

Bobby stepped bock involuntarily and an icy coldness pervaded his heart, anything to approaching merriment seemed so very dreadful at such a time and place.

"Little lady," said he, "you are in great peril, and I've come to help you to escape. Don't laugh, but pray to God that we may escape."

She was a beautiful little thing, plump of limb, and snowy white of skin, as her solitary little article of apparel, all dainty linen and lace, looped up at the shoulders with bows of blue riband, fully disclosed.

But yet, when for a second time she gave utterance to that ringing, hollow laugh, yet looking full at him with eyes having a strange wild light in them the while, Bobby Rogers shuddered.

"She's mad! Can't you see it? She's mad! These awful butcherings have turned her brain," said a voice at Bobby's elbow, and glancing round he saw little Evan ap Morgan.

"Oh Evan, I didn't wish you to run this peril," said Bobby, reproachfully.

"I couldn't desert a comrade, Bobby. A crowd of inhuman Afghan devils are on the top of the house, ay, and in the room above our heads too; for hark to their walking about."

"When they come down they will murder us all," said Bobby, "should they find us here."

"But why should they find us here?" cried Evan. "Why shouldn't we all three decamp at once?"

"And so we will. I wonder if she will come along willingly. We have no time to dress her, even if we could find her things. Oh Evan, she is quite mad."

She was not only mad, but speechless. Combined terror and horror had made her dumb as well as insane. When Bobby and Evan took her gently by the hand, and tried to lead her away, she resisted, however, yet laughing still.

Then their grasp was shifted from her

hands to her arms, and they tried, still with gentleness, to force her along, but insanity had lent to her nine golden summers, the strength of twenty accumulated years, and she clung to the window sill, still laughing hysterically.

At this moment, Evan ap Morgan exclaimed—

" It's too late, Bobby, it's all over with us ; the Afghans have won the day, and there go the remnant of our poor fellows as hard as they can tear ; only look at them."

Bobby did look, and beheld the Kentish Buffs, or at least the handful that were left of them, rushing away like mad, and thousands of hooting and yelling Afghans in hot pursuit, shouting out—

" Death to the Ghiours ! Death to the Ferringhees."

" They are gone, and there is no hope of our being able to overtake them, since there are hundreds of fierce Afghans between us already," said Bobby.

" Then what shall we do, Bobby ?" said Evan.

" We must hide ourselves somewhere about the premises, and steal away to the cantonment or the Bala Hissar, when the Afghans are gone."

" But this girl will betray our whereabouts by her laughter," said Evan.

" We must risk that, or rather I must; for I'll sooner be cut into ten thousand pieces than desert her, poor lovely little thing," replied Bobby, hotly.

" Well, anyhow, old boy, I'm with you," said Evan ; " so come along quick as lightning."

It was all very well to say " come along," but where ? That was the question.

The next instant it was reduced to its very narrowest limits by the sound of the Afghans coming down from the roof, and the floor above.

There was but a wardrobe to hold them, and it would be a tight fit for the three.

To add to their peril the little girl began to laugh hysterically again.

" We must carry her, and try to keep our hands over her mouth," said Bobby.

Between them they managed both, but they'd a hard task of it.

However, they were all within the wardrobe at last, and its doors closed tight.

Scarcely had they effected this when three Afghans entered the room. They began to talk loudly, and as though they missed something.

But not a word that they said could Bobby or Evan make out. And they had quite enough to do to keep their little charge quiet.

How the cold sweat of deadly fear trickled down their faces the while !

But oh, horror of horrors ! a hand is suddenly laid on the wardrobe door.

Surely the next moment will see them discovered, and slain.

No, the fellow breaks his finger nails in the attempt, owing to Bobby holding it as close as possible, from within. He swears awfully at this.

Then a companion seems to chaff him on his misfortune, or at least, so the English boys guess from the tone of his voice ; but the next moment a third Afghan, with a growl, raises his matchlock, and thrusts the bayonet attached thereto, right through the door, its point going between one of the little girl's pretty plump shoulders, and Bobby Rogers's right ear.

Bobby can hardly repress a scream ; Evan ap Morgan nearly faints away.

Then the child breaks into a perfect peal of wild shrill laughter.

" Oh Lor' ! it's all up with us now," thought Bobby.

But instead of that, it was all up with the Afghans ; for the shrill laughter, appealing either to their superstitious terrors, or something else in their organisations, they gave vent to answering yells of astonishment and terror, and fled *en masse.*

How thankful both Bobby and Evan did feel at their departure. Their little charge, instead of bringing destruction upon them had saved them. Perhaps they would get clear away after all, who could tell.

They waited where they were until the Afghans seemed to have deserted the house altogether, and then they came out of the friendly wardrobe, and Bobby hunted about to find the little girl's clothes, in order to dress her.

In doing so he took care not for a single moment to expose even the dead face of her sister, as she lay covered up in the bed, lest such a sight might prolong her madness, and make it more difficult to eradicate.

Girl's clothing of some kind suitable to her age he found; they managed to attire her in them, and Evan proposed, as she still seemed determined to resist, that they should bandage her eyes, and thus prevent her from seeing the accumulation of horrors that certainly would greet them otherwise, directly they got outside the bedroom door.

CHAPTER IX.

HIDDEN IN THE CELLAR—THE HOUR HAS COME.

THE little girl did not seem to object to the bandaging of her eyes, but they had to fairly lug her out of the room and down the stairs to the basement story.

Bobby and Evan had a faint idea that they would be able to get away there and then, but one glance from the front windows at the state of the street, which was very far from empty yet, warned them that they had better stay where they were.

To find some safe hiding-place within the house was evidently their wisest course, and they presently did find one which Bobby declared would suit them exactly, in the wine cellar, for they were able to lock the door from within.

It would have been far from a wise place to seek shelter in had an English mob been engaged in the burning and sacking business; but the Afghans hold all intoxicating drinks in detestation, so there was very little chance of their being sought for amongst the casks and bottles, and even their pretty charge's shrill laughter, if heard issuing from such a spot, would be taken to be that of a ghoul or some other evil spirit, of which the superstitious Afghan recognises nearly three hundred varieties.

"Evan, we must stop here till night comes again before we venture forth, and even then we shall have to disguise ourselves as much as we possibly can, or we'll never get out of this horrid town alive," said Bobby, when they had grown a little accustomed to the darkness.

"And when we get out, if we ever do, we may find the cantonments overrun, and all our soldiers and people murdered. What's to prevent it?" growled Evan.

"God can prevent it," said Bobby Rogers, solemnly; "and He can deliver us, too. I think we ought to pray to Him to deliver us, Evan, or it may not please Him to do so. I don't think I should be so frightened after we'd done that."

The two boys did as Bobby had suggested, drawing the little girl down on to her knees between them, and it's astonishing how comforted they felt when they had done. Bobby declared that he hardly felt terrified at all.

It was so dark down there that they could hardly see each other's faces; not sufficiently, at all events, to know what they were like; and this was a great loss to the two boys, for each felt that could he but only now and then glance at the almost divine beauty of the little girl whom they had saved, the time would pass thrice as quickly, and that he would gain from its contemplation both heart and confidence.

Strange to say, ever since they had offered up that prayer for protection, her shrill and almost demoniac laughter had ceased.

She still seemed to lack the power of

speech, but she was evidently more composed and tranquil.

Presently, as she sat on Bobby's lap, he felt her head droop on his shoulder.

"She's asleep," said he. "Let us take off our jackets and wrap her in them."

No sooner said than done, and no fond mother could have been more tender over her babe than were the drummer-boys over the little girl under their charge.

But a moment after Evan touched his comrade on the arm.

"Hark!" he said, "there are footsteps overhead. The bloodthirsty Afghans have discovered us!"

The boys stood prepared to resist at all risks any intrusion on their hiding-place.

Presently, however, they heard several fierce exclamations which they took for oaths, and then the footsteps retreated.

The Afghans had retreated, and they returned to the contemplation of the girl.

"I hope she'll wake up in her right mind, though, if she does, what we'll say to pacify her about her father and mother, and brothers and sisters, I'm sure I cannot tell," said Bobby.

"I wonder if the seeing her friends killed, or the blow on her pretty head took away her senses?" conjectured Evan. "Either was enough to do it. I wonder we aren't mad too."

"And so do I, Evan. But hush! she sleeps and breathes quite softly. Don't let us speak above a whisper or we may disturb her."

So the two boys sat and talked in murmurs, hoping first that the Afghans wouldn't return and burn the house down over their heads, thus burying them alive, then wondering whether every European in the city except themselves had been massacred, and counting up how many they knew resided there.

And next interchanging hopes and fears as to whether Jack Vere, their staunch friend—the only officer, in fact, who took much notice of them—had escaped with his life.

But they could come to no definite conclusion on the matter

They had plenty of time to weigh all the *pros* and *cons*—poor little fellows!—during the long weary hours that ensued.

They felt every time they heard the banging of the metal ghurries, the beating of the drums, and the blowing of the Afghan horns, that their countrymen must indeed be weak when their vengeance was so tardy.

Once Bobby crept out of the cellar and up into one of the rooms, whose windows overlooked the street, to reconnoitre.

And then he saw through the closed but bullet-riddled window-shutters a sight that filled him with horror, for a crowd of Afghan boys were playing football with a human head.

It was broad daylight and the streets were full of people, all armed to the teeth, and continually passing to and fro.

And whilst the horror-stricken English lad continued to gaze, a procession came rushing past, some on horseback and some on foot, bearing in their midst, on the points of tall tasselled spears, the heads of more massacred English, some of them those of women, as their long floating hair clearly proved.

Bobby went back to the cellar with a heart far more ill at ease than it had been before. What would become of them? What would become of them, but death?

The little girl was awake now, and Bobby left the cellar-door open for a minute to have a look at her.

Her beautiful eyes had no longer the wild glare of insanity in them.

He spoke to her but could elicit no reply, nor could Evan when he tried.

She looked sad and pale, and as though stunned and bewildered.

At last they got a shake of the head—that was all.

"Perhaps it's better as it is, just now," said Bobby; "perhaps she can eat if she can't speak. I'll pay the larder a visit, Evan, and see what's in it."

A murdered female servant was in it with the door lying in splinters around her, as though she had taken refuge there and tried to barricade the Afghans outside, but alas! vainly.

Bobby shuddered with horror, and Evan's heart sank, for perhaps in a few moments he and his two companions might share the same fate.

NOTICE.—Another Coloured Picture for binding with the work will be Given Away with No. 3. Other Gifts to follow.

PORTRAIT OF YAKOOB KHAN, AMEER OF AFGHANISTAN,
Ally of the British Government.

On the shelves, however, Bobby found a portion of a cheese, a loaf of bread, and some meat, which he hastened to appropriate.

Rejoining his companions in the cellar he laid out the feast before them on the head of a small cask; but the little girl could not be induced to eat.

She shook her head sorrowfully when the food was offered her, and set her little white teeth so firm that there was no getting anything between them.

"We must eat to keep up our strength, for we may want it in her service as well as our own," said Bobby; "and I don't think a portion of a bottle of wine would do us any harm. It would certainly give us more courage and strength."

"But how are we to get the cork out, Bobby?" quoth Evan ap Morgan.

"We won't trouble about that. We will knock off the neck of the bottle," said Bobby.

This was done, and the two boys made a very fair repast.

They felt stronger both in mind and body when they had done; but the day proved a long and a weary one, hiding away, and with such an awful uncertainty as now appeared before both our little heroes.

At last night came down upon the city once more, yet still they had to wait some hours for the streets to empty themselves.

Then and not till then they would have some hope of escape.

They ventured to find and to light a candle down in their gloomy hiding-place, after making quite sure that not the slightest pencil of light could be seen from outside the locked door.

They could better endure the slowness of the passing time now, as the lovely face of the little girl cheered them, for neither of them could fancy even angels' countenances to be more lovely; and when at last Bobby muttered—

"The good God will not at all events let her fall into the hands of murdering Afghans," Evan responded—

"No, I will never believe it."

And thus the hour drew on when their attempt at escape should be made.

CHAPTER X.

THE AFGHAN TIGER AND BRITISH LION PUPS

BOBBY and Evan donned their jackets, shakoes, and belts, slung their drums, put out the candle, opened the door, and led the little girl between them up the cellar-steps and into what was evidently the dining-room.

She made no resistance now, nor screamed nor laughed.

She seemed to be in a kind of half-trance or state of atrophy; perhaps happily so.

"Oh Evan," said Bob, suddenly, "it never struck me before, but we cannot hope to escape in these clothes. We should be mad even to attempt it."

"Well, I was thinking that if we were to rub ourselves all over with soot, we should have a far better chance of getting away."

"Yes," retorted Bobby; "suppose we were to blacken our faces, hair, and hands, stick on our shakoes awry, pull off our shoes and stockings, and blacken our feet, and then march boldly through the streets drumming away like mad, only, of course, very badly, you know. Shouldn't we be taken for young Afghans having a lark in dead drummers' clothes, eh?"

"But she wouldn't look much like going in for a lark, no matter how we dressed her," said Evan, indicating their little charge. "We couldn't make her ugly enough to pass muster for an Afghan child, no matter what we did to her. Do you think we could, Bobby?"

"Oh Lor', no! She would betray us anyhow; and if she only betrayed herself, hy it would be all the same, for what-'er happened to her should happen to e."

"Same here, Bobby," remarked little van ap Morgan. "But there goes twelve o'clock, and we have no time to spare. The streets may be quite empty."

"No, no, Evan. At all hours the homeless and houseless are wandering about them, and they would be the first to seize upon or denounce us. Stay! I have an idea there must be long gardens at the backs of these houses, and they must lead in the direction of the fortress of the Bala Hissar. Depend on it, that was the way the young gentleman escaped the mob who came flying over the parapet of the bastion on to the terrace-walk just as we were waiting for the order to march; and what one can do others can do," said Bobby.

"Now, that's not a bad idea of yours, Bobby, blest if it is," quoth Evan.

"No; I think we may be able to manage it—that's if I do not get horribly frightened," said Bobby. "However, let us take a good look out at the back and see our landmarks. The Bala Hissar is a conspicuous object enough."

"All right, Bobby. Shall we leave he little one here, or bring her along?"

"Oh, we may leave her here for a minute or two; she will be quite safe."

So the little girl was told to remain where she was, and not to move till they returned; and to make doubly sure of her not quitting the room while they were away, Evan, who went out last, locked the door behind him and pocketed the key.

They soon found their way out to the back of the house and into a kind of yard.

Beyond this, they perceived a long but narrow garden, bounded by low walls, and in a direct line with certain gilded domes and flat roofs.

"I think it will do," said Bobby, "or at all events, it will be safer than any other way."

Hardly had he uttered the words, when both thought they heard a groan.

"There is some poor fellow still lying wounded there," said Evan, in a whisper.

"Say rather, being butchered," exclaimed Bobby, as a shriek suddenly rent the air, coming from the same direction; "oh, aren't I frightened! But we must help him."

And away dashed Bobby, sword in hand, in the direction of the sound, as hard as he could tear, and Evan after him, in heart quite as terrified, though he didn't own it.

But they were destined both of them to be frightened still more, for hardly had they discerned by the moonlight a figure in a scarlet coat, and golden epaulets, lying amid the tall rank grass, than they also descried, oh, horror! a huge tiger standing almost over him, lashing his striped sides with his tail, and purring like a cat, while its cruel eyes flashed as do blood-opals.

For a moment Bobby prayed that the earth might open and engulph him, so terrified was he of this dread monarch of the jungle, from whom even the mighty elephant flies in mad panic.

But the next moment Bobby and Evan had recognised in the prostrate form on the grass, Jack Vere, the pet of the regiment.

He was bold enough then, and a certain brilliant idea struck him at the same moment, which he at once acted upon, for quickness was life.

"Drum, drum, drum like mad," he croaked, in a voice that he didn't recognise as his own, to Evan ap Morgan. "The assembly, no, no, no! The charge!"

Even as he spoke, round from his back on to his left hip came Bobby's instrument and the next instant the sticks were playing on the sheepskin like mad.

Evan ap Morgan followed suit, and joined in with rare precision.

The fierce beast, who had been in the very act of springing upon his prey, looked up at the two dauntless boy-drummers, and all at once, panic-stricken by the unaccustomed sound, gave a lugubrious howl, and then turned sharp round, and with his royal tail between his legs actually ran away.*

---

* Less than this has been known to frighten a tiger. A royal Bengal was once about to pounce on a lady, when she suddenly unfurled an umbrella in his face with the same result.

"Oh sir, get up and run with us into the house, or he may grow bold and come back again !" said Bobby, then trembling from head to foot.

Jack Vere attempted to do so, but no sooner was he on his feet, than he was down again, for he was hurt somewhat badly.

"Lend me a shoulder this time, and perhaps I'll succeed, Bobby," said he.

The Yorkshire lad at once did so, and by his aid Jack Vere was able to hobble into the house, whose back door the reader may rest assured was quickly closed and bolted, lest the tiger might make himself an uninvited guest.

"You've preserved my life, lads," said Jack Vere then ; "just, too, as I was making my way into the city in order to do my best to save yours, though with little hope of finding you still in the land of the living. He must have been attracted by the smell of the dead, doubtless, for he leapt over this garden wall not a score of yards in my rear, and in my hurry to escape from him I caught my foot in a hole, and falling down twisted my foot round, so that I fear I shall be of far less service to you than I intended to be. However, you are both alive !"

"I believe so," said Bobby ; "though I can hardly be sure yet, that big brute of a tiger has given me such a turn. Oh, I'm an awful coward, that I am !"

"I'm an awful fool to go spraining my ankle so as not to be one bit of use," retorted Jack ; "however, I can point you out the best way in which to effect your escape, and you must be gone at once, for the night wears apace."

"What, sir, and leave you here when you came all the way on purpose to look for us ?" retorted Bobby ; "by George ! it ain't my father's son as 'll do that, if

he is a coward. Nor will Evan ap Morgan, I am sure."

"No, I'm blest if I do," replied the Welsh drummer, sturdily.

At this moment a tumult of voices was heard in the street without, mingled with the banging of gongs and ghurries, and the beating of tomboys.

Then torches sprang into sudden life, and shed a lurid glow on a fast gathering crowd, all looking fierce and vengeful, and armed to the teeth.

"Ah, your drumming has done this. Exit tiger enter Afghan," said Jack Vere ; "they fancy that the troops are marching down upon them from some direction or other. A pity it's not April fool's day, isn't it ?"

"They'll make April fools of us if they break into the house and find us," replied Bobby ; "we had best hide away in the cellar again. We've got a capital hiding-place, sir, that I don't think they'll find out. You lean on me and I'll take you straight there, and you, Evan, bring down the little one."

"Little one !" quoth Jack, in surprise ; "why, what little one have you here ?"

"Well, she isn't exactly an angel, sir, though the Afghans were near making her one ; nor precisely a cherub, seeing as she has a body and legs, though her neck and shoulders are just as plump and white ; but she's the loveliest little girl that mortal eyes ever rested on. You'll see her presently."

And he led Jack on until the cellar-door was reached.

Bobby unlocked it and conducted his officer inside, and then down rushed Evan carrying the little girl in his arms and declaring that the Afghans were breaking into the house in a crowd.

CHAPTER XI.

SEARCHED FOR HIGH AND LOW—AN ALLY.

THIS was indeed true, as the noise of the violent breaking open of the doors and windows sufficiently testified.

And then ensued the heavy footsteps of the Afghans tearing about the house in every direction.

Fearful now was their position, for discovery seemed inevitable, and their murder equally so.

The drumming had evidently brought this hornet's swarm down upon them, and they assuredly would not leave them until they had stung them to death.

Even now they were coming towards the cellars "with feet quick to shed blood."

"My lads," said Jack Vere, "we've a moment to pray for those who are dear to us, for we are past praying for ourselves, in this world at least. It only remains for us to show how Englishmen can die."

"Oh, dear, what a fright I'm in," said Bobby; "but I won't show it," and he took a firm grip of his sword handle. "I think I'd be content to die if the little one could only be saved."

"The pain will be over in a moment, for, at all events, the Afghans, unlike other savages, do not torture their victims," responded Jack.

"Poor little soul!" said Evan; "and how unconscious she is of peril, too!"

This was true enough, for the child's mind was a perfect blank.

The day before she had been a bright, sparkling, merry little creature.

Nearer and nearer came the footsteps of the fierce Afghans, and Jack, Bobby, and Evan quietly drew their swords and awaited them.

Jack had to steady himself against a cask, behind which Bobby and Evan had quietly laid the lovely child down, hoping against hope that she might, at all events, escape discovery by the foe.

The next moment they would be in upon them, and then a glitter of steel, and all would be over.

But why didn't they come on?

Hark!

What meant that sudden shriek and confused scuffling?

Ah, the mystery was soon solved by an awful roar, succeeded by a series of angry growls and snarls, and a sound of falling bodies, whilst the shrieks were suddenly renewed with tenfold intensity, accompanied by the report of pistols and the clash of steel.

"The tiger is amongst them.* Gracious Heaven! the fierce brute has entered through one of the back windows, and is harrying them as though they were a flock of helpless sheep," said Bobby Rogers to Jack Vere, in a low and awe-struck whisper.

"Yes, the scent of blood has drawn him from his jungle home into the city. 'Tis said that they can smell human gore ten miles away," replied Jack, in the same low tone. "Thank Heaven! the tiger comes this time as a friend."

He was certainly doing battle with their foes, if that constituted friendship; but Afghans are not afraid of man, tiger, or devil, and to rescue their wounded and lacerated comrades they threw themselves on the fierce wild beast in dozens, attacking him with swords, knives, daggers and clubbed matchlocks, in grim defiance of his teeth and claws.

The tiger's roars were awful.

The cries of the Afghans were more fearful still.

They could hear each buffet that he

---

* A tiger who has once eaten a human being will run any risk to obtain another similar meal. Such a tiger has been known to enter an Indian town even by daylight.

"JACK VERE SEIZED UPON THE FLAG, AND TORE IT DOWN."

gave with his paws, and the squelch every time that his teeth met in human flesh, and the crack each time they crushed human bone.

But his foes were all too many, and at last he succumbed to a bullet that penetrated his right eye to his brain.

The Afghan battle yell announced his death, and Jack muttered—

"Now, lads, it's our turn ; show them that you are English born."

But the monarch of the jungle fought their battle in life as in death, for one of the Afghans declared, in a husky voice—

"Let us carry off our wounded and leave this place. The soul of the Sekunder Burnes was in that tiger,* and right thoroughly has he avenged himself. Those were ghostly drums that lured us hither. Let us go out and burn the accursed place to the ground, comrades."

This proposition was received with a yell of applause, and out rushed the Afghans to fire the mansion, and with it destroy the evil spirits or disembodied souls that had taken up their residence therein.

"We must try to get away before the house is set on fire," said Jack Vere. "There is so much dry wood in it that it will burn quickly."

There were no Afghans in the house now, so they unlocked and opened the cellar-door, and stole noiselessly out, one by one.

Right in front of them lay the tiger, a magnificent creature, of the largest size.

He was riddled by lead and slashed by steel in every part of his glossy body ; but he had amply revenged himself, for fully half-a-dozen dead Afghans lay around him, frightfully mauled.

They did not stay to look at him long, however, for they had to think of their own safety, and it was impossible for Jack to move along very quickly.

They never anticipated for a moment that the Afghans meant to fire the house in the rear as well as in front.

What was their horror, therefore, just as they thought that their safety was almost secured, to find that the garden as well as the street was thronged with their implacable and bloodthirsty foes, and that their retreat was utterly cut off !

For a moment they could not say a word to each other, their despair was so great ; for now the most awful of deaths stared them in the face—destruction by fire.

Or if they issued forth, by the sword.

Already, bundles of combustibles had been rolled up against the house on both sides, and these were soon set aflame by torches.

Up leapt the quivering, flickering tongues of fire towards the overlapping bamboo-thatched roof.

The roar was like that of a dozen blast furnaces in full operation, every room being as light as day, and the entire neighbourhood around also redly illuminated.

Down every street came thronging the Afghan citizens to witness the conflagration—men, women, and children, in countless legions—yelling, and dancing, and gesticulating like so many demons.

"It is all over with us this time," said Jack Vere, "without a doubt."

"Would the fire reach us in the cellars, do you think ?" asked Bobby.

"No ; but the smoke would suffocate us there, and if, by next to a miracle, we escaped that, we should be buried alive beneath the ruins, and I think I'd rather be burned up quick than die such an awfully lingering death."

"I wish we could kill her painlessly," said Bobby Rogers, indicating the little girl whom he bore lovingly in his arms, "and then put her body down in the cellar where the cruel flames couldn't spoil her beauty. It seems dreadful that she should be burnt as black as a coal."

"I'd die willingly if I could save her ; she is so very lovely," echoed Evan ap Morgan.

"I don't think we should be doing right to kill her ourselves, even to save her cruel pain," said Jack Vere, slowly and thoughtfully. "It would be like interfering with the will of God ; and, besides, God has delivered us so often that we ought not to lose faith in His protection up to the very last."

Hardly had the words escaped Jack's lips when Bobby started and exclaimed—

* The Afghans believe in the transmigration of souls.

"Hark, hark! Oh, is it true or am I going mad? No, no, no; my ears do not deceive me. It is the flourish of cavalry trumpets. The British vengeance is aroused at last. The sword is drawn and will not be sheathed until we are victorious. Evan—Mr. Vere! do you not hear it? Do you not hear that the English are advancing?"

"Yes, my boy," answered Jack, his voice almost stifled by the smoke that now rolled in eddying volumes through the rooms on the basement story; "but they must ride quickly to be in time to save us, so don't hope too soon."

"Oh, no, no, no, don't say that, sir. Surely God has sent them," quoth Evan.

It seemed as though He had indeed, for the next minute the onward rush of the horses could be heard, though they were soon drowned by the howls and yells of the surprised and terror-stricken Afghans.

Then, like a hundred blazing comets in the light of the conflagration, flashed suddenly on the rapt vision of Jack Vere and his companions the brass helmets of the British dragoons, with the black horsehair plumes streaming out behind them.

Jack Vere, little Bobby, and Evan, at that moment felt their hearts swell with pride at seeing their brave countrymen dash forward with such true British pluck, regardless of the great numbers against them.

CHAPTER XII

WITHIN THE BRITISH CANTONMENTS.

THE British dragoons were in grim earnest, there could be no doubt about that.

They smote hard and they smote true; their horses, as do all chargers of Indian breed, fighting just as savagely with teeth and hoof the while.

The Afghans scorned to ask for quarter, but had they done so they assuredly would not have got it.

British blood was up and British steel was not to be lightly sheathed.

So down went the yelling, hooting, and fiercely blaspheming horde of assassins, weltering in their gore, yet with their last breath, cutting and stabbing at the legs of the plunging, rearing, and snorting horses.

Now, lads, we must make an effort to join them now. There will be no getting out for the flames if we stay here longer," said Jack Vere in suffocating tones.

"Here, Evan, take the little one and shield her from the flame and smoke as well as ever you can. I'm the strongest and can best support Mr. Vere," said Bobby, then.

Evan strained the little girl in his arms, and thought how sweet it would be to die for her, and with Jack limping painfully, for even Bobby's shoulder was not a very staple support, they made the best of their way to the front door.

Jack had in secret feared to find it closed, but it was not.

Yet it was blazing fiercely, and it would be no joke passing out through it.

"Go first," said Jack, to Evan ap Morgan; "the little girl must be our first thought. When you get up don't look back to see how we fare, but think only of yourself and your precious charge, and attract the attention of the dragoons as soon as ever you can, or the Afghans will settle you."

"All right, sir," said Evan, and although he had to use both arms to carry the child, and so was utterly unable to protect himself or her out he boldly rushed.

Not so easily did Jack Vere and Bobby Rogers manage the perilous passage, for Jack could not do more than limp, try as hard as he would.

And though the little drummer volunteered to carry him out on his back, Jack feared that did he stagger and fall with the burden, there would be no getting up for either of them.

Never had their peril been so great as at this moment, for they had to push their way through the Afghan horde, whilst next to powerless to protect themselves ; for Jack could not fight unless propped up against something, and Bobby could do very little with his officer's weight resting heavily on one shoulder, whilst of course Evan ap Morgan with the child in his arms was more helpless than either of them.

Happily the Afghans were at that moment thinking more of how they were to keep their own heads on their shoulders than how to take off other peoples.

The crowd was dissolving itself as quickly as possible, in a dozen different directions, the British troopers still continuing to hack and hew till even their pipe-clayed gauntlets were splashed red with Afghan gore.

It is a wonder our three friends, circumstanced as they were, were not pushed down and trampled to death under the feet of the surging crowd, and Jack Vere would assuredly have met such a fate but for the sturdy strength of Bobby Rogers.

Hasty cuts and thrusts were more than once made at them, too, but happily without effect ; and at last, after what seemed to them an age, the attention of some of their countrymen was attracted, and Evan ap Morgan at the same moment catching a riderless charger by the rein, led it up to Jack Vere, and begged that he would mount it.

"Ay, ay, sir, and I'll give you a help up," said a stalwart dragoon, as he dismounted for the purpose. "Here, Arnold, Thomas—this to a couple of comrades, whom he perceived close by—take each of you one of these drummer-boys up behind you. What, laden with a girl as well as a drum? Well, give me the child, and I'll carry her as tenderly as though I were her mother, poor little thing."

At this moment "the recall" was sounded on the British trumpets, so that it was a case of look sharp or be left behind.

However, Jack, once in the saddle, was quite independent of his sprained ankle, and Bobby and Evan were up behind the two friendly troopers like monkeys, and clinging just as tightly to them, too.

And then back went the dragoons by the way they had come, only alas! about a score less in number, and their serried ranks doomed to be thinned still more, by a murderous discharge of firearms from the flat roof of the houses on either side of the street, to which the Afghans when worsted, had promptly repaired to avenge the massacre of their comrades.

There was no getting at them there, and so the dragoons could not in any way retaliate, except by a desultory discharge of their pistols.

Speed would be the only friend of the dragoons now, for speed baffles the best aim, and gets danger more quickly over as well, and the spur was used as freely as the sabre had been, and the fierce blood-horses almost flew.

Then, in another five minutes, the frowning archway of the Kohistan Gate rose to view ; the gate itself had been battered down by a couple of long 9-pounders an hour before, to admit of the entry of the dragoons into the city.

Before it a fringe of Afghans were drawn up to dispute the passage, out of the British, armed with swords, matchlocks, and spears.

But the dragoons with a yell of fierce joy at again seeing foes whom they could reach with their swords, went straight at them, and cleft a bloody pathway through them.

Then they were on the open plain.

The yellow walls of Cabul, and the towering cliff and fortress of the Bala Hissar in their rear, and two miles in front of them the long line of British cantonments.

The dragoons deemed that all danger was past now, and drew rein in order to breathe their horses, but hardly had the intervening space between Cabul's walls and the cantonments been crossed, than they perceived a rapidly advancing cloud of dust a mile away on their left, which quickly resolved itself into a superb body of cavalry.

On they came, with plumes waving and lance points and caps of steel flashing in the light of the full moon.

Their coats of chain-mail glinted and scintillated like rippling waves, and each polished shield blazed itself a perfect moon.

Of the standards that lazily unfolded themselves above their heads, one was green and the other crimson (the colour of the brother who perished by the flood, and the colour of the brother who perished by the sword) ; and as they came on, at least ten thousand little bells jingled musically from the gorgeous harness of their matchless Arab horses.

No sooner did these wild horsemen of the mountains perceive the little troop of British cavalry crossing the plain in their front, than as with one accord they brandished all their crimson tasselled spears, and then with frantic cries of " *Allah akbar! Allah akbar! Deen! Deen!*" they set spurs to their horses and came down on them like a thunderbolt.

Tired, jaded, weary with smiting, and decimated in numbers, the dragoons would have fled to the shelter of the cantonments had there been time ; but the headlong speed with which the Afghan horses were bearing down upon them rendered this impossible.

The only thing to be done was to charge them.

So the British trumpets rang cheerily out, and drawing their swords afresh, the dragoons went at them.

The shock was fearful, the struggle for a brief instant Homeric.

Then the resistless power, valour, and impetus of the British horsemen made itself felt, and they swept through the very centre of the Asiatic host, as a hurricane sweeps through a forest laying everything low in its course.

The wild horsemen formed again in their rear it is true, and pursued them, uttering the most fiendish cries of rage.

But presently some 9-pounders opened on them from a battery within the cantonments, and the iron missiles, fired with rare precision, soon sent them to the right-about with more haste than dignity.

Five minutes later the north cantonment gate was opened to permit of the dragoons riding in, and they found themselves safe among friends.

Safe ? Alas ! only comparatively so, for " the cantonments were a mile in length by a quarter of a mile in breadth, surrounded by a rampart and ditch of such trivial height and breadth that an Afghan could have cleared with the facility of a cat ;" and were there not a hundred thousand Afghans within a radius of three miles hungering to do so ?

CHAPTER XIII.

WITHIN THE CANTONMENTS—INTERVIEW WITH THE GENERAL.

THE British cantonments—fourteen hundred yards, or nearly a mile in length, by a little more than a quarter of a mile in breadth—were, in fact, streets of huts for our soldiers and camp followers.

Directly Jack Vere, with Bobby Rogers, Evan ap Morgan, and the little girl they had saved from the massacre, found them-

selves within the cantonment walls, th felt that—for a time, at least—they we safe, though the perturbed and anxiou faces of those by whom they were surrounded were hardly calculated to make such an impression upon them.

Though it was still night the entire encampment seemed to be astir, and directly the little girl was perceived a dozen ladies of all ages came forward ready to act a mother's or sister's parts towards her, so that the three youths had sorrowfully and reluctantly to let her go.

Then every officer almost wanted Dick and the little drummers to be his especial guests.

But they were saved the trouble of making a choice of entertainers by a sudden summons to the presence of General Elphinstone.

The general was in bed, and his reception of Jack Vere and his companions was not over and above polite, to say the least of it.

"What is this cock-and-bull story that I hear about your doings in the city?" grunted he. "Come, let me hear the matter from your own lips."

English Jack at once complied with this ungracious command, and without any bragadocia gave the old general an account of what had transpired in Cabul and at the Bala Hissar.

The narrative did not, however, allay his evident ill-temper.

He could hardly be brought to believe that the Afghan population had done such infernal cruelties, and accused Jack several times of exaggeration which the high-spirited youth could hardly submit to.

When, however, he came to relate how Shah Soojah in his terror had made up his mind to poison his entire harem, and the means by which he, Jack, had induced him to abandon his fell design, the old general lost all control over himself.

"What you dared," quoth he, "deceive the Afghan king? You dared to affirm that succour was at hand, when we have actually no hope of its arriving? You yourself, sir, shall return and tell him that our position here is most precarious, and it ill becomes an officer of junior rank to increase our difficulties in a way you have done."

"I only thought of our poor women, sir," quoth Jack.

"And what were they to you, sir? What were they to you, allow me to ask?"

"Well, I suppose the safety of the weaker sex should be something to every British youth and man, and there are

more than two hundred of them, all young and all beautiful," replied Jack.

"You will return to Cabul and the Bala Hissar without loss of time," said the general, tartly. "A court-martial shall decide on your conduct. Consider yourself under arrest."

Jack bowed to the old general, who, however, seemed of opinion that second thoughts were best, for he said—

"Stay; you will not be in arrest. Return to your quarters and confer with the senior officers of your regiment how you had best correct your misstatement to the king. Do you hear me, sir?"

And the old man frowned.

"Yes, sir," said Jack; "and of course to hear is to obey, though the consequence, I expect, if I have to return to the king, will be the loss of my head. His majesty is somewhat bloodthirsty."

"Have no fear. Have no fear of that. If the Afghan king dares to act so cruelly by you, by Jove! he shall be— yes, he shall be severely upbraided. Get you gone then, and let Shah Soojah know that you have been mistaken."

And the old general waved his hand in token of dismissal.

So English Jack Vere went forth from his presence, and Bobby Rogers and Evan ap Morgan, who had not dared to say a word, followed close at his heels.

"Well, this is a fine thing," quoth our hero, when the three had got out of earshot of old Elphinstone's sick chamber; "I'll be hanged if it isn't a very fine thing. The general might just as well have sent me into a den of lions as to make my apologies to Shah Soojah. The bloodthirsty villain will slice off my head as certain as possible, and all our commander-in-chief's upbraiding will never stick it on again."

"We must hope for the best, sir. We are willing to die with you," said Evan ap Morgan.

"It's not we, but I, this time, my lad. You must remain in cantonments. There's no earthly need for you or Bobby to return to Cabul."

"And do you think we should permit you to return there alone, sir?—no fear!" interposed the Yorkshire boy. "I may be an awful coward, and I know that I am, but duty's duty, and my drum shan't be missed on parade if I can help it."

"Nor mine either, Bobby," echoed Evan ap Morgan. "I'm blest if it shall ! o, no! We are British lads, I hope."

"But, my boys, I don't exactly under-and you," said Jack.

"Why, you see, sir," said Bobby ogers, "I—I should be afraid, you know, o go back with only Evan. I would rather fight, if fight I must, by your side, sir. I—I should feel a great deal safer along with you, sir. We'll go with you, fight for you, if need be."

"I believe your real thought is that I should be a deal safer along with you, too. Well, if you are resolved to go with me, and I find on inquiry that the dangers of the passage are not perilous, I will take you there."

"We will go with you, sir, whether they are perilous or no," replied Evan ap Morgan, boldly.

And Jack Vere could shake neither of the little British rascals' determination.

It was daylight now, and when the three clambered on to a gun carriage and looked over the strongly fortified city of Cabul, it seemed to be empty enough, save for the dead bodies, victims of the recent cavalry skirmish, that at one portion dotted it pretty thickly.

"The revolt seems to be over," said Jack. "The shah's native infantry and cavalry have, doubtless, restored order in the city, for the royal guard keep the Kohistan Gate, and we can return to the Bala Hissar without encountering danger on the way."

"Oh, I'm sorry for that," growled little Evan ap Morgan, "for we shall have no adventure."

"I'm sure I'm thankful enough," replied Bobby Rogers. "I've had adventures sufficent during the last two days and nights to last me for an entire year ; but then I don't profess to be brave or to care about glory like you do, Evan."

"You know how to do your duty though when the danger arises, Bobby," said Jack Vere, encouragingly. "You have quite as much true courage as Evan, only it is of a less showy order. There is not much fear of your ever really showing the white feather."

"Thank you, sir, for your good opinion of me, I'm sure," replied Bobby, highly delighted. "I'll try to deserve it—I'll try very hard to deserve it, Mr. Jack, and if I have to fight, well, sir, I will fight, though there may be a dozen Afghans before me."

"All right, my lad, all right ; and now we must set out," said our hero.

Yet, when a group of officers saw Jack and his two little drummer-boy companions about to set forth to return unto Cabul, they gathered around them and asked the reason of their sudden departure.

Jack stated the cause.

And after submitting to a score of hearty hand pressures, and having to decline a drain from many a proffered flask, Jack Vere was suffered to take his departure, and away he went out of cantonments on to a road of danger and death with Bobby and Evan, one on each side of him.

CHAPTER XIV.

ONCE MORE IN CABUL—A DEATH TRAP

IT was a cool and invigorating morning, the sky without a cloud, and the snow-capped summits of the Hindoo Koosh mountains reflecting in bright rose tints the rays of the pale wintry sun beyond rose the frowning rock and fortress of the Bala Hissar, where the Kentish Buffs were quartered, surmounted by the Union Jack of old England.

Our three friends passed on with tolerably blithe hearts, for at all events the insurrection seemed to have been put down, the city being as silent as the grave, and the guns of the royal fortress equally still.

And yet Jack, somehow, had his misgivings ; he felt sure that some terrible danger was near at hand.

PRINCE ACKBAR KHAN IN HIS YOUTH.
Principal Conspirator against the English in 1843.

"JACK WRESTED THE TORCH FROM THE FELLOW AND FELLED HIM."

The gate is reached and the Gholandazees present arms.

It is all right then.

Jack Vere touches his shako brim with the forefinger of his right hand, and closely followed by Bobby and Evan, whose little brass drums are slung on their backs, enters the city as jauntily and easily as though they were going on parade.

Jack heard not the sound of the chuckling, and with difficulty repressed laughter of the mock Gholandazees in their rear who are merely wild and fanatical "fighters for religion," dressed up in murdered men's clothes, and placed there purposely to deceive the British in their cantonments.

But Bobby and Evan both distinguish it, and close up upon Jack with their suspicions still more aroused.

And it does not look as though the city were so very quiet either, now that they are actually within the walls, for they can hear the sounds of riot and debauchery borne to them on the wind from many directions.

And on some of the housetops, they can see the spiked heads of Europeans grinning horribly in death.

Jack Vere feels that at all events those ghastly emblems would not be there if Shah Soojah, our miserable puppet king, had in reality regained his rule over his revolted capital, and he begins to dread that somehow or other they are in a trap, with little chance of escaping out of it with their lives.

He tells nothing of his doubts and fears to Bobby or Evan, as he still hoped against hope that they were unfounded.

The streets they are traversing are deserted save by a pariah dog or two, and if this state of things continues for some ten minutes, they will have gained the outworks of the Bala Hissar and the protection of its guns.

But it is not doomed so to continue, for hardly have they left the Kohistan Gate a quarter of a mile in their rear when, round the corner of the long, narrow street they are traversing, turns a huge war elephant, covered in the most gorgeous trappings, and bearing in a state houdah on his back a swarthy native chieftain and a white officer clad in a light green uniform, with massive silver epaulets and wearing a silver helmet, on which was a two-headed eagle with wings expanded.

"By George, that's a Russian!" was Jack Vere's mental ejaculation.

And then he began to think of the terrible danger they were all three in, for the huge elephant took up the whole breadth of the narrow street that he was coming down, and on glancing back over his shoulder, Jack perceived that up it by the way that they entered was now coming an armed rabble of ferocious-looking Afghans.

They could not retreat or advance, therefore, without coming in contact with foes, for that those on the elephant were enemies they sufficently evinced by the way they brandished their weapons and shouted out—

"Death to the British dogs! Death, death!"

Even the officer in green and silver did nothing to allay this demonstration or cool the blood thirstiness of his Asiatic acquaintances.

He merely smiled and sat still, whilst the steel-capped Afghan noble plucked a pistol from his belt with either hand, " grinning like a Cheshire cat the while," as Bobby Rogers afterwards expressed it, and the mahout perched atop between the elephant's ears urged the unwieldy beast forward with his short iron probe or spear until it roared in its passion.

Well, here was a foe that they had never calculated on, one who would trample them out of shape with his huge feet, or take them up and brain them against the wall on either side with his flexible trunk, added to which there was the grinning Afghan chief to pepper them with his pistols or slash at them with his scimitar, and the Russian officer to perform something equally disagreeable if he had a mind, whilst in their rear a group of armed Afghans, who must have seen them and dogged their footsteps, were coming up at a run to see the sport, and, if occasion demanded, to take an active part therein as well.

" Here's an end to us at last," thought Jack, drawing his sword through instinct, though what he should do with it he didn't exactly know.

Bobby and Evan followed his example, and Bobby suggested—

"Couldn't we crawl under his belly and between his legs and come out on the other side?"

"He'd trample or gore us all to death whilst we were about it," replied Jack. "What shall we do?"

"I'll have a good slash at his trunk, and then, perhaps, in his pain he'll upset all those grand people on his back and give them a trampling instead, which'll be a comfort, anyhow, even if he serves us the same the very next moment," said little Evan ap Morgan, half-crying, yet as angry and spiteful as a young wasp.

"Here he comes," cried Bobby; "I'm dreadfully frightened, but I'll fight and help you till I'm killed, Evan."

And the noble little fellow stepped before Jack Vere and Evan.

The next instant the elephant was upon them, roaring lustily.

CHAPTER XV.

BEAUTY TO THE RESCUE—THE ESCAPE.

EVAN would not be behind Bobby, so setting his teeth hard, leapt forward ere Jack could restrain him, and made a fierce slash at the elephant's trunk, but the sagacious animal lifted it for an instant out of the way, and then lowering it again, caught the little Welsh drummer-boy around the waist, tossed him up as high as the housetops, and seizing him once more as he descended, shook him to and fro, till he lost breath and reason as well.

Meanwhile the Afghan chief had discharged both his long, single-barrelled pistols at Jack and Bobby, with what would have doubtless been deadly aim, but for the disturbing movements of the colossal beast beneath him, one bullet as it was grazing Jack Vere's right cheek, and the other carrying away Bobby's white wool epaulet, whilst the Russian officer clapped a gold-rimmed glass to his right eye, and surveyed the scene with close interest.

Evan's shriek of terror at this junction, caused Bobby to bring round his drum from his back to his side, and thunder on the sheepskin like mad, for he argued to himself that as it had frightened a tiger, so it might an elephant, and cause the immense brute to drop his little comrade to the ground.

But the Indian war-elephant knew the sound of drums well enough, and the noise seemed to increase his rage.

He began to trumpet his passion, and to dash the hapless Evan still more furiously about in the air, seeming to delight in his screams and his terror, though at the same time he refused to advance, and trample to death his victim's companions, considering perhaps that it would afford him more pleasure to destroy all three in detail.

But this did not seem to suit the impatience of the brute's riders.

"Urge him over them, whether he will or no. *Inshallah!* whose dogs are we that two accursed Feringhees should bar our path?"

"Death to the British curs!—death, death!" shouted the wild, Asiatic warrior, giving the mahout a knock across the ear with the flat of his velvet-sheathed scimitar, an attention which he hastened to pass on to the elephant, the flaps of whose big ears stretched back till they entirely concealed the mahout's legs.

Whack, whack, whack; thump, thump, thump! went the iron handle of the sharp goad or spear, and the animal evidently began to think that he was misbehaving himself, and he was just on the point of braining Evan ap Morgan against one of the walls, previous to trampling or goring to death his companions, when a little window let deep into the wall of one of the Afghan houses opened, and a bare white arm showed itself in company with a little delicate hand, that grasped a long-barrelled pistol.

Bang !

Then a puff of red fire and a flash of white smoke, and the elephant dropped Evan, and began to rear and plunge, trumpeting the while in anguish, for the bullet had entered his huge head somewhere.

"Come ; quick, quick, or it will be too late !" then cried an appealing voice, and Jack, casting one hurried glance at the window, perceived that the rough whitewashed stonework framed one of the most lovely faces that he had ever looked upon.

The next, however, he had sprung forward, and from under the very feet of the prancing and maddened elephant had plucked forth poor little Evan ap Morgan happily still alive, though as pale as a ghost.

"Bravo ! brave—brave !" ejaculated the same silvery but excited voice. "Pass him in ; I'll pull him through, and then be quick—oh, so quick !—or it will be too late."

Jack Vere did as he was bidden quickly enough, for, in truth, not a moment was to be lost.

He pushed the unconscious drummer-boy through the window—or rather aperture in the wall, for there was no glass in question—lifted Bobby Rogers up and then followed as quickly as ever he could himself, the elephant laying hold of and dragging off one boot as he did so, though happily not his leg along with it.

"Now secure and bar the window. I'll help," said the musical voice of their deliverer. "Another minute and you'd have been cut to pieces by the Afghan rabble."

That was true enough, for the whooping, howling cut-throats were by now close by, and lest the reader may fancy that they have been a long time coming up we must inform him that the incident it has taken us so long to describe took place in a couple of minutes at the most, and that the street was a long one.

Still there was not a moment to be lost, the more so as the fierce Oriental warrior, notwithstanding the continued plunging of the elephant, kept shouting—

"Seize the accursed Kaffirs and bring me their heads ! By my father's beard, they shall hang at my tent door until the vultures have picked them to the bone !"

"Oh, dear, dear ! they will get in before we have fortified the place and murder us," said the same sweet, musical voice, though with something of terror and anguish in its tone. "I'll help you with that bar. It's as heavy as lead, I know, though I took it down all by myself."

And in the deep gloom—for it was all but pitch dark now that the shutter was closed—Jack Vere felt a soft shoulder suddenly come in contact with his chin as he bent forward, and sweet, warm, fragrant breath upon his cheek.

The next instant the great clumsy iron bolt was shot into its sockets, and the window was fortified for the time.

And as they paused to breathe the fugitives could hear a deep, leviathan-like groan, followed by a heavy thud, and knew by it that the elephant had fallen.

"My dear young lady, your shot was a deadly one—it has killed the monster. I vow you are a regular little Joan of Arc, and have saved all our lives," said Jack.

"For the moment. But we are far from out of danger yet. This house is an empty one. I've been hiding in it ever since the dreadful massacre last night. How I escaped that I don't know. It is all like a hideous dream to me. I wonder I'm not mad."

"And so do I, for I was a witness of most of the horrors myself," said our hero.

At this juncture the yells of the savages outside swelled into an awful chorus, and then all at once the sound of fierce blows came against the closed window and door.

"They will be in upon us directly," said Jack. "Now, by Jove, what are we to do ?"

"I think I know," said the young girl ; "though I've only been in this place a few hours, I have discovered an underground passage leading into a temple of some sort. It may not be generally known."

"By George, no!" replied Jack. "Do lead the way, my dear young lady—for I know not what else to call you—and we will follow as closely as your shadow. Here, Bobby, help me up with poor Evan on my back and then toddle on in front."

All this was done in the darkness, and then their deliverer said—

"Give me your hand, Bobby, if that is your name, and your other hand or your coat tail to your officer, and then we shall all keep together."

"Now come on, for we have no time to lose."

Jack was sorry now that he had told Bobby to precede him, for he would have liked to have had that little hand in his own grasp and the possession of Bobby's coat tail in no way made up for it.

There was no help for it, however, and so on they went in the darkness ; their guide proceeding with the confidence of one who knew well her way, and invariably telling them to step up or down.

"She's a little brick, and no mistake," thought Jack to himself. "How I do long for a glimpse of light in order to catch sight of her again. I hope that we'll escape, if only for her sweet sake.

How noble it was of her to risk her life for us !"

And while he was thus communing with himself, the Afghans were banging away at the door and window-shutter with muskets, clubs, and bayonets.

A second later the crashing and rending of the wood was heard distinctly.

"Good Heaven ! they will be amongst us in another minute," gasped Jack.

They were going down a flight of rough uneven steps whilst he spoke, but their fair guide, never pausing, answered quietly—

"I think we shall be in time, though."

"What pluck that girl has got," quoth Jack, again to himself.

And hardly had he done so when he heard the striking of a match in front of him, and then a little earthern lamp glared into sudden life, lighting up the exquisite face and form of the girl, and revealing the fact that they stood in a little gloomy subterranean passage, in one corner of which stood on end a tall cask or barrel.

"Move that aside and you will see a hole big enough for all to crawl through. It will lead us straight into the temple that I told you of," said she.

Jack uttered an exclamation of satisfaction, and bounding forward moved aside the barrel.

CHAPTER XVI

THE TEMPLE OF THE GOD BOORA PENNA—THE FOE "THEY COME!"

THEN the fair girl crept through, lamp in hand, and Jack carrying in Evan ap Morgan for a few yards, put him down, and then with Bobby Rogers's help drew back the barrel until it re-covered the hole, after which Evan was picked up again, and they followed the lovely lamp bearer until they emerged from out the narrow earthly passage into a rock-hewn temple, at the further end

of which was a hideous idol having three heads and eight arms, and handling a sword.

The temple but for this huge and hideous stone monster, and a kind of flat altar in front of it, surrounded by a circular stone trough, was empty, but their guide walked fearlessly up to the idol, and even screwed herself behind it, beckoning to her companions to follow.

This they did unhesitatingly, and the next instant actually found themselves within the grim image, and able to look up into the interior of each of its three heads.

To their infinite surprise there was hung all round the inside of the idol weapons of various descriptions, though of strange and barbarous shapes, and some of them seemed to be encrusted with blood, whilst in its centre stood a small keg on which their fair guide had already seated herself, lamp in hand.

Jack Vere now perceived that she was about sixteen years of age, and even more lovely than he had at first imagined.

In form she was *petite* and slight, but of most perfect modelling, and her bare neck, and shoulders, and arms were plump and white as snow.

Her face was fair and oval, her eyes of the deepest violet, shaded by long dark, lashes, even whilst her hair was of the brightest gold, floating around her gleaming shoulders and descending to below her little handspan of a waist in a cascade of undulating ripples.

She was attired entirely in black, and looked as pure and interesting as she was lovely.

"And now let us thank you for our preservation, my dearest young lady, for we all assuredly would have been slain but for your courage and devotion," said Jack Vere, putting down the still unconscious Evan, and kneeling deferentially before her.

"Do not be so demonstrative, though," said she, "it looks theatrical. I have but acted as a soldier's daughter should do by soldiers; so do not say any more about it."

"Oh, but I must. You have acted so generously, so heroically. I really must tell you, for I may not have much time to do it in, how sweet it will be to pour out the last drop of my blood in your defence," persisted Jack, raising one of her little hands to his lips.

"Same here, miss," said Bobby Rogers, saluting; "I'm an awful coward, but I think I could fight for you, blest if I don't, just the same as I would for Master Jack there."

"I like your compliments the best of the two, my boy," said the young lady, smiling on the little drummer; "it doesn't seem so high flown though I daresay he's equally sincere."

"I will prove my fidelity if the Afghans permit me to live long enough," quoth Jack; "Bobby, you just see to Evan, will you. I am afraid the brave little chap is much hurt. He's your charge, remember."

"Poor boy. I hope he will soon recover. I don't think the Afghans will find us out here," quoth their preserver.

"I trust not, but from whence do you draw your conclusions?" asked our hero.

"From the idol that encloses us, and which tells me that this is a secret place of worship of the Khouds, a race abhorred by the Afghan Mussulmen, though 'tis well known that Cabul holds hundreds of these dark believers," was the reply.

"By Jove, you are a deeply read little philosopher and angel in one," said Jack.

"To prevent you calling me by names that cannot pertain to me, I will tell you my right one," said the young girl, rather proudly. "I am Rose Trevor, an orphan girl; my brave father having been slain in battle and my beloved mother having died of jungle fever all within two short months. Twelve hours ago I was the governess of Lady Burne's children, but now she and they are dead, and alone and friendless in the world I have already many times wished that I had perished with them."

As she finished speaking the poor girl set down her lamp and pressed her tiny hands before her face, but the tears trickled through her fingers and fell on her black dress, so intense was her grief.

"For Heaven's sake don't cry," said Jack. "Look here, Rose, I'll be a brother to you if you will accept me as one, and not pay you any more compliments, since you don't seem to like them, though, 'pon honour, I meant what I said."

"You speak more like a real friend now," said the poor girl, placing a hand in one of Jack's, who felt that he would have given the whole world to raise it to his lips and kiss it, but he contented himself with a warm grip, and then relinquished it again.

Bobby Rogers meanwhile did his very best to restore to consciousness his little comrade, Evan ap Morgan, and soon he was completely successful.

Evan had been much more frightened than hurt and save a few severe bruises he was all right.

"And—and have you killed the elephant?" was his first exclamation.

"Lor', no, Evan; we had enough to do to prevent the elephant from killing you. We'd never have done it either, but for that young lady. She saved us all, she did."

"Dear me," quoth Evan, not yet quite in his senses. "It isn't an angel, is it? She's exactly like one, isn't she, only I think prettier, prettier than the pictures at least?"

"There, Rose," said Jack, "you see I aren't the only flatterer. But what are you sitting on? You seem out of character as the presiding genius of a rum keg."

"It's a little powder barrel, Jack," was the reply, and the fair girl blushed as she called him by his Christian name for the first time; "I found it here when I first crept inside the idol, and having some matches with me, I resolved to blow myself and the hideous monster to atoms, rather than fall alive into the hands of the ruthless Afghans."

"Halloa! Joan of Arc again, though I don't mean to say that you did not resolve rightly. However, I with you think that they will not find us now, for they must have o'errun the house long ere this, and I quite concur in the opinion that the existence of this horrid temple has been kept a secret from the entire Mussulman population, who have as great a horror of false gods as us Christians."

"Especially such a one as this," responded Rose, with a shudder, "for unless I greatly mistake, this idol is the god Boora Penna, whom his deluded followers believed to have created all things by casting eight handfuls of earth around, one with each hand, I suppose, and to whom are offered human sacrifices."

"God of Heaven! how horrible!" ejaculated Jack. "Hence, I suppose, the stone altar and the deep trough around its foot. These men must be worse than Afghans."

"Yes, far worse," replied Rose Trevor, with blanched lips. "I have heard papa, who lived more than half his life in India, tell of their sacrifices in the city and in the forest; in the city, by cutting the throats of their victims, and in the forest by holding them over a slow fire. You may be sure that these weapons are stored here, ay, and this keg of powder as well, in order that they may be able to sell their lives dearly, should they be surprised at their awful practice by the followers of the prophet."

"Why, Rose, you are a perfect little Encyclopædia of Indian lore," said Jack.

"I have always taken a strange interest in the weird and the horrible, and hence, perhaps, I dreamed I was seized, lifted up, and crushed to death by an eight-armed, three-headed idol, just such as this one, only a few nights ago. No sooner had I looked round this temple than I recognised it as the one in which the idol of my dream stood."

"God grant that your dream comes not true," retorted Jack. "But then it cannot, or in it you would have seen me so crushed to death first, ay, and these two boys too, for I am sure that they as well as I would perish in your defence."

"Ay, that would I, at all events," quoth Evan ap Morgan, valorously.

"And I twice over, though I am such a coward," echoed Bobby Rogers.

"I hope I shan't have to put your gallantry to the test, my poor boys," said Rose, patting each of the little drummers on the head in turn, and then an expression of terror passed over her face as she placed a finger on her lips and said,

"Hark! hark! a great crowd is surely coming this way. Heavens! we are lost!"

And she was right, for the murdering Khouds were coming to their temple.

CHAPTER XVII.

ACKBAR KHAN AND THE RUSSIAN AGAIN—AN INFAMOUS BARGAIN.

THE next few minutes seemed like hours of agonised suspense to the four fugitives, for the footsteps and the voices were drawing nearer and nearer, and they could not doubt but that they were those of their pursuers, the fierce and remorseless Afghans.

"Blow out the lamp, Rose, or its light may betray us," said Jack, as calmly as he could.

"And if they discover us, shall we yield ourselves calmly up?" asked Rose, obeying him.

"No, dear, for that would be to invite insults, torture, and lastly, a horrible death. Give each of us a match. Bobby, turn the powder-barrel up. Evan, pull out the plug. Is it full? Oh, yes, I can feel that it is with my finger. Rose, you can guess what I contemplate doing."

"Yes, Jack, and be, it so. I have a match in my own hand, too. I am a soldier's daughter."

"Well spoken, dear. My first thought is to save you from the unclean touch of these devils' stepsons ; my next that the more of them we kill the less there will be left to massacre our brave fellows at the Bala Hissar and in cantonments. But now hush !—not another word !"

It was high time to subside into silence, for the intruders upon their privacy, whoever they were, were already entering the temple from the subterranean passage they had just themselves traversed, and the rock-hewn cavern was already aglow with the red light of their torches.

Then the fugitives in the idol discovered that there were eyelet-holes in different parts of the hideous god's body, doubtless intended for the priest who was performing the hanky-panky within to catch a sight through of his auditorium without.

They found these holes very useful in the present instance, for they enabled them to see everything that passed.

It was a dusky and a savage-looking multitude, indeed, that were streaming into the cavern.

They seemed to Jack Vere to be darker of hue than ordinary Afghans, but he soon ceased to notice this in boundless surprise at seeing that the Oriental chief and the green uniformed Russian officer whom they had last beheld on the back of the rearing and pain-maddened elephant were in their midst.

It appeared as though they were prisoners, too, for both looked pale, angry, and evidently ill at ease ; and those of the mob who were immediately around them had their weapons drawn, and appeared occasionally to menace them therewith.

This was strange.

What could it all mean?

Were the Afghans quarrelling amongst themselves ?

It was a greater puzzle even than that of such a grand Russian officer being in Cabul.

But the mystery was soon to be solved, and in a most simple manner, too ; for suddenly from out the crowd stepped a gaunt, big man, naked but for a white cloth around his loins, and with the eye of the Braminical god Siva—that eye that by winking once is said to have involved the world in darkness for a thousand years—painted in the centre of his forehead.

In his right hand he held a bare creese or long-bladed knife.

"Ackbar Khan, son of Dost Mohammed, whilom King of Afghanistan," said he, confronting the mailed Oriental chief ; "we have not brought you here to slay you, but that you shall listen to us."

"Could we not have listened to you outside this dark abode of Eblis?" replied the person addressed.

"The captain of thousands would not listen to the leader of hundreds."

"And so you brought me hither, thinking that you could compel me to listen to you? Well, say on, for he who is in the tiger's den must humour even its cubs."

"Thou wilt have to do more than humour us; thou wilt have to swear, ay, even on the Koran, that when thou hast driven those accursed British out of thy country, and installed thyself on the throne of thy ancestors, thou wilt permit us Khouds, the servants of Brama, to worship our gods in our own style, without molestation."

"I would rather die a thousand times than thus make infamous terms with the pagan and the unbeliever!"

"Fool!" hissed the Russian between his set teeth, and in the Persian tongue, which he rightly guessed that the followers of Brama would not understand. "Promise these fools whatever they ask, or we will never get out of their hands alive. Think you not that Allah will forgive the breaking of an oath made under pressure; for what saith the Koran—'Al harbu khudatum'—all war is fraud. Do I not quote truthfully?"

"Yes," replied Ackbar Khan; "I will swear to whatever they require; but I will make mental reservations in my own mind, and what is more, I will hold the holy book in my gloved hand and bite my thumb after having taken the oath, when it will cease to be binding."

And into the eyes of the wily Asiatic there came a sinister gleam.

He smiled, though, and promised all that was required of him, and confirmed those promises by the most solemn oaths.

But he took the book in a gloved hand, and he surreptitiously bit his thumb after.

"Now, oh Ackbar Khan," said the priest of Siva, "we are sure when thou comest to the throne of receiving justice at thy hands; say therefore what dost thou most desire."

"The destruction of every Feringhee dog in Afghanistan," was the retort.

"The very many of them we can deliver over unto destruction. Will that please thee?"

"Ay, verily, that will it. But explain, for it strikes me very forcibly at present,

that the followers of the prophet are capable of accomplishing their destruction."

"With the support of Russia—the moral support, I mean," interposed the officer in green.

"Ay," echoed the Afgan prince, with a laugh, "the moral support that takes the form of an unlimited supply of gunpowder and arms, together with a few thousand Cossacks, disguised.

"Hush!" quoth the wily emissary of the czar; "hush! It is not well that the secrets of the council chamber should be spoken of without its doors, especially to aliens."

"Providence has not saved us, and conducted us hither for nothing, Rose," whispered Jack, within the idol, to the most interesting of his three companions. "We have already heard much that will be most useful to our commander in-chief, and we shall hear more, but we must be as still as dormice."

His arm was around her waist, his short crisp curls against her rippling waves of gold.

But he pricked up his ears, and started, when he heard the priest exclaim—

"We worshippers of Boora Penna hold the key that unlocks the cabinet of the Bala Hissar. Without us, the conquest of the royal fortress and palace would cost thee five thousand men, but with our aid not a score. What thinkest thou of that?"

"Bismillah, prove but the truth of thy words, old man, and the protection of the Kings of Afghanistan shall be spread over thee and thy religion now and for evermore," exclaimed Ackbar Khan.

"May Brama confirm thy resolution, oh prince. There stands the god. Wouldst thou know what he predicts of thee?" said he, advancing towards the idol with some of his followers.

Jack and Rose saw him and stood with matches in their hands, prepared to blow themselves into eternity rather than fall into the clutches of those fiends.

"I would rather know how thou intendest to instal us in the Bala Hissar," responded Ackbar.

"Humour the priest; curb your impatience. Never lose a chance of turning into friends those whose alliance may be useful to you," whispered the Russian officer in the Afghan chief's ear.

"Ah, is that thy plan?" exclaimed Ackbar, regarding his colleague for a moment with angry suspicion, then he said to the priest of Brama—"Let your god speak!"

"Thou shalt hear and judge for thyself," said the priest, a gleam of satisfaction lighting up for a second his deep-sunken and bloodshot eyes. "*Hooleadroo, gokla ootradoog!*"

The last three words were uttered in a loud voice, accompanied by a stamp of the foot, and Jack and his friends in the idol found to their horror, that some one was pushing a way into it from the back, and the next instant would assuredly be amongst them.

"Shrink close against the walls," whispered Jack; "be still as death; hardly dare to breathe, and leave the rest to me."

There was no time to say more; the person or thing, which ever it was, was in their midst.

Ha! it breathed, it shook itself, it muttered, and "things do not mutter," Jack thought.

It was a rhyme that the creature was murmuring to himself, and Jack caught the words.

It was in the Afghan tongue, and freely translated, ran as follows—

> "Thy house, oh prince, shall proudly shit.
> The bulwark of thy gallant line;
> And glory crown thy lance and sword,
> And conquest hail thee for her lord.
> Nations shall follow in thy lead,
> Thy kingdom stretch from hill to water,
> If thou wilt honour Brama's creed,
> And wed thyself to Brama's daughter."

CHAPTER XVIII.

JACK INDULGES IN PROPHECY.

THE invisible being who had come amongst them—for it was too dark to obtain the slightest glimpse of his person, repeated this doggrel rhyme in the manner of a schoolboy muttering to himself a lesson to be sure that he is perfect in it before he goes up to the master's desk.

It was a wily prophecy, indeed, to come from the mouth, or rather from the belly of the god, for it promised as a reward of his doing so, that his dominion should extend beyond rugged Afghanistan, and over the greater portion of British India; and Ackbar Khan, the son of Dost Mohammed, was as ambitious as he was brave and bloodthirsty.

But Jack Vere was resolved that the idol should utter no such words, but instead, some of a very different meaning, so ascertaining where the verse mumbler's mouth was, from the direction from whence his foul breath came,

Jack clapped one hand upon it in a twinkling, and just as rapidly clutched with the fingers and thumb of the other the throat that was a little way below, garrotting its owner into unconsciousness.

Then Jack kicked his legs from under him, and dropped him on the ground, lastly tearing off his own silk scarf, and effectually gagging him with it, lest he should too quickly come to.

"Kneel over him, Bobby, drawn sword in hand, and whisper to him, should he show any signs of recovery, that at the slightest attempt to speak or move, you will slice his head off," murmured Jack in the little Kentish drummer-boy's ear. "And now hush!" he added, "till I've composed an Afghan prophecy, and made the god spout it."

The audience outside were evidently getting impatient that the god should spout something, for they were murmuring amongst themselves, and the old

Khoud priest with the eyes of Siva in the middle of his forehead, again bellowed—

"*Hooleadroog gokla ootradoog!*" which our hero didn't understand, but took it to be a petition to the god to prophesy.

He had taken from the grasp of the man he had just garrotted something that he had first imagined to be a species of bell-mouthed blunderbuss, but which he discovered to be a huge, horn-shaped tube, which he at once saw was intended to be used as a speaking-trumpet.

So he raised it to his lips, and roared forth the following—

"Thy cause, on prince, shall like a meteor bright,
Flash but to set in dark and endless night.
Beware the bear, who'll use thee as a paw,
Then cast thee helpless in the lion's jaw ;
That lion who shall turn in all his might
On those who've put his feeble cubs to flight ;
With teeth and talons he shall rend and tear
The foolish puppets of the Russian bear !"

Jack was almost frightened himself at the roar with which his words issued through the trumpet, and from the mouth of the hideous idol. That was nothing to the tumult that ensued within the temple.

"Curses on thy false deity and on thee also," roared Ackbar Khan, in a paroxysm of rage to the priest of Brama, though his bronzed face grew white as marble the while, for he was deeply sunk in superstition like all his race ; "will not rich gifts induce it to prophesy better things for me and mine than that ?"

"Doubtless, doubtless," retorted the astounded priest, as pale every whit as the Mohammedan chieftain.

He could not account for the blunder that Boora Penna had made, save by the supposition that its human inmate had been seized with the real gift of prophecy and been forced to give it utterance.

He proceeded to stammer and contradict himself all in a breath, until Ackbar Khan exclaimed passionately—

"How is the Bala Hissar to be won from these ghiours with the loss of only a score of men ? How is the place to be won ? I have taken my oath, now fulfil thine."

"Well, prince," began the Braminical priest, "there is a subterranean passage leading from this temple to the very summit of the highest ramparts of the Bala Hissar. In thy father, Dost Mohammed's day, rememberest thou not a rugged hole in the dell close to what they now call the Flagstaff Battery ?"

"Yes ; well, we used to call it the Cobra's Nest, so many of those deadly snakes dwelt therein."

"The British dogs have no great curiosity that way either, and doubtless for the same reasons," replied the Bramin. "Yet, you see that low browed arch over yonder ? Well, a narrow subterranean leads from thence underneath the city, and upwards through the solid rock into that very hole. Now do you see how the Bala Hissar is to be won and the British dogs killed ?"

"Ay," replied the Mohammedan prince, exultingly ; "and it shall so be won, and Shah Soojah, with his mock court and his British allies, shall all be put to the sword, I swear it ! The rocks of the Bala Hissar shall trickle over with English blood this night, and I will seat myself on the throne of my sires with the head of Shah Soojah for a footstool, and that despite the prophecy of thy god."

"The god will prophesy happier things, no doubt, when gifts have been laid upon his altar."

"And they shall be so laid—not out of gratitude to him, but to his priest. Khoud, my first act of sovereignty shall be to place thee in one of a pair of scales, and fill up the other with bags of gold until they exactly balance ; and every one of thy followers here assembled shall be weighted against bags of silver in the same manner. By Mahmoud, no man shall say that Ackbar Khan is ungrateful towards those who served him."

"Good," muttered the Russian officer, with a chuckle. "And you can make your gratitude come cheaper by weighing one man at a time in the scale minus his head, and then you can take your money back again."

"I mean it," said Ackbar, "by Allah and the holy prophet I do ! Stay you all here whilst I go and assemble the most trustworthy of my followers. The Kussilbashes I cannot trust, but I can lay my hands on three thousand men who will follow me to the death. Do you trust me ?"

"THE HUGE SNAKE JERKED HIS VICTIM UP INTO THE TREE."

There was a moment's silence, and then the chief priest, with the eye of Siva painted on his forehead, answered aloud for himself and his followers, saying—

"We trust thee."

A minute later and Ackbar Khan and the Russian officer, to whom he had addressed not a word since the prophecy of the idol, quitted the subterranean temple together.

CHAPTER XIX.

ROSE'S DESPERATE PROJECT—TOM DEFYING HALF A HUNDRED.

CONFOUND them, I wish they'd all gone!" muttered Jack. "But they evidently don't intend to leave the temple empty for a moment."

"We should attempt it nevertheless, Jack," whispered Rose; "warn your comrades, for if three out of the four of us lose our lives in the undertaking, yet that fourth might be the means of saving the whole garrison; and there can't be less than a hundred and fifty of our countrymen there."

"Rose, you are a little heroine. But if one of the victims should be your darling self?"

"Why shouldn't I have the privilege of offering up my life for my brave countrymen as well as a boy, Jack?" was the calm, quiet response.

"Oh, because you are so much more beautiful! Because we are of tougher mould and made to fight, and if need be, die in the defence of those who are dear to us," said Jack.

"There's a girl or a child being cruelly used even now, and in this very temple," replied Rose, with a finger to her lips; "hark how she screams! What can they be doing to her?"

They glanced through two or three of the little peep-holes in the idol, but could see nothing to account for the heart-rending screeches.

Upon Rose applying her eye, however, to one that was situated in a crease in the belly of the god, she beheld a sight that thrilled her with horror, and she fell back, half fainting, into Jack's arms.

Holding her in his embrace he glanced through the hole in turn, and saw the brutal Khouds in the act of sacrificing a white child on the altar of their deity.

She was a fair, lovely little thing of about six years of age, stripped nude as she was born, and her rounded limbs gleamed white as snow, as she writhed on the black marble slab in the still blacker clutch of her Braminical tormentors.

Two held her down, whilst a third drew her head back by its wealth of bright auburn hair, and a fourth pulled a long curved sacrificial knife from his striped cummurband and prepared to inflict a red gash across her little white throat.

Not a moment was to be lost if she was to be saved.

But how could she be rescued?

There were at least five hundred armed Khouds in the temple, and to boldly confront these in the poor screaming child's behalf would be sheer madness.

But luckily Jack bethought himself of the trumpet, that had already performed such marvels, and raising it to his lips he bellowed through it in rhyme—

"Away with her, the sacrifice is nauseous to my eye;
In the pathway to the Bala Hissar place her to starve and die!"

"Bravo, Jack! A good idea, and they are obeying the supposed command of their deity," said Rose, placing a hand on Jack's shoulder; "one man is carrying away the pretty little thing in his arms

Let him gain the subterran   and we will follow him."

"Follow him! How, Rose? We shall be hacked to pieces," rejoined Jack.

"No, I don't think we shall," replied Rose, quietly; "we must creep forth suddenly and make a bold dash for the subterranean, and in the following manner. You must glide forth first, seize the torch out of the hand of that Khoud who is standing clear in the shade of the idol. The instant you grasp it you must wave it wildly round your head, and make a screen of fire and smoke, sheltered by which we will come forth, Bobby and Evan carrying a keg of powder with bung-hole upwards, and I in its rear with a lighted match in my hand. You will gain my side, as quickly as you can, still grasping your torch, and then we will all walk backwards to the subterranean; you, Jack, yelling out what is in the barrel, which doubtless they know already, and that you will ignite it with one dash of your torch and blow ourselves and them up together should they dare to press on us or try to get in our rear. The subterranean gained we shall have but one foe behind us, the man with the child. You comprehend me?"

"Yes, capital. Not a moment is to be lost, dear Rose, for I believe they are approaching to inspect the interior of the idol. One kiss, Rose, and I'm off, to succeed or die."

He snatched the kiss from the sweet lips of pretty Rose, and the next instant had bounded out at the back of the idol, and was stealing with velvet tread towards the nearest torch-bearer.

He gained him unperceived.

He wrested the torch out of his grasp with one hand, and felled him to the earth with a straight English blow of his fist.

He dashed the flaring, tar-dropping flambeau round and round his head, causing the Khouds to recoil precipitately before it; and then glancing round and perceiving Rose and the two boys retreating, crab-fashion, towards the subterranean passage, the old priest of Brama had pointed out as leading upwards to the Bala Hissar, he sprang backwards with rapidity, gained Rose's side, and threw his arm round her.

The Khouds, recovering from their momentary consternation, sent up a frightful yell of rage directly they saw the small number of their foes, perceived where they had come from, and guessed how they had been hoodwinked in the matter of the prophesying idol.

Then, drawing their weapons with one clang and clash, they made a dash forward, determined to capture, and torture, and then slay the daring English.

Happily they carried no firearms of any description on their persons, and those inside the idol were of no use without the powder-keg that our friends had captured.

And over this powder-keg, the bung of which Rose held loosely, just in its receptacle, ready to draw it forth at an instant's notice, Jack Vere kept waving his flaring torch and shouting at the top of his voice—

"Come on, cowardly cut-throats, if you are tired of your lives! for rather than be taken, we will blow your temple, and your god, and yourselves to the clouds in our company."

"What say you, cowards?—do you accept the challenge?"

No, they didn't accept it.

Those black devils knew what Britons, when driven to desperation, were capable of—even British youths such as those who now braved and defied them.

And the five hundred cowered before our brave British lads.

Despite the dreadful peril Rose Trevor was as rigidly calm, yet as terrible in her anger, as one of the marble furies— even her snowy and expanded chest disdaining to rise and fall quicker than was its ordinary custom, whilst Jack Vere towered a head and shoulders above her, looking like a youthful Mars

Little Bobby and Evan retreated, standing with a hand each for the support of the powder barrel, and a hand each for the grasping of their swords, their cheeks meanwhile puffed out to the amplitude of cherubs.

Their foreheads were drawn down and wrinkled in frowns, until, indeed, their little twinkling eyes were scarcely visible.

And in this manner the dauntless four retreated, facing the hooting, howling, spitting, face-making, weapon-brandish- ing, but non-advancing enemy, until they were hid from the view in the windings of the dark passage.

CHAPTER XX.

THE RETREAT THROUGH THE SUBTERRANEAN PASSAGE—ATTACKED BY COBRAS.

WELL, Rose," said Jack, when they found themselves alone in the subterranean passage, though not knowing how soon they might not be pursued by matchlock-men, who would be able to shoot them down from, to themselves, a safe distance, "your scheme has succeeded admirably."

"Yes, Jack," replied Rose, calmly. "But now I think we may right about face, for we shall get on quicker than marching backwards."

"You are a heroine, Rose, and no mistake. It's almost a pity you aren't a boy, 'pon my word it is ; but then, perhaps, your courage would not be so remarkable," quoth Jack.

"I'm sure I was frightened enough, and my heart beats now like anything," interposed little Bobby. "I'm an awful coward, there's no gainsaying it—I haven't the pluck of a flea; but I'll fight."

"Oh Lor', Master Jack, take hold of this end of the keg for an instant in Heaven's name !"

And before Jack, Rose, or Evan could guess what ailed him, he had relinquished his hold of the barrel, and dashed forward through the subterranean passage as hard as he could tear.

"He's running away. Well, I didn't think he'd come quite to that," muttered Evan.

"There's no running away in that noble little fellow," retorted Jack.

At this minute there came the clash of steel from a little way up the passage, and the fugitives could see something black as ebony fall, and something white as snow whipped away from it by something in red.

A minute later, however, Bobby rejoined them, carrying in his arms the lovely little girl whom the Khouds had been going to sacrifice on their altar, covering her with kisses as he came along.

"Beautiful little creature," exclaimed he, gaspingly ; "I saw the black rascal hold her out with one hand and then draw his long knife to kill her. Look what a bruise his beastly black fingers have made on her pretty arm ! But I was in time, and I killed him, and oh, what a pleasure I did take in killing him, to be sure ! How could ever a devil have had the heart to hurt such as her ?" and the gallant Bobby kissed her again.

The child was in a swoon and knew nothing of all this.

"You are a little hero," said Jack ; "why the fellow who had charge of her was six feet high, my lad."

"I did not stop to count his inches or those of his knife," retorted Bobby ; "if I am an awful coward I wasn't going to let a pure little white dove like that be hurt by a monster, if I could prevent it by sacrificing my own life."

And Bobby looked at his brethren thoughtfully.

"You're no coward, my brave little fellow," replied Jack Vere, hardly able to repress a smile ; "but she is too heavy for you, and you don't seem to know how to hold her. Give her to me, for I can carry her with one arm, and you can return to your side of the powder-keg."

"Don't drop her, sir," said Bobby,

"for goodness' sake ; nor grasp her too tight, nor press her hard against your buttons or belt, or they will mark her—and she is so soft and white."

"All right," answered Jack, " I'll be as tender with her as though she were a butterfly or a dove. But let us get on, for no one knows how soon those fellows may be after us."

And so the retreat was continued, Jack carrying the little girl, who being as plump as a partridge was weighty though small.

The subterranean seemed endless, and in some places was so narrow that they had to proceed in Indian file.

At last the rugged pathway began to have a rise in it, and soon it grew to be a steep one, and the whole party knew by this that they were ascending inside the rocky cliff on which the royal fortress and palace of Shah Soojah were built.

Nothing had occurred yet to bar their way, save the clambering over the body of the Khoud whom Bobby had killed, nor were there any signs of their being pursued, for the disciples of Brama had evidently a wholesome fear of gunpowder.

Jack Vere had never yet thought of the cobras-de-capella, whose nest the priest of Brama had mentioned.

But yet the Cobra's Nest had to be passed on the way out.

It was to be hoped that the horrid reptiles had left their own lodging, or if not that, at all events, they would be in a sound sleep ; yet Jack knew from report that the cobras-de-capella were the most restless of snakes.

Well, he could hope for the best, that was all, and there was no occasion to terrify Rose.

Yet a slow and protracted hiss convinced Jack that the grim guardians of the subterranean were at hand, and would not let them pass.

"Rose," said Jack, in a murmur that he essayed hard to prevent being tremulous, " look straight before you, and go on without pausing, whatever happens ;" and then turning to the two boys he added—" You may drop that powder-keg now ; it can be of no further use to us,

but grasp your swords still, and look out for snakes—poisonous ones, my boys."

The opening out of the subterranean was now reached.

Rose passed on and was safe ; but just as Jack was about to follow her example, two hideous monsters glided out from cavities on different sides of the dark passage, and with sparkling eyes, quivering tongues, and inflated hoods, advanced simultaneously upon the young ensign.

Evan forced his way through, just as Jack dashed his torch in the face of one and caused it to recede ; but in doing so, a leg of the child he carried slipped under his arm, and revealed its dazzling whiteness to the view of the other monster.

He drew back his head to strike, disclosing his long and poison-laden fangs as he did so.

Bobby slashed at him with his sword, but his tough scales turned the edge of the weapon aside, causing it to drop from the drummer-boy's hand.

But Bobby neither ran away nor stopped to pick it up.

Jack Vere had not seen this second foe ; he was still confronting and making dabs with his torch at his other antagonist.

The child was still in imminent danger, and without a thought of his own deadly peril, Bobby flew at it bare handed and clasped it round the throat.

Boy and serpent rolled over together.

Hardly could Bobby prevent the horrible head from approaching his own.

Rose, turning suddenly round and perceiving the peril of her friends, uttered a piercing shriek, and ran back towards them.

"Catch the child ; I'll throw her to you, but come not a step nearer," sang out Jack.

" Oh, don't, sir ; don't. She'll fall and get hurt so," bellowed Bobby, still struggling like mad with the serpent, whom he felt to be rapidly getting the better of him.

But at this instant some one came bounding down into the little dell, passed Rose sword in hand, and in an instant off went the head of Bobby's adversary.

"'THIS IS YOUR WORK; YOU HAVE POISONED HER. WRETCH!' JACK EXCLAIMED."

Whilst Jack retreated out of sight, and springing up the bank he placed his beautiful little charge in Rose's hands, who kissing her first, next promptly rolled a fold of her dress over her smooth and gleaming body.

Then Bobby and the discomfited Evan came up out of the semi-darkness, one on each side of the young British officer, who had dashed so chivalrously to their rescue, and in whom Jack Vere now recognised his comrade Willie Dunbar.

"Why, where have you all come from?

We thought you dead; killed in the massacre last night," said he.

And then he doffed his shako to the young lady.

"We've come up a path which a few thousand Afghans will be traversing at our heels presently," said Jack. "When we've got a thirty-two pounder gun loaded with grape looking down the hole, and the garrison under arms, I'll tell you all about it.'

And Jack grasped Dunbar by the hand and wrung it warmly.

CHAPTER XXI.

JACK'S INTELLIGENCE, AND HOW IT WAS RECEIVED.

WILLIE DUNBAR was indeed surprised at what his friend Jack Vere told him.

"Why I'd no idea that that place was anything more than a snake-hole," said he.

"On the contrary," replied our hero; "it is a subterranean passage more than a mile long, and at its opposite extremity is a Braminical temple in which the followers of Ackbar Khan are doubtless at this instant assembling in their thousands."

"Come away to Major Tomlinson, then, without loss of time," said Willie Dunbar, "for I would not say if the enemy once gained a stand on the ramparts of the Bala Hissar that the shah's sixth foot and household cavalry would not at once join them."

"Well," said Jack, "we British must be ready to fight now. Come along, Rose, we are all in the same boat, and must keep up our hearts. Shall I carry the youngster again?"

"No, for you've nothing to wrap her in, and the air is cold and chill up here. Is there no officer's wife or grown-up daughter in the palace barracks?" replied Rose, wistfully.

"Why, no," said Willie Dunbar; "but there is Sergeant Baker's good woman, and she would answer much the same purpose, I should think, for she's a kindly sort of soul."

"Would you take this young lady to her?" said Jack, eagerly. "I would do so myself, only did I not at once report myself to Major Tomlinson as the bearer of such important news I should subject myself to a court-martial. Rose, dear Rose, you will not think me unkind, will you?" grasping her hand, fondly.

"I shouldn't like you at all, Jack, if you were to neglect duty for my sake; but there!" and she put up her rosebud lips to be kissed.

We need not tell with what rapture Jack's heart beat as he accepted the mute invitation, and a minute later, she was tripping away by Willie Dunbar's side, still bearing her lovely little invisible burden.

Jack Vere sighs at the disappearance of its bearer; Bobby and Evan then hurry to the officer's quarters and impatiently our hero demands to see Major Tomlinson, the commandant.

The major is in bed, rather fatigued from the hot work of the night before.

His head is wrapped up in a bandage and a glass of brandy pawnee is at his bedside.

He greets Jack as one risen from the dead, as do the little drummers' friends and acquaintances in the common barrack-room, whither they have repaired.

Jack has no time, however, to listen to congratulations on his safety, the moments are too precious, for it will never do for the followers of Ackbar Khan to catch them napping; and so stopping Major Tomlinson in the middle of a long-winded speech, he tells him briefly what has happened in the temple of Boora Penna, and how that the foe may be expected at any moment on the battlements of the Bala Hissar.

Major Tomlinson is out of bed like a shot on hearing the intelligence.

"Ackbar Khan, the son of King Dost Mohammed, in Cabul, and secretly supported by Russia," quoth he. "Then we may make up our minds that we are done for, Vere, for we had no earthly right to dethrone his father, and this young prince is just one that the warlike population will gather round."

"But have we not his father and brothers as prisoners, and hostages for his good conduct at Calcutta?" inquired our hero.

"And what would a younger son of Ackbar Khan's stamp care, think you, for the execution of his father and his elder brethren at our hands?"

"Come with me," said Jack, "we must to the artillery quarters at once, and beg a gun."

Major Anstruther, who was at the head of that branch of the service on the Bala Hissar, issued orders that a nine-pounder gun, for he hadn't the means or appliances at hand of moving a heavier piece of ordnance, should at once be placed in position to cover the entrance of the Cobra's Nest.

This was at once done, heaps of ammunition piled up beside it, and a formidable guard placed over it, many of the men being armed with hand-grenades, to be thrown in amongst the advancing foe directly they should show themselves.

These arrangements were almost complete, when who should suddenly appear on the scene but the king's shazadah, or master of horse, glittering in velvet and cloth of gold.

He had come to inquire the cause of the busy gathering at this point of the defences, which the king Shah Soojah had noticed from one of the windows of his zenana.

Major Tomlinson immediately explained to him the intelligence that Jack had brought, and a close and suspicious observer might have noticed a snake-like glitter brighten up for a brief second the eyes of the shazadah, and then die out again, leaving his dusky face as calm and inscrutable as before.

"Ah!" said he; "the same young officer who told a strange and improbable story to his majesty, and assured him at its close that there was no fear of our being able to hold our own, for that large British forces were rapidly approaching Cabul under Sahibs Pollock and Sale."

"Why, I've heard nothing of this!" exclaimed Major Tomlinson. "Can it be possible, I wonder?" Why didn't you rejoice us with the good news, since you possessed it, Vere?"

"I—I was premature—that, that is to say, I was in error. I have been sent back from camp especially to explain away my misstatements, that is to say, my mistakes to his majesty," stammered Jack, growing red and pallid by turns.

"You had better go at once, then—you had better accompany the shazadah," replied Major Tomlinson; "and when next we meet, tell me how you came to make the mistake."

Jack thus urged had no choice but to obey.

Sol Tal stamped his spurred heel upon the pavement, and declared, haughtily, that "the kings of Afghanistan had never yet accustomed themselves to be kept waiting."

So Jack tucked his sword under his arm, and with as good a grace as he could summon, strode on by his side.

CHAPTER XXII.

JACK'S PREDICAMENT—"OFF WITH HIS HEAD!"

AGAIN Jack thought that glances of hatred and malice were bent upon him by courtiers, officers, and guards, as he passed through the halls and corridors.

At last the presence chamber of the bloodthirsty puppet was reached, more bloodthirsty, arrogant, and unscrupulous through knowing that he was a puppet, and considered a necessary evil by the British.

He was seated on a pile of gold-embroidered, Persian silk cushions, and smoking a magnificent hookah, but at his crossed feet lay his drawn scimitar, and by his side his pistols, their stocks incrusted with gold and inlaid with gems.

His eyes lighted up when they rested on Jack, and he said impatiently—

"Ah, you have been sent to tell me the meaning of all this bustle and excitement on the ramparts—this movement of guns and activity of troops—wherefore is it?"

Jack told him in as few words as he possibly could, but Shah Soojah did not seem to be at all comforted by the preparations made to receive his rival hotly.

"If Ackbar Khan is in Cabul, backed by Russian influence and Russian gold, Ackbar Khan's cause will prevail, be assured of that," said he. "Our only hope lies in the immediate arrival of those British armies, under Sahibs Pollock and Sale, of whose approach you told me yesterday. How close think you they are now?"

"The young sahib seems to have deceived you in this matter, your majesty," interposed Sol Tal, bluntly; "I heard him own the British."

"*Inshallah*, what is this I hear?" exclaimed the Afghan king, springing to his feet and scowling malignantly; "a wilful misstatement, and to me? By the beard of the prophet, the insolence of the act passeth all understanding! Pray, young sahib, was the tale of the thirteen shroud-draped conspirators another of thy imagining?"

"Undoubtedly," muttered Sol Tal; "truth is a stranger to this boaster."

This uncalled-for remark, however, was resented by the monarch by throwing one of his high-heeled slippers at his prime minister's head.

The shot was a good one and brought the tears to the shazadah's eyes and a rubier fluid to his nose.

"Silence, slave," roared the monarch; "now, sir, give us the length and breadth of thy falsehoods, and that, too, without subterfuge."

"I am unaccustomed to lie, your majesty," said Jack Vere, haughtily; "the story of the shrouded conspirators and the severed hand that I told you yesterday was true. The latter must have been stolen from me after I entered the palace, as likely as not by the shazadah there."

"By Allah, by the blessed prophet, by the holy water in the well of Zuzul and the black stone of the Kaabaa, I swear 'twas not I who did it."

"Ah, dog, then you half admit that it was done?" roared his master.

"No, your highness, no. I know naught of it. The accusation was so sudden, so unexpected, that I was taken off my guard——"

"Silence, slave, before the sharpness of your tongue whips off your head," roared the incensed monarch again; "remember you are not at present under examination, whereas this young Englishman is. Now, sahib, you have told me one tale was true, but why did you lie to me in the other, eh?"

"I—I was driven to it, your majesty, in the hope, thereby, of prolonging the lives of the ladies of your zenana, whom you had cruelly resolved to slay lest they should fall into the hands of the foe," stammered Jack.

"By Allah, then no reinforcements are marching to the aid of Sahib Elphinstone? It is all a myth, a delusion; speak and answer me truly."

"Alas! we know of none, your majesty, though we still hope," sighed Jack.

"And Ackbar Khan, the son and heir of Dost Mohammed, is in Cabul, and with him a Russian chief of note. Always those Russians. Sahib, we are all lost. Ackbar Khan would never have thrown his sword into the scale unless he was assured of victory. Why there is a price upon his head—a lac of rupees. Would he dare to show himself here, think you, unless he was sure that every Afghan loved him too well to attempt to win it? Answer me!"

"I cannot because I cannot read Ackbar Khan's thoughts and fears. Methinks I have heard that he is brave, and he struggles for a prize well worth the winning," answered our hero calmly.

"Worth the winning? Ah! I have not found it worth even the acceptance."

"Your majesty, a little courage and all will yet be well," responded Jack.

"Courage! Do you accuse me of want of courage, ghiour?" screamed Shah Soojah, foaming at the mouth with rage. "By the blessed Koran you shall see how an Afghan king can die! I will have my courtiers, and captains, and commanders slain, and then I will give my palace to the flames, and perish amidst its ruins."

"Rather than face your foes like a man? Bah, that is not our way."

It was a bold speech of Jack's, but it seemed to be wrung from him.

Shah Soojah gazed at him with dilated eyes and frowning brow for an instant, and then he roared out to his shazadah—

"Give me your sword, and then pinion his arms. I am independent of the British now. They are too few and too weak to save me from my foes, and so at least they shall no longer insult me; that I am resolved. I will afford myself revenge at last. I will have his head. I swear it!"

The shazadah handed his monarch the sword quickly enough, but he did not evince half the haste to throw himself upon Jack.

"Wait a minute," said the king, to his great delight; "beat that gong to summon the Mother of the Maids. There are matters still more pressing than the death of an unclean dog to be attended to."

The gong was struck, and in almost immediate answer thereto, a curtain at the further end of the chamber was raised, and in glided a female so closely veiled that naught could be seen of her but her eyes.

"Zuleina, the hour has come," said the Afghan monarch. "You know what I mean. Let it be consummated without loss of time. Go!"

"She shall not go until I know what has to be consummated, at least," exclaimed Jack, in a voice trembling with suppressed passion. "If you mean to destroy in cold blood all the beautiful inmates of your harem, I will, at all events, offer up my life in the attempt to prevent it."

He made a dash towards the veiled female as he concluded, but with a cry she retreated.

He pursued her, but Shah Soojah raised a whistle to his lips and blew it, and the consequence was that when our hero raised the curtain behind which she had disappeared, his passage was barred by a dozen huge slaves at least, all armed with long pistols and tremendous scimitars.

"Bring him hither," roared Shah Soojah; "bring him hither and hold him steady while I whip off his head at a stroke! Do you hear me, dogs?"

They did hear, and were by no means slow to obey.

It was a job after their own hearts, and Jack was easily overmastered by such a number.

He gave himself up for lost.

But just as Shah Soojah was about to draw back his keen Damascus blade to strike, three British officers suddenly entered by the way that Jack and his guide had done, and the savage monarch stayed his hand.

CHAPTER XXIII.

A DESPERATE LEAP—THE MARCH OF THE LIGHT BOBS.

JACK recognised those who had entered the presence chamber of the king in an instant.

They were our envoy, Sir William McNaughten, in full Windsor diplomatic costume and court sword; Brigadier-General Shelton, the second in command of the troops in cantonments, and Colonel Cameron, the Scottish leader of Shah Soojah's irregular native horse, who performed the part of master of the ceremonies.

All three naturally stared to see a young British officer in the grasp of half-a-dozen of the king's hideous guard, and the monarch himself almost in the act of taking off his head, though he certainly sheathed his weapon with a smile on their entry.

"Your young countryman may thank your opportune arrival for his life," said he, not at all embarrassed. "He deceived me, lied to me, and what is more, acknowledged it, so you will own that I had good cause to be angry. However, he is forgiven. Go, sin no more, and may Allah protect you until you are amongst your own people!"

"Yes, go," Sir William McNaughten added in Jack's ear. "Your regiment has just received orders to march into cantonments. The game is up here, and we have only to think of saving what we can. It is rumoured that ten thousand Russian Cossacks are in Ackbar Khan's train, disguised as Afghans. We commence our retreat to-morrow, and have sought this interview with the king, in order to invite him to accompany us. His people would tear him in pieces the instant we were gone if we left him behind."

Oh, sir," quoth Jack, in the same undertone; "as a chivalrous British gentleman, secure the safety of the poor women as well. There are **two hundred, at least,** of them in his zenana, all under twenty, and all, according to report, beautiful. Yet he has just ordered the old hag, who goes by the name of the Mother of the Maids, to poison them all, or at all events I know that was what he meant."

"I will see to it—I will see to it, be assured," said the envoy; "but repair you to your regiment at once. Few officers are left alive."

Jack saluted and departed, with Sol Tal again as his guide.

Jack soon became aware that the shazadah was leading him altogether wrong.

He thought at first that it might be by a quicker means of exit, but at last found himself led into a spacious chamber that had no outlet at the other end.

And when half-a-dozen fellows came rushing in after him, with howls of rage and delight, and brandishing naked swords and daggers, he knew that his murder was contemplated.

To stop there would be to be killed.

The only possible means of escape seemed to be a leap out of one of the long lines of windows.

It was his only chance, however, so drawing his sword, and making a thrust at his treacherous conductor's gold-laced, ruby-dotted breast, and then a couple of slashes at the bare tawny throats of two Afghans who attempted to bar his course, he tripped up another, and thus clearing his way, crossed the room at a run, and gathering himself together rose at the leap.

Through the glass he went like a shot, making a precious clatter and din, and the next instant he had alighted on the topmost of the long flight of steps leading down to the terrace-walk on the ramparts.

Jack Vere went down those eight separate flights of marble steps somewhat swifter than they were in the habit of being descended, but some jezail bullets took the descent quicker still, one going through his shako and another carrying away an epaulet.

He would assuredly have been hit, but for the gathering shades of evening.

"Hang it, this is warm work," thought Jack.

He found his regiment paraded in heavy marching order, when he reached that part of the broad ramparts where the barracks were situated.

Our hero's whole thought and anxiety began now to centre on Rose Trevor, whom he saw in the centre of the regiment, along with the sergeant's wife, who carried the little girl they had rescued.

She was warmly clad and muffled up now, as was Rose.

It was impossible for Jack to get near enough to Rose to speak to her, for he had to keep on the flank of his company, but he greeted her with a wave of the hand, as did Bobby Rogers the lovely child, and both greetings were smilingly acknowledged.

As they waited there for the order to march, Shah Soojah's 6th Native Infantry, about nine hundred strong, and the troopers of his native cavalry, five hundred more at the very least, looked down upon them from the heights above, and gibed and taunted them at deserting the cause they had come to Afghanistan to uphold, calling them dogs, cowards, and so forth.

"By George," Jack heard Captain Faulkner say to Major Tomlinson, "these fellows who have eaten salt with us would feel even a greater pleasure in cutting our throats."

"I wish the envoy would make haste and rejoin us," was the reply; "I shouldn't wonder were these rascals to spring at our throats, without a moment's warning."

"For Heaven's sake, Tomlinson, don't prognosticate still further misfortunes! they are already falling as thickly around us as these accursed snow flakes," said Captain Freeman.

This was not enlivening conversation to have to listen to, and Bobby Rogers, looking up to his friend and protector, Jack, said with a shudder—

"Oh, isn't this awful! Hark to the mob out on the plain! I believe that thousands are waiting to murder us. We are not to play our drums even, only fancy that!"

"Well, Bobby, it wouldn't exactly be sensible to attract them towards us, and thus openly invite them to cut our throats, would it?" said Jack, as cheerfully as he could.

"No, sir, only I always feel bolder when I'm rattling away at my drum. I do hope Miss Rose won't get hurt, or the little one. I wish I knew what her name was. She looks very pretty, don't she, sir?"

"She looks a beautiful little thing, certainly; but hark! there is six o'clock striking, and here comes the envoy and the brigadier. Cameron stays behind with his regiment, of course, for he has been in Shah Soojah's service for years," said Jack Vere, half to himself.

The faces of the envoy and of the brigadier were very grave, as the ranks of the Kentish Light Bobs opened to receive them.

When they had closed in around them again, like a hedge of gleaming steel, the order was given to march, and away they went as one man, the colours cased, and with no music but the dull tramp, tramp, tramp, of their feet down the winding pathway.

Then the great port, or gateway, is reached, a massive iron structure let into the thickness of the rock, with cannon ever loaded and pointed outwards.

But the gates are thrown open, and the British infantry issues forth, the Afghan soldiers of Shah Soojah banging them to in their rear, and derisively cheering them the instant that the rearmost file of the gallant British have marched on.

The instant that cheer is heard it meets with a thundering response from thrice as many throats, and the streets, which a moment before looked as though empty, suddenly swarm with dusky faces and forms, all pressing on, on, for the Bala Hissar!

A Coloured Picture for binding with the work is Given Away with this Number.

ENGLISH JACK AMONGST THE AFGHANS. No. 6 "BOYS OF ENGLAND" EDITION. PRICE ONE PENNY. PUBLISHED AT 173, FLEET STREET E.C.

"'ROSE, DEAR ROSE,' SAID JACK, WILDLY; 'RECALL THOSE WORDS! YOU SHALL NOT GO.'"

Demon-like are the faces with their great rolling eyes, and gleaming white teeth, or rather fangs, for they looked as though they could rend and tear, whilst swords and knives, jezails, and match-locks are raised on high, and the very heavens seem to echo with the cry and shout of "Death to the English!"

"On—on to the palace!"

But at the first taste of cold British steel they broke in front, and suffered the head of the column to push on, making up, however, as they swept on and past, by striking and thrusting wildly with their hiltless swords, and long double-edged creases.

Scores of them were slaughtered with the bayonet, but our troops forbore to fire, lest the noise should attract thousands more of the black fiends to the spot.

And thus the English soldiers pushed on and on through the streets, losing many of their number on the way.

CHAPTER XXIV.

WOUNDED AND ALONE—A STRANGE FOE, AND STRANGER ALLY.

ON reaching the Kohistan Gate they found it open and unguarded, and so the column pressed in, and on gaining the plain, they could see the lights of the British cantonments only a couple of miles across it, beaming forth a dim and foggy welcome.

They naturally thought that the worst was over now, and the order was issued for the drums and fifes to play a quick-step, in order to give spirit to the troops.

But hardly had the music struck up when it was drowned by yells so loud and deep, that it made the blood of our gallant fellows run cold.

The next instant, the solid ground seemed to shake 'neath the thundering gallop of countless horses, and the dusky snow-laden sky, to be full of flashing spear-heads and brandished scimitar blades.

The cries of "Allah Ackbar! Allah Ackbar!" showed them clearly by whom they were attacked; next they heard their own officers shouting to form rally-ing square.

Then it was waving spears, grinning, fiendish faces, oaths, battle-cries, and pistol shots on all sides of them.

One glance to assure himself that Rose was in the very centre of the compact ring of British steel, and out of reach of the Afghan lance, and Jack Vere fought like a tiger.

And roared very like one, too, in his encouragement of his men.

There is no need to tell our readers that the Kentish Light Bobs fought well —for when did British Infantry ever fight otherwise?—and the royal artillery-men, who were all mixed up in their ranks seconded them nobly.

Yet, what can hundreds do on an open plain, when assailed by thousands, and though Jack Vere in common with the rest fought like a paladin of old, he at last sank to the ground beneath a blow from an Afghan, in whom he recognised Ackbar Khan.

* * * * *

When Jack Vere recovered conscious-ness he found himself apparently amidst a heap of dead.

He put his hand up to his head and withdrew it covered with blood.

Then he looked around him, and saw the full moon looking coldly down from a cloud, a solitary date-tree rising spectre-like up out of the plain near at hand, and single mounted figures crossing it to and fro in different directions

Jack presently perceived that they were Afghan horsemen riding about and spearing the wounded.

Scarcely had he made the terrible discovery when he heard the quick pad, pad, pad of a horse's feet fall upon the plain, and glancing round saw that one of the villains was approaching him at a gallop, doubtless having noticed him raise himself on to his elbow.

Jack picked up his sword, but it was broken short off at the hilt.

He then felt for his pistols but found them uncharged, and the Asiatic horseman was approaching him lance in rest with the fleetness of the wind.

Another minute and he would be pinned to death.

There was no time to look around, for the Afghan was already upon him.

A most unexpected ally was to be raised up, or rather to drop down to the assistance of our hero, however, for just as the dusky warrior shot beneath the outspreading branches of the date-tree like a thunderbolt, and just as his cruel lance-point, already gore dripping with innumerable murders, was within a few lengths of his head a huge corkscrew-shaped bough seemed to fall on him, and curl round him and lift him out of his saddle with irresistible force.

"Good God, it's a boa-constrictor!" exclaimed Jack to himself, as the hideous monster, holding his victim firmly in his embrace, looked him in the face, with distended jaw.

Jack couldn't move for the life of him; he was awe-struck.

The Afghan's horse dashed past him with the fleetness of the wind, and actually shrieking in its terror, but Jack could only listen to the cracking and snapping of the bones of his late rider, as the at least thirty feet long snake crunched him to pulp in its folds.

The victim's face lost all resemblance to humanity; blood spouted out of him, even through his clothes in different places, and last of all the boa-constrictor jerked his head and body, with the mass of dead humanity that it enclosed, up amongst the topmost branches of the tree.

Where it lay in a huge heap, supported by three great forked boughs, licking its prey, and uttering a kind of harsh purr, preliminary to supping on it.

Jack Vere struggled to his feet, and then looked wildly around him.

The other horsemen had moved further away. There was no deadly danger near at hand. He glanced towards the cantonments.

They were still a good mile and a half away, while the city walls were but a quarter of a mile distant on his right.

A cold bleak wind swept over the plain.

The snow soon covered the heap of dead amongst which Jack had been lying as with a pall, for they all seemed to be dead; there was not a movement amongst the lot.

Suddenly Jack caught sight of a little fellow lying on his face, with a sword in his hand, and a drum slung upon his back.

A dead Afghan had fallen across him.

In an instant he had recognised Bobby Rogers, and, weak as he was, plucked him forth.

He placed a hand alternately on his pulse and heart.

Both beat.

"Bobby," said he, giving him a shake, "you aren't nearly dead yet. Open your eyes and say what's the matter!"

"Don't; leave me alone; it ain't time to get up yet, never fear," was the grumbled response.

"I'll be shot if he hasn't been asleep," muttered Jack. "Well, that is strange."

"Halloa, Mr. Vere, is that you? Then we aren't all killed?" said Bobby at this juncture.

"All killed? No, of course not; though I thought that you were, my boy."

"Oh Mr. Vere, I fought as well as I could—I did, indeed, though I am such a coward. But one of our fellows knocked me down in falling, and he was such a heavy man that I couldn't get up again; and so I suppose the cold made me go to sleep; I don't know."

"Yes, Bobby, that was it. 'Twas a big fellow that lay across you. I could only see your head and the drum, and could hardly drag you free of him. However, you are on your pins now, and, I must say, very much alive indeed."

"What's that great thing up in that tree, Mr. Jack? I declare it's moving."

" Oh, never mind it," replied our hero, with a glance of affright towards the topmost branches of the tree. " We must try to get on to the cantonments, Bobby. Will you be able to walk so far, do you think, my boy ?"

" Well, I will try, sir, though my legs are tired and stiff, I own," was the retort.

" Oh, that's from their having been lain on. It will wear off with every step you take. Now, then, off we go. Oh !"

Jack reeled and would have fallen, had not Bobby somehow kept him up.

" Oh, sir," said he, gazing towards the camp, " we'd better lie down again, for here comes a lot of the enemy this way all on horseback.

CHAPTER XXV.

FRIENDS OR FOES—THE PYTHON NO LONGER AN ALLY.

AS may readily be imagined, Jack Vere was not slow to take Bobby Rogers's advice, for they were by no means in a position to bid defiance to the approaching Afghan cavalcade.

It was coming straight towards the spot where they lay crouching in fear of their lives—a score of savage-looking warriors, with turbaned or steel-capped heads, and tasselled spears, which in the moonlight gleamed like frosted silver.

At their head rode a slim, youthful figure, with long waving hair, and a boy who, to Jack and Bobby's infinite surprise, had a drum slung on his back.

" Rose and Evan," ejaculated our hero, when they had approached a little nearer ; " and oh, horror ! they are in the power of the Afghans. Better that Rose, at least, were dead."

" Ah, Master Jack, that it would be, for they'll torture them to death in the end, for certainty. Oh dear, isn't it awful, and my poor chum, little Evan, too ! We shall surely be killed, too."

" Yes, Bobby ; for they'll spear all they see to discover whether there's any life left in them ; and I daresay we shan't be able to help making some sound the first time the cold steel goes through us."

" Well, sir, I'll be as brave as I can, for the honour of old Yorkshire. By George, sir, there's someone calling us

by name ! It's Evan ap Morgan that is doing it."

" And Rose, too," echoed Jack. " Oh Bobby, killed or not killed, I must go to her when she calls me ! I daresay the villains have promised that they won't kill us, and that she believes them, poor dear, being all goodness and kindness of heart herself. However that may be, she calls and I obey her as though she were my guardian angel."

" And I, too, sir ; for perhaps she has still the little white-skinned angel girl in her arms, and I might be able somehow to die for her, who knows ?" and the boy and the youth staggered simultaneously to their feet, both embued by the magic power of love.

Each expected to fall beneath a dozen spear thrusts ; but each expected to catch a glimpse of her he loved best in the world ere he fell, and that was enough.

But they did not so fall, for each was bewildered and surprised to be received by a joyous cry from Rose, and a triumphant shout from little Evan, and the next instant the fair girl had leapt from her horse and thrown herself in Jack's arms.

" Jack, Jack, these are not foes but friends," said she, breathlessly. " It was my idea to have them dressed up so, in order that they might succour and carry in our wounded without inviting an attack from the Afghans, who continually scour the plains. The general approved it, and there were enough and to spare of dead Afghans close up to the cantonments' walls, to supply the disguises. Those who wear them are brave British dragoons, and I and Evan led them straight to this spot. Didn't we Evan?"

"Yes, miss; and you recollected it better than I did, a precious sight!"

"Oh Jack, I saw you fall, though not before you had killed, at least, three of the foe. I wanted to stay behind and take my chance of life with you; but they wouldn't let me; and then I thought that none could carry the child so gently as I could. But I resolved to come back and recover you dead or alive."

"How good, how noble, how generous of you!" said Jack, raising her hand to his lips.

"No, only comrade like. And we are comrades, ain't we?"

"Yes, dearest, through life," rejoined Jack, "if you will only let it be so."

Ere Rose could make any reply, there was a cry of horror amongst the dragoons.

Then they divided to right and to left, forming an avenue, and down this avenue Jack and Rose saw coming, in at least forty feet length of undulating ripple, and with his huge head at an altitude of ten feet from the ground, the horrible boa-constrictor that had devoured the Afghan chief.

In vain the dragoons, seeing the fearful and imminent danger that threatened the girl and youth, made furious digs at it with their lance-points as it passed along.

Their horses would seldom let them get within reach of the monster, so that the mere skin-deep wounds that he now received, only irritated him still more, and he uttered a kind of roar, not at all like a wild beast's, as he opened wide a mouth big enough to take in a man.

Jack threw his left arm round Rose's waist, for there was no time to get away; and with his right he drew a sword he had taken from one of the dead, and stood on guard, determined to make a fight of it.

He could feel the heart of her he loved palpitating against his own, and that braced his nerves as nothing else would have done.

They would die in each other's embrace anyhow.

The dragoons could evidently render them no assistance.

Evan ap Morgan had been pitched over his horse's head, and had fallen headforemost into his own drum, so that he was eclipsed, as it were, and couldn't extricate himself, struggle as hard as ever he could.

But Bobby Rogers on the other hand had crept upon the other side of Rose, determined with his three feet of Sheffield steel, forged by his own father, to do that father and his native town honour.

In far less time than it has taken to tell all this, the python was upon them, his hideous mouth open wide enough to take them both in at a gulph—a fearful and terrible foe indeed.

But as that huge head swooped downwards, Jack smote at it so heartily, that it uprose again with a stream of blood trickling from its leathery under-lip.

Then Bobby Rogers flew at it in turn, striking at it, wherever he could reach, with all his might and main, being too frightened, as he afterwards expressed himself, to leave off.

And upon this, Jack, letting go of Rose, advanced on it again, whilst at the same instant one of the dragoons, having at last managed to dismount, also rushed up to the leviathan, and drove his sharp lance through its head, till it came out a yard on the other side.

It was a case of keeping clear of its coils then, for four or five minutes, so fearfully did he lash himself about on the ground; the end of it, however, was that the horrible reptile at last succumbed to superior numbers, and thought fit to give up the ghost.

"Oh Jack," said Rose, "I thought it was all over with us then," and she shuddered.

"Well, dear," quoth our hero, "and so did I. Bobby here did certainly half the killing. Bobby have you made up your mind to eclipse the deeds of Jack the Giant Killer, eh?"

"Lor', no sir; I'm too big a coward

for that. Fancy me tackling a giant with three heads. Why, I'd run a mile rather than set eyes upon such a monster."

"I'd sooner confront three giants with three heads apiece than another monster like this," said Jack; "but see, they have begun to search for the wounded. I wonder if any more poor fellows are alive?"

No. All else had been despatched after they had fallen, the majority having had their heads sliced off by the razor-keen Afghan knives, for it is against the Afghan creed to give quarter.

So at last the dragoons betook themselves to their horses again, and with Rose and Jack riding double, and Bobby and Evan ditto, they bent their way back to the British cantonments.

CHAPTER XXVI.

COLD AND HUNGER—WHAT WILL HAPPEN NEXT?

DAY was just dawning, and the appearance of the British cantonments was miserable and wretched in the extreme.

Sleet and snow lay thinly on the ground.

No wreaths of cheerful smoke rose in the keen frosty air, for every fragment of firewood had been long since used up, and it was evident that the troops, especially the Sepoy infantry, who had never before in their lives seen frost or snow, were so benumbed by it, that they could hardly grasp their weapons.

It was pitiful to see the sentries at their posts, shivering in their thin summer clothing, and already showing by the gaunt angularity of their frames, how near they were to starvation.

From the long lines of huts, too, as they rode along, came the wailing of children and sobbing of women.

"Are those Afghans in your fort?" asked Jack Vere, of one of the disguised dragoons, who rode at his side; "surely I must be mistaken, yet I thought I saw black faces."

"Alas, sir, you are right," said the man; "they captured it yesterday from us, and with it our stores for the next six weeks. We have rations but for four days and a half left in camp now, and when they are gone, God alone knows what will become of us."

"Why, that was a commissariat store, and within fifty yards of the cantonment walls! However came General Elphinstone to let it fall into the hands of the enemy?"

"Everything's of a piece here now, sir. The general is in his dotage, and through an extra twinge of the gout, or something of the kind, didn't reinforce the garrison until it was too late. The Afghans swarmed into it hundreds at a time, and its garrison of twenty-five men were put to the sword. We are now quite at the mercy of the barbarians, sir; for Ackbar Khan has stuck up decrees all over the country threatening torture and death to all villagers supplying us with food. We are in a very bad way, sir."

"You are, indeed. Why those fellows in that fort can look right down into our cantonments and look all over them, and if they only had some light howitzers up there, they could knock down these rows of huts like houses built of cards."

"That could they, sir. And they are near enough to chaff and taunt our poor fellows as well. They hold out all sorts of tempting food towards our half-famished sentries, and eat it themselves, and sometimes they will shout—'Look out for a loaf!' and then instead of bread thrown over the cantonment wall, the gory head of one of our poor fellows who held the place against them. Oh, sir, it's down-right awful," and the dragoon frowned.

"And is there no talk of falling back on Jellalabad?" asked Jack, eagerly.

"Plenty of talk, sir, but very little do. The wretches hold out to us that the vultures and the jackals are waiting to pick our bones in the Cabul Passes. 'Here comes your winding-sheet—do you think it'll be big enough?' they yelled last evening directly the snow began to fall, and they've been at it ever since, the fiends."

"We'll alter the colour of it with their blood before it enfolds us anyway," said Jack; "it shall be a crimson and not a white one, by Jove, it shall!"

"Bravo, sir, and so I say," replied the trooper. "Ah, sir, if we had Sir Robert Sale here, he'd get us out of the mess even now, someway. But as it is—well, sir, as it is, all hope is passed."

The party had by this time come to a halt, and nothing was left but for Jack Vere and his companions to dismount and go their way.

The former they did, but then the question arose which way they were to go, which was decided by Rose saying—

"Your regiment, or what remains of it, dear Jack, is cantoned over there in the next row but one on the right; but I was to repair on my return to the general's villa, where are Lady Sale and Lady McNaughten, with my other hap-less companions."

"Then I will escort you, at all events as far as the general's," said Jack.

"If you please, miss, is the little girl there too?" asked Bobby, rather sheep-ishly.

"Yes, and getting on nicely. You must come up and see her later in the day."

"And—and is she a young lady, miss, or a soldier's daughter?" stammered Bobby.

"She's the youngest child of Captain Foster of the dragoons," answered Rose.

"Oh, then, she'll never think of me."

"I should think that, on the contrary, she'd be grateful to you as long as she lived," answered Rose. "Do you think that officers' daughters are less grateful than soldiers'?"

"Oh, no, miss; but I don't care about her gratitude. I want her love!" blurted out Bob.

"Well, she will love you very dearly, no doubt."

"Ah, that will be nice, miss, though I don't think you know exactly what I mean."

"Oh Miss Rose," put in Evan ap Morgan, at this juncture, "can you tell me anything about another little girl that we saved, that we brought in last night. She was frightened into being mad, I believe."

"Yes, I've seen her, too, and you'll be glad to hear that her reason and memory are returning. She takes notice of things and calls them by their right names."

"Hurrah! that's fine!" said Evan. "And you think she'll get all right again?"

"The doctor says as much, my boy," replied Rose Trevor, with a smile.

"Now that you've had so many ques-tions answered, you must trot off to quarters," said Jack. "I shall see you both during the day."

With this promise poor Bobby and Evan were forced to be content, and, knowing that Jack Vere was their officer as well as their friend, off they went with-out a murmur, first, however, favouring Rose with a military salute.

As Jack and Rose wended their way through the huts towards the general's house, many and many a scene of painful distress did they witness.

Troop and baggage horses falling to the ground from very weakness.

Half-starving women and children hunting amidst heaps of dirt and refuse for bones that even the parish dog had passed over as worthless.

At last their destination was reached, and what was Jack's surprise to behold outside the general's residence a troop of mounted Afghans, clad in splendid ap-parel, and evidently forming the body-guard of some great chief.

"What can this mean?" quoth our hero, in amaze. "Can you guess, Rose?"

"No, Jack, no; but it looks like the shadow of coming evil. My heart seemed to stand still when my eyes rested on those men."

They entered the villa by a side door, and Rose, who seemed to know the house by heart, led Jack straight into a room in which some half-dozen ladies were seated, with expressions of blank despair upon their countenances.

"Well, I have succeeded ; here he is," said Rose, as they entered the apartment.

Its occupants all smiled upon her, but sadly.

They all shook hands with Jack, and the two senior ladies patted Rose on the cheek and head, and called her "a brave, dear girl."

Seeing, however, the frightened look in their faces, she asked them what was the matter, and they replied that Ackbar Khan had come into camp under a flag of truce, and to demand, they thought, the surrender of all the English ladies into his hands, as a condition of allowing the army to depart unmolested for the frontier of India.

"The villain !" exclaimed Jack. "Were I General Elphinstone, I would give him his deserts by blowing him from the mouth of a nine-pounder gun !"

"Hush ! lest he may hear you," said Lady McNaughten. "Just draw aside the folds of that curtain ever so gently, and we will be able to catch a glimpse of this human tiger."

CHAPTER XXVII.

THE CONFERENCE AT THE GENERAL'S VILLA.

JACK VERE did so, and Rose crept behind him and peered over his shoulder.

They were thus enabled to look through a narrow slit of window pane into the adjoining apartment, where old General Elphinstone, his second in command, Brigadier Shelton, and Sir William McNaughten, sat on one side of a plain deal table and Ackbar Khan and two fierce-looking chieftains on the other.

Prince Ackbar, a perfect model of a man and warrior, for he was upwards of six feet in height, and broad-chested and muscular in proportion, was gorgeously attired in camise of scarlet cloth covered with gold lace and pearls, which he wore over his closely-fitting coat of ringed mail, which glittered like silver and yielded to every motion of his form.

His helmet, or cap of steel, was bright enough to serve for a looking-glass as well as a head-piece, which no doubt it did, and in his thick sash of twisted silk were thrust an ivory-hilted scimitar, whose velvet sheath flashed with gems, a poniard, and a brace of superb pistols, which in friendly times had been the gift of Sir William McNaughten.

His two companions wore the high fur caps with red flaps from which they derived their name, Kussilbash, meaning literally red cap, and their stalwart forms were attired in blouses of scarlet stuff.

The countenances of these three Asiatics wore an expression of savage exultation.

And those of the three British officers corresponding ones of doubt.

Old General Elphinstone sat with his bandaged gouty foot resting on another chair ; Brigadier Shelton's dark brows met in a frown as he hacked pieces out of the edge of the table, with a somewhat formidable clasp knife, and Sir William McNaughten betrayed his agitation by tearing into minute fragments a sheet of paper he held in his hands.

"Well, sahib, your answer?" exclaimed Ackbar Khan, after a pause.

"Kindly state your proposition over again. It so astounded us at a first hearing that we could hardly grasp it in its entirety," rejoined Sir William Mc-Naughten.

"By the prophet, methinks it is simple enough," was the savage rejoinder. "It is your only chance of saving your army, yourselves, and your families from extermination. Do you hear me, from extermination, for the confederated chieftains have sworn that no man, nor woman, nor boy, nor girl, nor child, nor babe of all your host shall ever live to quit Afghanistan."

"But our men are brave, they are unconquerable, and as a single ship rides out a gale in which she is assailed by the buffets of ten thousand waves, so shall our one army, though small, push on, no matter by how many it is attacked on the way," said Brigadier Shelton, giving such a dig at the table that his knife-blade snapped off short.

"An omen," laughed Ackbar Khan, pointing towards it; "an omen; for so is snapped off British rule in Afghanistan, and you are doomed to destruction."

"How are we doomed to destruction?" demanded Shelton.

"Cold, and hunger, and starvation will destroy you in the narrow mountain gorges; your troops will be slain in scores and hundreds by rocks hurled down upon them from above, fair women and helpless children sharing the same fate! What think you of that my brave British?"

And the monster smiled grimly.

"For Heaven's sake cease, or rather tell us again how we can avoid all these horrors," said Sir William McNaughten, for he had a wife and children.

"A secret alliance with me, Ackbar Khan, son of Dost Mohammed," rejoined the prince. "I alone can save you and yours from the feast of vultures that your foes have planned in the Cabul Passes."

"So be good enough to state your conditions again," said General Elphinstone.

"They are these. Shah Soojah is to remain on the throne as king, but I am to be appointed his prime minister, and master-of-horse, and my followers alone to form the garrison of his palace and his body-guards. This until the spring, when you shall withdraw your troops from Afghanistan. When they have departed, Shah Soojah will have to look to me for protection in the same way as he looked to you; and on regaining your Indian territories your government shall settle on me an annuity of four lacs of rupees."

"And when we have gone you will murder the King Shah Soojah, and seat yourself on the empty throne," said Sir William McNaughten, bitterly.

"It is not likely. I am a humane man, and why should I thirst after the nominal power when I shall grasp the real? Besides, should I be so tempted, you can cease paying the annuity," said Ackbar.

"And the king, he will be a mere puppet in your hands," groaned Elphinstone.

"Has he been more than a puppet in the hands of you British? *Bismillah!* he refused to accompany your troops back to India but a few hours ago; he seems rather inclined to prefer to entrust his precious person to us Afghans, eh?"

"Say rather he was alarmed at the perils that would beset the line of march," said Shelton.

"Anyhow, he declined to go with you —to perish with you! Ah, ah! you must accept my terms; you daren't refuse, or history will write you down idiots and madmen."

"As ambassador and plenipotentiary of the Queen of England I agree to them," said Sir William McNaughten; then, with feverish haste and anxiety, he added—"could we bring a quarter as many men into the field as you Afghans, I would snap my fingers at you and bid you defiance; but you outnumber us by twelve, ay, by twenty to one. Your hand on this unhappy compact, prince."

"Stop, stop! in Heaven's name what are you doing, McNaughten?" gasped Elphinstone and Shelton in a breath; "have a care! The glory and honour of England!—think of that!"

"It has not been prostrated by me," said the envoy, proudly; "the glory of England cannot be upheld by an army of shadows; but duty to England demands that when a gigantic sacrifice of human life would achieve no useful end, it should be avoided."

"Well said," grunted Ackbar Khan; "you have passed your word, the alliance is made, and it cannot be departed from. Now, listen to me, you must break off with the Barukzyes and the Douranees who have always meant to betray you."

McNaughten nodded assent.

"Then," said Ackbar, "I and those upon whom I can rely, all chiefs of note, will meet you, Sir William, and you General Elphinstone, on the bank of the river hard by the mosque of Baben of either, when the sun marks high noon. You will there ratify in public the contract that you have just made with me in private, and as an earnest that you have broken off all relation with the Barukzyes and Douranees your troops will, whilst you are thus engaged in conference with us, attack and recover the commissariat fort, yesterday captured, and now held by the Barukzye chief, Ameer Dollah. Is this also agreed to?" and the speaker glanced disdainfully round.

"How can he whose head is in the tiger's mouth disagree to anything?" answered the envoy.

"I am glad that you know your position," sneered Ackbar Khan. "It is well."

"I cannot come to the conference on the river's bank," said General Elphinstone.

"By the prophet's beard, and why not, old man?" asked the Afghan prince.

"Because of my gout, to be sure. Do you think I can move about with a leg like that?"

"Bah, you can be borne there in a litter, easily enough," retorted Ackbar Khan.

"Well, then, I do not think fit to go. The army must not be left without a head."

"Ha!" exclaimed Ackbar Khan, with a glance of keen suspicion; "then I must have some security that you are in earnest with me, some satisfactory security"

"But I will come to the meeting in General Elphinstone's place," said Shelton.

"*Bismillah!* that is all very well, but it is not enough. But I will have security for your good faith. I will take some lady of rank away with me as a hostage."

"Perhaps no lady will be willing to go," suggested Brigadier Shelton, roughly.

"*Inshallah!* then she will be a fool. I shall not harm her, and by her refusal she will sacrifice the lives of all. By the prophet, am I or am I not in position to make my own terms? Are your lives so valueless that you can afford to trifle with them?"

"You know the names of many of our ladies, prince," said Sir William McNaughten. "I have such faith in your honour that even were you to name my own wife, I should say to her, 'Go with Prince Ackbar.'"

"Thanks for your good opinion of me, Sir William," answered the fierce Afghan; "but I do not feel inclined to deprive you of your wife. Let me think over the names of a few ladies whom you have in cantonment here."

He knitted his brows and seemed for a moment to be lost in thought. Then he raised his eyes so suddenly, and in the direction of the little window that communicated with the other room, that Rose Trevor, who had just taken Jack Vere's place against the glass, had no time to withdraw her lovely face until it was perceived.

And then the fascination of the Afghan prince's great, cruel, yet brilliant eyes, held her there in a species of fascination as the serpent holds the little trembling bird.

"I will have her," said Ackbar Khan, pointing in the direction of the window.

CHAPTER XXVIII.

ROSE AND JACK HOSTAGES TO THE FOE.

ROSE TREVOR heard the words, and saw the motion of the savage warrior's hand, as also the baleful lighting up of his cruel eyes.

She felt faint and giddy, and sank half fainting into Jack Vere's arms.

"What is the matter? Oh, what is the matter?" exclaimed the other ladies.

"The villain Ackbar has chosen her for a hostage," replied Jack. "But she shan't go alone. I will accompany her, that I am determined."

The three British gentlemen's gaze had also followed the direction of Ackbar's finger, and each had recognised the blanched but lovely face of poor Rose.

"Oh, she is but a child," said Brigadier Shelton. "She would not answer your purpose. She is not of sufficient value."

"I am the best judge of that," said Ackbar Khan. "I intend to have her."

"She is alone and friendless in the world. I'd rather break our compact than consent," retorted the envoy.

"And so reserve her for the wolf, the jackal, or the vulture? Pah, where would be the kindness of that? Keep your word with me, and she shall be returned unharmed."

"And if we refuse to let you have her, what then? When there are so many ladies of rank and consequence to choose from, what can you select this fair, innocent, young girl for but with motive of evil?" inquired the old general, with disquietude.

"That the thought of the dire evil that will befall her should you break your word, should force you to keep it."

Ackbar Khan leant his elbows on the table, rested his chin in his hands, and laughed loud and boisterously.

But before that laugh was done, the room door had opened, Rose had glided noiselessly in, and approached to within a few feet of the fierce Afghan warrior.

"I will go with you, I will trust in you. Surely you will not have the heart to harm one who throws herself on your protection, Prince Ackbar?" said she.

Ackbar Khan sprang to his feet with a clatter and clang of all his weapons, and took three steps towards the beautiful girl with a wild gleaming in his eyes.

But before he could get any nearer, Jack Vere had rushed into the room in turn, and encircling Rose's waist with one arm had half slung her round so as to interpose himself between her and the barbarian.

"Rose, dear Rose," said he, wildly, "you are mad, recall those words! You shall not go."

"And why not?" was the reply; "who is so fit to go as me? I have no father, no mother, no sister, no brother. I shall save, perhaps, a mother from being parted from her children, or a child being wrung away from her doating parents. Besides which, by my acquiescence, I may save the lives of all. I go on a good, a holy mission; thwart me not, Jack!"

"Anyhow, if you go, I will go with you, that I am resolved," said our hero.

"Ask Ackbar Khan if you may; surely he will not, cannot, object."

Jack at once complied with her request, but the prince did object in a very decided manner, indeed.

"Stop, prince," quoth our hero, desperately; "before you refuse, remember the temple of Boora Penna, and the prophecy of the god. Ah! will that alter your determination?"

Ackbar Khan turned of a perfectly livid hue as Jack spoke.

For an instant he grasped the hilt of his scimitar, and then withdrew his hand as though he had laid it on red-hot iron.

"JACK VERE SEIZED UPON THE FLAG, AND TORE IT DOWN."

"'NOW YOU SHALL SEE THE DISGUISES WE HAVE BROUGHT,' SAID THE BOYS."

Then he said in gasping, uncertain tones—

"Come if you will ; I suppose two hostages should be more satisfactory than one."

Rose looked thankful indeed for this permission ; the colour even returned to her pallid cheeks, and she thanked Jack by a loving glance of confidence.

Of course neither the commander-in-chief, nor the brigadier had the heart to say Jack nay, though they of course knew that he could not have obtained the requisite permission from the commanding officer of his regiment.

" I'll manage all that," said Brigadier Shelton, alluding to this very patent fact. " Go along with her, my boy, with a good heart, and act the part of brother to her ; I'll see that you don't get into difficulties through your generous action."

Jack thanked the speaker, of course, but Ackbar Khan looked anything but amiable over the matter. He said, however, briefly and curtly—

"At the river side, just below the Mosque of Baber, at high noon, then ; play me false but in the slightest, and though you may see these young people's faces again, be assured that they will have parted company with their bodies."

He rose and bowed, and his followers did the same.

Then Ackbar Khan signed to Jack and Rose to accompany him, and they went out of the governor's villa in a group, Rose warmly thanking our hero for his devotion on the way.

"Pooh, 'tis nothing to what you did for us in Cabul," said Jack ; "and besides, I love you, and 'tis sweet even to die for those we love, or at least I should think it sweet."

A couple of horses were brought up for their use, such bags of bones, that they could hardly hold themselves upright, far less carry a load.

Ackbar Khan smiled grimly as he looked upon them.

" *Bismillah!* this is the beginning of the end," said he, under his thick, drooping moustache.

Then he continued still more *sotto voce* as he beheld Jack assisting Rose into her saddle—

"Accursed son of a dog, does he think that he can shield her from me ? Fool ! she shall be mine, all mine, for she is as fair as the full moon, bright as the morning star, and beautiful as any houri in the paradise of the faithful. Ay, I will bend her to my will in all things, and should she persist in thinking more of this beardless boy, I will send his head up to her table, and toss his body to the dogs, for I have drawn these sons of burnt fathers into a precious snare, and that girl shall be the sole being out of their number who shall live to see the end of the month ! I have sworn it."

And so saying Ackbar Khan mounted his horse, and rode after them.

CHAPTER XXIX.

JACK FINDS THE OWNER OF THE SEVERED HAND.

MANY pitying and sorrowful glances were bent upon Rose and Jack by the British soldiers, as surrounded by the Afghans they rode through the cantonments.

Indeed, had not the savage warriors been surrounded in turn by a guard of our 5th Native Cavalry, by way of escort, in all probability they would have been attacked and the white youth and maiden been torn from their custody by force.

Happily Bob Rogers nor Evan ap Morgan had an idea of what was going on, or they would have created a pretty disturbance in a futile attempt to accompany Jack and Rose.

At last one of the cantonment gates was reached and thrown open, and the escort of Indian cavalry having drawn up in a kind of half-moon order, the Afghans defiled through it out into the plain, and the gates were immediately closed in their rear.

Then as they rode away, such a shout of hatred and defiance arose to the dull, grey, leaden heavens from the half famished British and Sepoy troops who lined the walls of the compound, that it must have been clearly heard even in revolted Cabul.

Rose and Jack dreaded that their captivity was to be inside Cabul; great was their relief, therefore, when they found that they were to be, at all events, for the present, confined in a small round fort, in shape somewhat like the martello towers on England's southern coast, rising as sheer upwards from the flat as a castle does on a chess-board

It stood at about a hundred yards' distance from the south-east angle of the city walls, and had four brass guns mounted on its ramparts.

'Twas evidently garrisoned by followers of Ackbar Khan, for at a summons from his horn the outer gate was thrown back, a rude kind of portcullis raised, and a strong interior door, barred, banded, and bossed with iron, opened in the thickness of the wall itself.

Having dismounted, Rose and Jack were driven up a spiral staircase that circled round and round this inner wall to the top, until they came to a door.

They were told to enter, and having done so, they found themselves in a small, dimly-lighted chamber, the furniture consisting of a charpoy, or native bedstead, a rough wooden table, and a couple of still rougher three-legged stools.

The view from the narrow slit of a casementless window, to Jack and Rose's great joy, if they could feel joy in so terrible a position as they had voluntarily placed themselves in, commanded the whole of the British cantonments, about a mile and a half distant, the Mosque of Baber, and the winding course of the Cabul river; whilst the hateful city of the same name was hidden from their sight.

Scarcely had they made themselves acquainted with this fact, than they became aware by the jingling of spurred heels upon the floor, mingled with the clattering of arms and armour, that some one had entered the chamber in their rear.

Glancing round simultaneously, they perceived that it was Ackbar Khan.

What could he want? He did not leave his helpless prisoners long in doubt upon that subject.

"You are here, and it is well," said he, seating himself, whilst Jack and Rose stood hand clasped in hand before him. " In my forbearance and mercy, I asked but for one hostage—the other thrust himself upon me. It was the will of Allah."

Here he fixed his keen searching gaze full upon Jack, and continued—

"The fool who thrusts himself unsolicited into the tiger's den, must beware of his teeth and talons. So you are they who hid themselves within the idol and dared to prophesy in his name. You have half admitted it."

" I was determined to accompany this young lady at whatever cost, and I knew no other way of frightening you into a consent," answered Jack, boldly returning the Afghan's fierce glance.

" Frightening me ?" retorted Ackbar Khan. " By every word in the holy *Kulma*, the creed of our prophet, I agreed to your accompanying your companion, not through any terror of what you might disclose, but in order to be avenged on you for befooling me. You, girl, too, shall suffer for the part that you took in the matter, though in a different way. By the prophet's beard, I swear it !"

" Remember we are hostages, and as such our persons are inviolate by the law of nations," said Jack ; " you cannot, you dare not break your plighted faith."

" Can I not ; when the Koran declares that the faithful shall be bound by no compact made with dogs and unbelievers ? I tell you, ghiour, that by your daring escape from inside that accursed idol and your retreat through the subterranean, you defeated a most brilliant plan for gaining an almost bloodless possession of the fortress of the Bala Hissar, and the persons of the king and all his followers. Do you think that I will not exact vengeance for this?"

"Was it not natural, prince, that we should seek to preserve our lives by the only means that lay in our power? Discovered by accident, too," rejoined Jack.

"But it was not the first time that you had thwarted!" exclaimed Ackbar Khan, now actually foaming at the mouth with passion. "Do you remember the ruined temple on the Bala Hissar itself—the thirteen shroud-cloaked men, the oath of vengeance over the altar fire? The eavesdroppers, and the severed and stolen hand? Ha, ha! you did not think that you would encounter those conspirators again, least of all where they would exact retribution. Yet they are here, here in this fort, all of them, and their mission is nearly accomplished. Ha, ha, ha! do I surprise you?"

"No," said Jack, "because we know that you are now a friend and ally of our people, and that you will not break your plighted and princely word."

In heart he thought nothing of the kind, poor fellow, but he felt that their only hope lay in giving Ackbar Khan credit for virtues that he did not possess.

But the wily Asiatic seemed to read his thoughts, and retorted, with a grin—

"Have I not told you that by the law of the prophet, it is sinful to make any term with unbelievers? Know in plain words that I have befooled your dotard general and his unscrupulous advisers, and that when the sun marks high noon, I shall reap the fruit. You will be able to see all from this window. I have chosen the chamber on purpose; and now I will introduce you to him who will be your gaoler during my absence. He is an old friend."

He rose to his feet as he concluded, strode across the floor, and throwing open the door, yelled down the funnel-like cavity without—

"Osman Abdallah! Come hither!"

Then other footsteps could be heard ascending the circular stairs, and a minute or two later, there stalked into the chamber a warrior, taller and broader than Ackbar Khan himself, and with a most savage and forbidding expression of countenance.

He wore a shirt of ringed mail, and a steel cap with a chain neck-flap, like his leader.

Like him, too, he carried a whole armoury of weapons, thrust in the rich twisted cashmere shawl that girt his waist.

On his left wrist, secured thereto by a silver chain, he carried a hooded hawk, for falconing is as favourite a sport in Afghanistan at the present day as it was with us in the middle ages, perhaps even more so.

"Osman Abdallah," said Ackbar Khan, "here are two caged English birds. Watch over them that they do not break through the bars of their prison-house. Thou art still a good gaoler, Osman, though a hard fate debars thee from being also a warrior."

"Curse that fate!" retorted Osman Abdallah, gloomily, whilst an old sword gash that crossed his face obliquely from his right temple to his left cheek-bone, almost severing the bridge of his nose in two, gleamed in hues of red and purple, as the hot blood rose to his cheeks; "curse that fate! say I. By the prophet, could I but come across the author of it, I would rip his heart out of his still quivering form, and cast it reeking to my dogs. By Heaven, and by hell, I would!"

Ackbar Khan replied—

"You need not feed your dogs to-day, Osman, for they shall have the heart, and you your revenge, perhaps, ere the sun goes down. Ask that stripling there what he has done with your hand, for 'twas he who took it."

"Ha! and he is in my power," came with a joyful gasp from the rage-panting chest of the savage chieftain; "I thank thee, Ackbar Khan, for this. I can bear my loss now with fortitude," drawing his right arm from where he had hitherto kept it behind his back, and surveying, with something of exultant satisfaction, his red, raw stump of a wrist. "Ha, ha, ha! he shall be held down on his back by half-a-dozen of our fellows, and then I can manage to cut him open down the chest myself, ay, and to pluck his heart forth also, and when I have spat at it, how the dogs will enjoy it—how the dogs will enjoy it to be sure!"

He glanced at poor Jack with eyes of fire as he concluded, thrusting the mutilated stump right up against his face; but all Jack's attention was taken up by Rose, who, poor girl, had fainted dead away, despite her usual courage.

Jack bore her across the room, and placed her on the rough bedstead, even shaking up the coarse straw pillow, so that her gentle head might repose the softer.

But the calmness of his conduct enraged Osman Abdallah against him still more.

"Curse him!" exclaimed he; "does he think that we are playing with him?"

"We will soon convince him to the contrary," said Ackbar Khan, with a cruel smile.

"And the girl. Of course you will slay her, too?" remarked Osman Abdallah.

"No, no, for has it not been prophesied that of their four thousand troops, and nine thousand camp followers, Azael, the Angel of Death, shall lay his icy hand on all, save one? She shall be that one, for she is white as a lily, bright as the morning star, and as lovely as the houris of our prophet's paradise."

"Hush, Ackbar, blaspheme not," said the other villain, with an expression of horror contorting his already sufficiently hideous countenance. "Blaspheme not, I say. And thou intendest to make this maiden thy wife, is it so?"

"Even, as you say, after the vulture and the jackal have picked clean her kindred's bones."

"Well, take her. I envy thee not as long as I have the other's bleeding heart."

"A compact, Osman. Shield her from danger and harm during my absence, and his heart you shall have, ere the sun goes down. Thy hand on it."

And thus the two Afghan villains exchanged hand-shakes over one of the most infamous compacts ever entered into beneath God's bright sun.

And having done so they quitted the chamber in company.

Jack heard bolts and bars being shot into their places, and a rusty key being turned in the huge lock, and then their footsteps descending the spiral staircase until they were out of hearing, when he threw himself down on his knees beside the bed on which Rose still lay unconscious.

CHAPTER XXX.

ROSE'S CODE OF SIGNALS—ARE THEY UNDERSTOOD?

HOURS seemed to Jack to elapse ere Rose recovered consciousness, but at last she opened her dark, heaven-lit, violet eyes and looked upon him.

"Oh my poor Jack," she said; "and you have placed yourself in this terrible peril for my sake. But fear not, Heaven will not suffer your noble and chivalrous generosity to be punished so fearfully as these demons intend."

In this manner she tried to comfort him all she could.

So each endeavoured for the sake o the other to bear up as well as possible, and presently they repaired to the window to gather some few grains of comfort, if they could, from gazing towards the distant encampment of the starving British.

"I wish we could apprise our friends of the treachery that Ackbar Khan contemplates," said Rose, presently; "is there no way, dear Jack, in which we could do so, or escape?"

"Alas, no," sighed our hero; "escape is a sheer impossibility from this place; even had they not taken from me my sword and pistols our position would have been equally hopeless."

"But," said Rose, "I have an idea; the waving of a red flag on some of our lines of railroads at home means danger, and a green one caution, whilst white signifies all right. Is it not so, Jack?"

"Yes, you are right, Rose, there. But how can we turn that fact to good account?"

"Well, there is our window and opposite it is our camp. Suppose we wave my white handkerchief out of it to attract attention, and when they have seen that show my green scarf to signify there is danger brewing, and then your red silk sash to intimate that danger is imminent. Might it not be effectual, think you?"

"I fear not, Rose, for who would think of English railway-signals at such a time?"

"We thought of them, and so the same idea might strike others. God might put it into their heads to be struck by them and to apply them as well," answered Rose.

"Well, my dear, we will put it to the test. There can be no harm in that."

They proceeded to do so, and before the white handkerchief had been fluttering out of the window for many minutes, the prisoners had the satisfaction of seeing several field-glasses and telescopes directed towards it from the cantonment wall

Then the green scarf and the crimson silk sash were substituted, each being allowed to flutter for a few minutes in turn.

There was little fear of these signals being seen by the Afghans on the ramparts, as they projected beyond the round walls of the fort a matter of a couple of feet at the least, with tourelles and embrasures.

The green and red signals were re-garded as curiously as the white had been, but suddenly Rose grew convinced that those who gazed at them were trying to understand them in vain, and her glance wandering rapidly around the room she perceived a large sheet of white paper in the open grate.

It was soiled and dirty enough, but it was unwritten on, that was the great thing, and looking up at Jack, she said, with emphasis—

"Do you think if 'treachery' was written in big letters across that sheet with blood, they would be able to make it out from the cantonments?"

"By Jove, Rose, they might, though I hardly think it possible," was the reply.

"It is worth the attempt, anyhow," replied Rose, rolling up a sleeve and revealing an arm exquisitely rounded, and as white as snow; "there is a bit of broken glass. You can cut deep enough with it, I have no doubt, and I fear you will have to use a finger for a paint-brush, for I see nothing else that will answer the purpose. Make the characters as large as ever you can, that's the chief thing."

"All right, Rose, I'll mind what you say, only the blood must be from my arm; I would not deface yours at any cost. Oh, this is the bit of glass, is it?"

Jack stooped to pick it up, and in doing so brought his nose by accident against the edge of the table.

There was quite blood enough after that, though obtained in a most unromantic manner; so the word "treachery" was written across the sheet of paper, in as large letters as possible and held up to the window.

Rose and Jack saw many telescopes pointed towards it, but from the length of time each took up in its regard they feared that at that distance no one could make it out.

They were right, for neither was it decipherable from so far away nor had anyone in the British camp guessed at the meaning of the red and green signals either.

CHAPTER XXXI.

CAKES AND LEMONADE—POISON AND THE SWORD.

AND hour after hour passed away, and still our hero and heroine sat hand in hand at the narrow window, looking out across the plain towards the cantonment, and all the while the sun was climbing up higher in the sky, until at last it was nearly above their heads.

Then they knew that the hour was at hand.

It was indeed, for one of them, though neither happily guessed it.

Presently they could hear distinctly the clanging of the guard-house ghurries from the distant camp, proclaiming the hour of noon, and ere the brazen clangour had died away, they saw a gate of the cantonments thrown open, and a group of British officers ride forth, the envoy in his Windsor court uniform being conspicuous amongst them, and head their horses towards the Mosque of Baber.

"Heavens!" exclaimed Rose, excitedly, "there are only six of them altogether. Our warning must have been misunderstood."

Scarcely had she given utterance to the speech, when the gates of the fort were thrown open beneath the window at which they sat, and they saw Ackbar Khan, followed by at least a score of Afghans, gallop forth and take the same direction.

" Why, his personal attendance should have been limited to six men, also," said Jack.

" Yes, but see also how many of the savages are converging from the direction of the city and different parts of the plain towards the same spot. Sir William McNaughten and his slender escort will be surrounded by hundreds. Oh, can he not see his danger?"

" He knows that matters cannot be worse, and that by Ackbar Khan's al-liance alone can they be made better. He stakes everything on the last throw of the dice, Rose."

At this moment the door of their prison chamber opened, and in stalked Osman Abdallah. Behind him came a black slave, carrying on a tray a dish of cakes and dates, and two silver cups full of what seemed to be lemonade.

" Here is food and drink," said he, surlily, " I may not give you wine, because its use is forbidden by the prophet. But what I may give you, you are welcome to, whilst you live, at least."

With his solitary hand, he took one cup and gave it to Jack, and then in like manner handed the other to Rose Trevor.

Being parched with thirst, each tossed off the contents of a cup at a draught.

Osman Abdallah's face gleamed with an expression of triumphant malice as Rose put her empty cup back upon the tray. He smiled like a fiend, and that smile could mean nothing but evil to Rose.

The vilest treachery was at work.

But a moment later the face of Osman had become as emotionless and inscrutable as ever, as he invited them to partake of the cakes and dates in turn.

They had neither any desire to eat, and Osman Abdallah motioned to the Nubian to retire, and followed him out of the chamber as he had followed him into it, like his very shadow.

Then bolts and bars were shot into their places again, the key turned, and the prisoners were once more alone.

" What does this sudden and unexpected kindness and consideration from Osman Abdallah portend?" remarked Rose Trevor to Jack Vere.

" Indeed, I cannot guess. I know the draught was very grateful."

" Oh Jack, suppose the lemonade was poisoned?" exclaimed Rose, suddenly.

"No fear of that, Rose. I wish it had been, since it would have saved me from being disembowelled alive, and you from even a worse fate—being wedded to Ackbar Khan."

"But whilst there is life, there is hope, Jack. Don't let us think of those things."

Rose looked at him so piteously, so entreatingly, that Jack shuddered.

The fact was, each was thinking of the approaching sufferings of the other, not of his or her own.

And Osman Abdallah, what was he thinking of, as he descended the spiral staircase in the rear of the Nubian tray-bearer?

These were the words he muttered—

"And he would save her, because her features happen to be cast in a pleasing form. Ha, ha! and to think that Ackbar should prove such fool in this one thing. But I have saved him from his thrice accursed weakness, and she will die like the rest, die in such agony that he himself will be disgusted when he looks upon her. Ha, ha, ha! Allah is great, and Mahomet is his only prophet."

The villain had scraped a root somewhat resembling in look that of the Turkish rhubarb into Rose's cup of lemonade, a root that though entering the human body in particles no larger than grains of the finest sand, take root afresh instantly, and, nourished by the inner warmth, expand and throw out shoots, which elongate themselves into tendrils, that in turn grow, and grow and grow a quarter of an inch a minute, and curling and twining around the internal organs, cause in a few hours a death of fearful agony and suffocation.

This terrible Indian poison is known as "the root," and by no other title.

Its power is dreaded by all, but understood by few.

It is one of the secrets of the Braminical priesthood, and is seldom communicated to outsiders; the method of the cure, never.

British surgeons, with the sanction of government, have offered fabulous sums for an effectual antidote, but they have never become possessed of one.

All unaware of the death that she had literally swallowed under the name of lemonade, Rose Trevor now concentrated her attention on the two bodies of horsemen who had by this time met in front of the Mosque of Baber.

Jack was equally and just as fearfully interested.

"Look! Ackbar Khan's followers are laying horsecloths upon the snow," said Jack.

"And now they seat themselves thereupon cross-legged, and invite McNaughten and his companions to do the same. Surely they will not be so foolish as to dismount," retorted Rose.

"Yes, but they are dismounting, and it is Afghans who advance and hold their horses. And look at that other horse, oh, what a beautiful creature, all housied and harnessed with almost more than Oriental magnificence. It is an English soldier, a dragoon, who leads him forward, and the envoy is patting him and apparently praising his good points. I declare he is presenting him as a present to Ackbar Khan, and see how the treacherous villain bows and scrapes and seems to be thanking him," said Rose.

"And well he may, for it is a princely present; though I daresay Ackbar Khan laughs in his sleeve at the thought, that gift or no gift it must have been his by the fortune of war ere long. Ha! an Afghan leaps upon its back and rides it towards the town. Now the real business will commence," said Jack.

"Sir William McNaughten stretches himself on the rug next to Ackbar Khan. Oh Jack, I'd as soon lie down by a hungry lion. The rest of the officers follow his example, except Captain Lawrence, who sinks on one knee and in a manner that seems to betray suspicion. The rest have each an Afghan chief on his right."

"Yes, so that their arms could be easily seized, whilst in the act of drawing their swords," replied Jack.

"Now the crowd of Afghans close in upon them. Cannot our poor officers perceive their deadly peril?"

"If they did they wouldn't show it. They know they are in the trap now, and that apparent confidence and cool effrontery are the only means to escape therefrom. Ah, the Afghan chief attempts to wave back the crowd. That looks well. Ah, and they lash out at them because they will not obey. That looks better," added Jack."

"Hark!" said Rose; "there is the roar of cannon. And see, there is the rush of our glorious infantry from that further gateway to the left, towards the Commissariat Fort. They are your Kentish Light Bobs, Jack, and they are attacking the town."

"Then Ackbar Khan cannot say but what we have kept our word with him."

"He does not seem very pleased with it, though," said Rose, seizing her companion's arm ; " see, he springs to his feet ; he is gesticulating violently. He points towards the distant fort which our men are attacking, his companions do the same. One poor fellow seems to be remonstrating or else endeavouring to explain matters."

"Oh! hark to that low murmur of rage gradually swelling into a roar. Jack, I can look no longer."

Rose threw herself into Jack's arms and hid her face on his breast, sobbing convulsively.

But Jack was so excited at the tragic scene that was being enacted before his eyes that he had no words to comfort her.

He strained her to his heart, as he continued—

"Oh Rose, swords and knives are drawn by the Afghans. Our brave English fellows fight like lions, but what can six do against more than a thousand ?

"Sir William is down !"

"No, he is on his feet again, and hacking and hewing like mad !"

"He is done for now, though, for Ackbar Khan has passed a sword through his back !"

"Good Heavens! his head is off already, and raised on a spear-point, all reeking with gore. Hark how the demons cheer ! and list to that answering cry like a wail that comes from within the cantonments.

"All those gallant six Englishmen have wives and families there, who are no doubt looking over the walls at their barbarous and horrible murder."

"Jack, Jack, don't, don't! It is horrible ! I can't listen to more," sobbed Rose.

"There is no more to listen to," replied our hero, sorrowfully ; " their bodies are trampled in the dust, and their heads are all raised on high on the Afghan spearpoints.

"They wave them in the direction of the cantonments. With a grim sense of humour they are making them bow, I think. The demons! Why don't old Elphinstone give them a dose of grape and canister ? Ah ! they are just now out of range, the hounds.

"Rose, forgive me rattling on so, for my heart and brain are both on fire. Rose, why don't you answer me ? Rose, dear Rose, what's the matter ! Look up, you seem like one dead."

CHAPTER XXXII.

THE RETURN OF ACKBAR KHAN.

WELL might our hero ask the question, for on raising Rose's head from off his chest, not only did he notice that she was deadly pale, that might have been natural under the circumstances, but that her eyes looked dull and leaden, and that there was a light froth upon her half-parted lips, tinged of a vivid green hue.

"Rose, darling, Rose, what is the matter?" he repeated, anxiously.

"I don't know, Jack. I feel as though I were suffocating; and so sleepy—oh, so sleepy that I can hardly keep my eyes open. It has come over me so suddenly."

"Oh, my poor darling, you are very ill! I can see it," moaned Jack. "Oh, would that I only knew how to do you good; but I don't. Is the pain very terrible?"

"No, Jack; there is little or no pain; only the heavy weight and the sleepiness. Perhaps it is the jungle fever. Oh, would that it were, and that I might die of it!"

"Rose, I fear that death would be the only means of escaping from Ackbar Khan. You are certainly very ill, darling."

He bore her across the room and laid her on the charpoy, or native bedstead, for her limbs had suddenly grown too weak to support her.

Her eyes were closed now, her breathing had become more sterterous, and the green foam had increased upon her lips.

At this juncture the chamber-door opened again, and Osman Abdallah entered the room for a second time, looking somewhat alarmed and confused.

He, in truth, was curious to see whether the poison had begun to act, and he had suddenly recollected its one suspicious feature—the green foam on the lips—which, for his own safety, it was highly desirable that Ackbar Khan should not see.

"*Bismillah!* and is the maiden ill?" he exclaimed, as he suddenly turned round and pretended to regard the occupant of the couch with considerable surprise. "There is a handkerchief to wipe the green foam from her mouth with."

He tossed a perfumed 'kerchief of white grass cloth, elaborately embroidered, to Jack as he spoke, but expressed in his face neither glee, sorrow, nor surprise.

The very way that he had carried the handkerchief into the prison chamber across his arm, showed clearly enough that he had brought it hither for the very purpose that he had offered it.

Jack therefore regarded him very intently and said—

"This is your work. I did not think so at first, but I am convinced of it now. You have poisoned her, wretch! For what object, Allah alone knows; but it is the fact."

"Blame him not," said Rose, getting out the words with pain. "Be his motives what they may, he has saved me from Ackbar Khan."

Osman Abdallah glared wildly at both speakers, and then stammered forth—

"Poisoned her! By the prophet's beard, not I. Wherefore should I do so, when she is the chosen one of my chief and prince? She has fever, that is all. Keep wiping her lips of that green froth, and all will be well, I tell you."

"Are you so afraid then of Ackbar Khan seeing it?" asked Jack, sharply.

It was a random shot, but it told.

Osman Abdallah's face, notwithstanding its blackness, turned of a sickly bilious hue, for, as it happened, that was what he was intensely afraid of.

"I am my chief's faithful slave," said he. "His will to me is law; and besides, why should I pine after his share of the spoil? I am sure of mine. Let him keep his pale face Feringhee girl till, growing tired of her, he gives her to his slaves, and they in turn to the dogs or the jackals. I have my prize to-night. Your blood-reeking heart torn from your still palpitating body. Ha, ha! think of that."

"Make not so sure of that if Ackbar finds you have poisoned this poor girl."

"What, you would tell him? You will not wipe the green foam from off her lips? You will play the traitor—spy? Rather than be robbed of it, then, I will take it now. Ha, ha! now! Do you hear that? No time like the present, curse ye!"

With gleaming eyes, quivering nostrils, and teeth set hard Osman Abdallah drew his long Afghan knife, and sprang upon the young unarmed Englishman.

In another moment the long, cruel blade would have drank his life's blood, for the fellow was a monster in strength and stature, and our hero was weak, feeble, and dispirited.

But happily at this juncture Ackbar Khan himself rushed into the room, and seizing Osman Abdallah's arm, swung him aside with such force that he reeled right across the chamber and fell against the opposite wall in a huddled-up heap of rage.

"What is all this?" then demanded Ackbar Khan, in a voice of thunder.

"She is poisoned, and that man has done it!" replied Jack, calmly.

As for Rose, her eyes were closed, and she was in a state of insensibility.

"Poisoned!" gasped Ackbar Khan. "Has he dared?"

But then he perceived the light green froth on her lips, and added, in a deep tone of concentrated rage—

"By Allah and the Prophet he has dared! But if there is a priest of Brama in all Cabul, she shall be saved; and if one cannot be found, and she die, then, Osman Abdallah," turning fiercely on the murderous wretch, "I will have thee torn in pieces by wild horses, by Allah and the Prophet, I will!"

And crossing to the door, Ackbar Khan yelled down the staircase for aid.

CHAPTER XXXIII.

THE LEECH AND HIS PATIENT—A TERRIBLE THREAT.

OSMAN ABDALLAH had never seen his chief and prince in such a rage as he was at present.

After Ackbar had despatched three several messengers into Cabul, with strict injunctions to bring him back the high priest of the temple either by fraud or force, it mattered not which as long as he brought with him an antidote to the terrible poison of the root, he turned again upon the discomfited assassin and said—

"Dog and slave, if she dies through thy vile machinations, I will have thy life for hers."

"And why should she not die as well as the rest of her people!" growled Osman.

"Because Ackbar Khan, thy chief and prince, has conceived a fancy for her. Is not that sufficient reason, dog? Am I, or am I not, master here?"

"But there are many others in the Feringhee camp as fair as she," persisted Osman.

"What if there be, when a single specimen suffices me?" retorted Ackbar Khan.

"I would not have spared one. I would have destroyed them utterly."

"But I have taken a fancy to this girl—this child. I love her!"

"Well, well, it matters little, if you will cut her throat when your passion subsides."

"Your throat has a great deal better chance of being cut at the present moment."

"*Inshallah!* you threaten me thus because I cannot defend myself, because I have but one arm. Remember, that I lost the other in your service."

"I well remember it, Osman Abdallah, and to prove that I am not ungrateful, should this girl die through thy devilish machinations, instead of having thee torn limb from limb by wild horses, as I threatened, I will have thee merely despatched with a volley of jezail balls. Will that content thee? Here, guards, remove this man to a dungeon, and put trusty sentinels over him."

The Afghans who had rushed up the spiral staircase and into the chamber at the call of their chief, were not slow to obey him.

"BOBBY LEVELLED A PISTOL, AND SHOT THE MAHOUT."

Osman Abdallah had never been a great favourite with them.

They hustled him out of the room and down the staircase before them.

So that, after receiving many blows from the flats of swords and the stocks of pistols, he was at last thrust into a dungeon underneath the very foundations of the fort.

Meanwhile, the chief was stamping up and down the prison chamber of Jack Vere and Rose Trevor like a man possessed; at one moment interrogating the poor girl, or Jack, how they did, and the next breaking into volleys of curses at the conduct of Abdallah, or at the delay of the priest of Brama.

"If the messenger returns without him, I will have the dog's head—ay, and the heads of all his kindred as well; and if the Bramin refuses to accompany him, I will not leave one of his race or creed alive in the city, no matter what I may have sworn in his thrice accursed temple!"

But hardly had the words escaped his lips when lo! and behold, the Bramin and the messenger entered the chamber in company.

Ackbar Khan's face lighted up.

"Good; it is fortunate for you that you have so speedily obeyed my behest," said he. "Now, look at thy patient, Bramin, and tell me if 'tis in thy power to save her."

Then the fiendish-looking old man, with the great eye of Siva painted in the middle of his forehead, strode up to the charpoy, on which Rose Trevor lay stretched out, and with frowning brows, regarded her intently for a minute or two.

"Well, canst thou save her?" asked Ackbar Khan, impatient at the delay.

"If Brama wills it, that assuredly I can," was the calm reply.

"And without any impairment of her beauty? Because if her cure leaves her less lovely than she was before she took the accursed stuff, you may let her perish for all that I care," and Ackbar Khan laughed for a moment like an hyena.

"Her beauty shall be as great as it was before," said the Bramin.

"Then in that case," replied the Mo-hammedan chief; "thou shalt have this diamond as thy reward, and rich gifts for thy temple as well."

And he flashed before the enraptured gaze of the Braminical priest a gem that he wore on the middle finger of his right hand, which was as large as a bean and as brilliant as a star; a diamond, in fact, of immense value and beauty.

"My prince is as liberal as the great Mogul could be," said the Bramin. "I accept the gift, but I must have another, for vengeance is more precious than wealth."

"Make thine own terms, and then get thee to thy task as quickly as possible."

"I must have a human sacrifice to offer up on the altar of my god."

"And so thou shalt, in the person of that English youth. Thou shalt take him back with thee, bound with cords."

"I will freely offer myself as a sacrifice, if when this dear girl is cured you will send her back amongst her own people," said Jack, with a burst of passionate grief.

"Ah, ah, ah! do you think I want her cured for that?" laughed the fierce Mohammedan chief. "Fool, rather than return her to her people, I would give her to my hyenas."

"The lad is not the sacrifice I require," said the Bramin, calmly; "I must have the body and soul of him who administered the poison. It is a secret dear unto Siva and to Vishnu, and was learnt by fraud. The poisoner must be delivered up to me alive."

"But he is one of the most powerful chiefs of our cause," gasped Ackbar.

"It matters not. I must have him, or this girl shall perish of the poison."

"If you suffered that to be, you shall be sacrificed to my anger."

"Well, your highness, better that than, proving false to my creed, have to endure the tortures of the damned for millions of years."

"Save the girl, and the man and the diamond are both yours," growled Ackbar Khan. "But," he added, "if she die under thy hands, I will have thee flayed alive."

The priest with trembling fingers, took a small phial from one pocket of his ong, white gaberdine, and a small glass from another, and into the latter he poured thirty-three drops of a bright, golden fluid, having a particularly pungent odour.

Signing to Jack to raise the unconscious girl into a sitting posture, he with difficulty forced the thin rim of the glass between her lips, and poured the contents down her throat.

The effect was almost simultaneous. The grey tints of approaching dissolution receded from her lovely face, and a flush like that of the China rose came in their place; she gave a painful gasp, and her eyes opened to their full.

"Thank God, she is saved, she is saved!" cried Jack, joyfully.

"And for me," responded Ackbar Khan, bending upon him a look of malice. "I hope you rejoice for my sake, boy, as much as for her own."

"Oh Heaven!" gasped Jack; then— "Would that she had died after all."

Ackbar Khan laughed, but the Bramin said—

"Boast not of her recovery too soon, for she is by no means yet out of danger. All depends upon whether she hath strength sufficient to cast forth the tendrils of the root that are curling round her vitals.

"Ah," continued the Bramin, some seconds later, "the antidote was not given an instant too soon. Another minute or two, and the tendrils of the root would have caused suffocation; but she is at last safe."

"Enough that she is saved for the present," cried Ackbar Khan; "and here is the diamond that I promised thee."

And as he spoke, he drew the superb brilliant off his finger and gave it to the Bramin, who fixed it on one of his hooked talons with evident pleasure.

"And the man?" said he; "the poisoner who hath acquired, by bribery or by stealth, the secrets that belong not to his race?—wilt thou give orders, oh, prince, that he be delivered, bound and gagged, at the door of the temple of Boora Penna, at the end of the first hour of the night? For it would not be prudent for him to be borne through the city to his doom by daylight."

"No, nor shall he be; and, furthermore, there is no need, for the physician leaves not his patient who is dangerously afflicted. You will remain in this fort for a week, by which time, no doubt, the maiden will be out of danger."

"For a whole week? And who will perform the services at the temple?"

"There are other priests belonging thereto; let them do thy duties as well."

"But none save the high priest can prepare the sacrifices for the altar."

"Then the altar must await its sacrifices until thy return, for here thou stayest."

The wrinkled brow of the old Bramin grew dark as night as he listened.

"The maiden's recovery is not assured until I have offered a sacrifice and prayers on her behalf unto my deity," said he.

"By Allah and the prophet, in that part of thy nostrum I have no faith, old man," answered Ackbar Khan, with a laugh, "and by the blessed prophet, I mean to keep thee."

And as he finished speaking, Ackbar Khan shouted down the staircase again for his guards, who instantly came thronging up.

"Put this old man into the dungeon next to Osman Abdallah," said the Afghan prince to them; "and remember, that you will answer for his escape with your heads!"

The old priest's face assumed the expression of a very demon, as, swearing and gesticulating, he was dragged away down the spiral stairs to his underground prison.

"Now," said Ackbar Khan, when he was gone, as he fixed his malevolent gaze upon Jack, "I am going to spare thee until thou seest the massacre of thy countrymen out upon the plain yonder— ay, the slaughter of every man, woman, and child, and until the great fire has flickered and died out that will consume their remains, and then—Ha! wouldst thou know what I intend to do with thee then?"

"To kill me in like manner, I presume," said Jack, as coolly as he could.

"By Allah, a fool might have guessed that much; but it will take a clever guess on thy part to hit upon the manner of thy death," and Ackbar Khan laughed heartily.

"I am a bad hand at guessing riddles, nor do I care to attempt this one," said Jack.

"Then I will solve it for thee," replied Ackbar Khan, with a fiendish chuckle. "I shall have thee removed to the deepest and the darkest dungeon beneath the fort, and there thou shalt be cut in pieces bit by bit."

"Anyhow, tyrant, my troubles will soon be over," said Jack.

"No, no," retorted Ackbar Khan, "have no fear of that. I can cut a piece off each limb, day by day, without any chance of thy bleeding to death; for plunging a gory stump into boiling pitch will stop the gush of blood on the instant."

And with a roar of boisterous laughter, Ackbar Khan strode out of the room

---

CHAPTER XXXIV.

HOPES AND FEARS— A HOT SKIRMISH.

ROSE TREVOR had been in too dreamy and bewildered a state, though conscious, to understand Ackbar Khan's parting and terrible threat to Jack Vere.

But she shuddered when she heard the great bolts shot into their places, and the clattering chains put up, and turned upon her companion a glance so full of despair, that he tried to call up a hopeful look upon his own countenance in order to cheer her.

"You are much better, darling," he said. "You will soon be strong again."

"Ah, dear Jack, but not soon enough to save your life. You must escape without me!"

"I'll be cut into kabobs first," retorted our hero; "ay, be hacked into ten thousand little bits, rather than leave this tower except in your company, dear Rose."

"Then I must get well and strong, Jack. They say that a strong mind can do whatever it wills. I will—will get back my strength and energy in order to escape from hence."

"My poor Rose, you must be as weak as a little child," said our hero.

"At present, comrade, at present. But I will get over that, I am resolved."

She raised herself into a sitting attitude, and Jack supported her.

"Now, dear Jack, tell me something that will enliven me, that is if you can, Not about this dreadful country, but dear old England. Oh, you needn't look sad, you will see it again, and so will I. Our Heavenly Father won't desert us."

It cheered Jack to see her in such spirits, though he guessed that they were in a great measure forced. But to humour her, he did as she requested, and for more than two hours he told her tales of school life, and school larks, until he almost now and then forgot in what a terrible position they were both placed.

Darkness was just beginning to veil the scene when Rose suddenly exclaimed—

"Jack, I feel an immense deal better. I want to see if I can cross the room to my window."

"Oh, my dear, you must be altogether too feeble," said Jack, anxiously.

"Well, I can at all events try," was the rejoinder; and she not only tried, but succeeded.

"Now, Jack, let us sit down here and look for the good time that is surely coming," said Rose; "have faith, like me, Jack, and be assured it will come."

"Yes," quoth our hero ; "but how dismally the cold white snow is coming down. It will be the winding-sheet of our starving army—its winding-sheet and its shroud."

"God can cause it to melt, if he likes, and we are in his hands, Jack."

"True, dear. What a coward I must be to despond, when you are so brave."

"Oh, Jack, what's that? That sudden glow of light? Ah, it's out! No, it isn't. There is a flash of red flame. How it rises—how it spreads. The bridge is fired that crosses the Cabul river—in many places, too. Oh what a terrible sight !"

"Rose, I heard Brigadier Shelton say that the Afghans must not be let fortify or destroy the bridge, or that all would be lost, for that our only hope for escape was by retreating across it, and by blowing it up in our rear. What can Elphinstone be dreaming of to throw every chance of escape away, one after the other ?"

"Ah Jack, but their project is perceived. There are our guns speaking out, and there are the cantonment gates being thrown open, and our brave troops pouring out in a steady stream. See how the flames light up their gleaming musket-barrels and flashing bayonets !

"Hark ! I can hear a band playing the ' British Grenadiers,' too."

"Yes, Rose ; but nothing could save the bridge now, and so the sortie will be a wanton waste of life. Oh God ! would that Sir Robert Sale were only here !"

"Oh Jack ! let us wish our noble, gallant soldiers the victory. Ah, see, they are already engaged."

"And they are my own gallant Kentish Buffs," said Jack ; "alas ! there are no cavalry to support them now, for all the horses are eaten up. The guns are well served though, by Jove, they are ! and don't the Kentish men fight ! Each one is a match for half-a-dozen Afghans, but alas ! not for a score. There are the mail-clad horsemen of Ackbar Khan charging down on them now. Pray Heaven, some lucky ball may lay that archfiend low. Then, indeed, hope would re-dawn in my breast."

"Oh Jack, hurrah ! They recoil from the bayonets of the gallant Buffs in confusion !"

"Yes, yes, of course they do ; but our poor fellows are falling very, very fast ! Oh, why don't they recall them, or send out more to their support? It is murder !"

"Jack, the Afghan cavalry are on them again. Ah, they get a volley in their faces, and recoil for a second time ! Ackbar Khan is down ! Hurrah for that, Jack !"

"Dear Rose, you cannot be sure of him at this distance," urged our hero.

"Oh, yes, I can. I know his white horse, and his towering plume. Ha, and he cannot rise again, for there dashes off his riderless horse like mad towards the city. Hark how the men cheer ! It is at his fall ! So will we, too. Hurrah !"

"Why, Rose, you seem almost yourself, again," said Jack, delightedly.

"And so I am. That old man has quite cured me, I'm sure. But oh, Jack ! I wish they'd send out some more men to help those poor fellows of yours. It is awful."

"Yes, for they are bleeding at every pore, and can do no good, either, for the bridge is past saving. I hope poor Bob and Evan won't get killed, or many of the score of brave fellows, my father's labourers and tenants, whom I tempted in an evil hour to come soldiering. Ah, thank God ! here come others to their assistance at last."

"And the recall bugles are sounding at the same time, Jack. Yes, they are some Sepoy infantry, and some dismounted dragoons. I can tell the latter by their brass helmets. Oh, they will have a task to rescue them, they are so surrounded."

"They'll do it, though—that was a gallant charge. Well done, sepoys ; well done, dragoons, and, by Jove ! well done, big guns, too. Ha, it's all no good. Yes it is, though. They've cleft their way to their side. The Afghans recoil. Dastards, when they are three score to one at the very least. The gallant Buffs are saved. They retreat in good formation. Ah, Rose, a little rock can defy the roaring, on-sweeping waves of an entire ocean, and that little square of flashing bayonets deserves to be called a rock, don't it?"

"Yes, Jack ; and I'm almost as proud of your gallant regiment as I am of you. See, they have reached the cantonment gates. They are retiring through them, the rear ranks facing round, and still sullenly confronting the foe. Ah, the Afghans surge forward. They will be in with them.

"No ; they recoil from a withering volley, and now the great gates are slammed in their faces, and a big gun vomits forth grape and canister from behind it. They break—they fly !"

"Hurrah !" shouted Jack. "They will find it hard work to beat our English. Why, Rose, I am delighted to see you so much recovered. The Afghans have had a licking, though I don't believe we've gained any good by it."

"What, not by the fall of Ackbar Khan, the bloodthirsty assassin ?"

"Ah, that was a lucky incident I own, Rose, especially for us. But now will you not lie down again ? You must still be very weak."

"No, I'm not, Jack, and the time seems to pass less heavily sitting here. Let us try to think upon some plan of escape. We shall succeed at last, depend on it."

To humour her, our hero complied with her request, though he failed to see how by any means they could succeed in escaping from so strong a chamber as that in which they were immured, far less from the fortress itself.

And so half an hour passed away, by which time the blaze of the burning bridge having to some extent subsided, the two prisoners observed that the level plain around the fort was becoming the theatre of strange Afghan rejoicings.

Bonfires were lighted here and there, and groups were gathering round them, composed of men and women, and youths and children of both sexes.

The men and youths were mostly dressed in the uniforms of the British who had been killed in the recent or in previous actions, put on grotesquely,

and in a way to create the laughter of their fellows.

"By Jove, the fiends are in their own opinion commemorating a victory," said Jack.

"They ought to consider they've had an awful thrashing," replied Rose.

"And so say I," quoth our hero ; "but 'tisn't the case for all that. I only wish our gaolers would open the gates and either go out and fraternise with them or invite them to be festive inside. They would, but for fear of Ackbar Khan, I've no doubt."

Scarcely had the words passed Jack's lips than the carousers around the nearest of the fires held up bottles, and flasks, and skins containing some liquid or other, and seemed to challenge the guards on the walls to come forth and join them.

For some time the invitation was not responded to, but at last the garrison could resist the temptation no longer.

On its being roared out to them that there was no risk of a visit from Ackbar Khan, as he lay too badly wounded within the city to bear removal for that night, at all events, the gates were thrown open, the portcullis hauled up, and forth streamed the greater part of the garrison to take share in the drinking that was carried on, on the plain.

"Things are working round, Jack," said Rose, hopefully, when she saw this.

Jack replied that he "hoped so," though he couldn't see how.

"You will see," said Rose ; "it will end by their coming inside the fort, or, at least, some of them, and then we shall be made an exhibition of ; and when they go out, if they are all very tipsy, they may as likely as not leave all the doors open. Do you see, Jack ?"

"Yes, dear ; and I hope that all may turn out as you expect," retorted our hero ; though he couldn't help thinking— "If they do get drunk and come in, they may go out and leave the doors open behind them ; but it's a very sure thing that they'll cut both our throats before they do it."

CHAPTER XXXV.

MOMENTS OF SUSPENSE—UNBIDDEN GUESTS.

ANOTHER half hour passed by, and the carousals still went on all over the plain ; but at the end of that time a reeling, shouting crowd could be descried coming back towards the fort from the nearest watchfires, and in them the prisoners recognised the slender garrison, and fully as many outsiders as well.

"They are drunk with milk and the juice of jaggery berry, the only intoxicating thing that the followers of the prophet are allowed to indulge in. Now we shall see, Jack, whether my prophecy will be a true one," said Rose.

"Oh Rose !" was the horrified retort, " I fear that poor Bob and Evan are no more. To be sure, it may not be them, but the drums are of our regiment."

"Jack, Jack, what do you mean ? Don't—don't imagine such horrible things."

" Well, I may be mistaken, little comrade, and I pray to Heaven I am. But do you see those two horribly hideous little Afghan wretches, more than half naked, and wearing two brass helmets on their heads, and two drums in front of them, which they are banging into like mad ?"

"Oh, yes, Jack, I see them. I do hope they are not poor Evan and Bob's drums, for that would imply that they were dead."

"Yes, indeed ; for they would never have surrendered up their drums with life. But then, there are four other drummers in the regiment, and it may be two of them who have fallen. We will hope for the best, anyhow."

"We will, Jack ; and now I will lay me down and pretend to be still very ill indeed. Jack, you must be weeping over me when they come in ; for that they will come I am convinced."

"Yes, darling, of course," responded Jack, in want of something better to say, for he hadn't the least hope of the Afghans visiting their prison and leaving them in it alive.

And as it happened, none too soon, for presently the Afghans were heard stumbling up the stairs and indulging in curses and laughter on the way.

"Oh Rose, darling, be firm ; a terrible ordeal is before you," said Jack.

"I will be firm, comrade. Am I not a soldier's daughter ?" was the response.

The chains were now heard being let down and the bolts shot back.

The huge key was turned in the rusty lock, and the door was thrown wide open.

A group of hideous and forbidding faces at once filled up the aperture.

Every hand grasped a weapon, every mouth breathed forth insults, blasphemies, and threats of the most fearful nature.

And then they all surged tumultuously into the room.

Jack Vere made up his mind that it was all over with them.

He had no weapon wherewith to defend Rose from an attack, but he resolved that the first weapon that aimed at her life should take his own as he threw himself across her for a shield.

He gazed at the awful intruders as calmly as he could, and then his gaze involuntarily wandered to Rose.

She lay as calmly as though she slept ; true, her beautiful chest rose and fell violently, but this was but too natural under the circumstances.

The villanous Afghans would certainly have killed them had not the guards appealed to them to spare the prisoners, since terrible would be the anger of Ackbar Khan did they suffer harm.

This restrained them, and they committed no greater violence than spitting in our hero's face, devoutly wishing that jackasses might defile his father's grave.

and demanding of them whose dogs were they ?—a question which perhaps would have been rather difficult to answer.

At last, however, they all reeled and staggered away, forgetting, just as Rose had predicted, to secure their prison door behind them.

" Rose," said Jack, " you are a charming little prophetess. Look there !"

" Yes," was the calm reply ; " I told you it would be so. I had a presentiment."

" Well, darling, so far so good. But what do you suggest doing now ?"

" We must wait until our gaolers and their friends are far more tipsy than they are at present, and then we must dare all, dear Jack."

" What, darling? Do you mean we must boldly run the gauntlet ?"

" Indeed and I do. Jaggery and milk makes its votaries most helplessly tipsy, not so much in their heads as in their legs. I've seen the effect of it before now. Another half hour and not an Afghan will be able to stand on his legs."

" I'm glad to hear it, dear, and I hope they will remain so until we are within the cantonment walls. Would that there was some safer place that I could take you to," and Jack sighed as he threw an arm around her and kissed her.

Another half hour slid, oh, so slowly along, and the noise and uproar in the well-shaped courtyard and the various apartments below had increased to a perfect Babel.

Surely drunkenness could no further go.

" We will attempt it now, dear Jack," whispered Rose, at this juncture.

They were about to put their project into execution when they heard someone coming up the spiral staircase with firm step and alone.

Their room was dark, save for the reflection of the cold, white snow without, but that was sufficient to show them a colossal and shadowy form enter in at the open door.

Presently they heard a voice that they both seemed to know well, exclaim—

" Ah, and so the dogs have left your door open as well as mine ! It is well, since it enables me to secure my vengeance. Ha, ha, ha ! Die !"

Jack saw the flash of steel, as some weapon or other sprang from its sheath, and he immediately interposed himself between it and his companion.

There was no getting past the intruder and gaining the door undiscovered by him, since he stood right in the way ; and now Jack's keen eyes discovered that it was Osman Abdallah, the one-handed.

A formidable opponent, however, with that long, bright weapon that he grasped so firmly, for a youth to tackle unarmed ; and now he evidently perceived their exact position in turn, and with a fiendish laugh sprang towards them.

The next instant his long sword would assuredly have drank Jack's life blood, but suddenly he reeled and fell, and the shriek that he gave utterance to was drowned in a vigorous, yet most melancholy rub-dub-dub-dubbing, and then Jack and Rose became conscious that there were two other beings in the room.

This became more evident still when one of them struck a match and illumined a little bit of a fag-end of candle ; for its feeble light revealed the two hideous, coal-black, and half-naked young Afghans, in the brass helmets, and carrying the drums that Jack had feared might have pertained to poor Bob Rogers and Evan ap Morgan.

CHAPTER XXXVI.

TWO LITTLE DEVILS NOT SO BLACK AS PAINTED.

THE first thing that Jack Vere noticed about the hideous young intruders was that the tallest and biggest grasped in one hand in addition to his drumstick a long Afghan knife, from which the blood was dripping.

It was evidently he who had struck the blow at Osman Abdallah, which had saved his and Rose's lives. Struck hard, and true, and deep.

And yet what could he and his companion mean by the horrid din they were making, and the faces of more than Afghan hideousness that they were pulling the while?

He was surprised, bewildered.

But how were Jack's surprise and bewilderment increased, when all in an instant he beheld Rose dart from his side and rapturously kiss first one and then the other of the boy savages, thereafter turning towards him with her lips almost as black as their faces!

At the same instant the biggest of them ejaculated in tones that were joyfully familiar to him—

"Oh, Mister Jack, either polish him off or gag him, or we'll never be able to leave off drumming for the alarm he'll be giving, and it's more than half dead with terror, that I am. Oh, what an awful thing 'tis to be a coward."

"Bob! Evan!" gasped Jack; "and to think Rose recognised you first. I'll never forgive myself for it, my brave and plucky little fellows."

But whilst he was saying this he was not grasping his young comrades' hands, not a bit of it; but he was following Bob's advice by gagging and thus effectually silencing the bloodthirsty miscreant, Osman Abdallah, for he could not bring himself even to kill him in cold blood. Such a deed was revolting to his nature.

When he had put it out of the power of their grim and seriously wounded foe to give utterance to the slightest sound, by twisting the thick folds of his silk sash into his mouth and over his nostrils, and fastening it securely round at the back of his head, for he was far too severely wounded to be able to move, much less to rise, Jack did approach Bob and Evan, who had left off drumming, and shook them by the hand in turn.

"My brave comrades," said he, "how heroic of you, how good of you, to run such terrible risks in order to deliver us."

"Oh, Master Jack, don't talk like that," blubbered Bobby; "because we'll never all get away alive. I'm such a coward that I'm sure to break down in something."

"It was Bob who proposed coming," said Evan. "The plan was all his, for we knew well enough in what fort you were imprisoned, and directly we heard it given out that the army was to march ere dawn, Bob said he'd rather be cut to pieces than leave you behind."

"My brave Bob," said Rose, grasping his hand again and wringing it fervently.

"What's the good of telling such nonsense, Evan? 'Twas you who thought of stripping ourselves nearly naked, and then rubbing ourselves over with soot from the chimney."

"Yes, Bob; but your idea of black-leading ourselves was an improvement on that, and 'twas you who stole the shiny packets and the brushes out of the general's kitchen. 'Twas you who thought of packing the disguises inside the drums," retorted Evan.

"What, have you got dresses for us inside those drums?" exclaimed our hero, joyfully. "By Jove! that was a brilliant idea, for now there is a chance of our getting away."

"Yes," said Bob Rogers, grinning; "and what is more, I've got the black-lead as well."

"No wonder the drums sounded so

strangely then. But let us make haste and disguise ourselves, my brave lads, lest we be disturbed at our toilettes."

"Not much fear of that," laughed Evan, "for I don't believe that any of those below could get up these stairs by now. Not even on their hands and knees."

"That is famous," said Jack; "now tell us what you have got for us to put on?"

"You shall see," said the two boys in a breath, as they set to work to take off the heads of their drums. "We stripped the bodies of those who were killed in the fight, and only an hour after it was over, too, for we had no time to lose," added Evan.

"And did you two take part in that desperate struggle?" asked Jack.

"Yes," replied Evan; "and helped to beat the Afghans as well as our drums, for I think we gave them as good as a beating, considering how many they were."

"And so do I," said Jack; "Oh, those are the clothes that you've brought us, are they?"

"Yes," replied Bob Rogers, "for we were bound to select such as we could tuck inside the drums, you know. We thought our bare skins would pass unquestioned."

"'Twas certainly the safest kind of dress, or rather undress, that you could have worn," replied Jack. "Rose, dear, this is the suit I think will fit you. Retire into yonder corner and commence your toilette, then."

Rose immediately took the clothes and did as she was bidden; whilst Jack made a dressing-room for himself behind the half-open door of their prison chamber.

Short time did they take to attire themselves in the apparel that had been brought them to put on, and when they met each other again in the middle of the floor, they were agreeably surprised at the change in each other's appearance.

Rose had hidden away every tress of her beautiful golden hair beneath the folds of a red and white turban, and the loosely flowing costume that she had donned concealed the symmetrical proportions of her girlish figure admirably.

"The blacklead will make you perfect," said Jack, admiringly.

"And you, too," said Rose Trevor, surveying our hero in turn with a well satisfied glance.

Each then blackleaded the other's face, hands and arms, not without a little quiet laughter at the peculiar effect the change of colour had on their features.

"You'll do," said Evan ap Morgan, in high glee. "You look as thorough cut-throats and villains as any of them. No, I don't mean that, exactly. You know what I mean."

"Yes, yes," replied our hero; "of course I do. Were we only armed now, all would be well."

"We dared not bring weapons," said Bobby, "or at least any of a size that would have been noticed. Here, however, are a pair of double-barrelled pistols and a little short-bladed dagger to match," and he drew them out of the folds of his cummerbund.

"Are the pistols loaded?" asked Jack, delightedly, as he surveyed the little weapons, which were not much longer than the middle finger of his right hand.

"Mr. Dunbar said that they were, when he gave them to me, sir," replied Bobby, "and he bade me tell you if we succeeded in getting near you, which he didn't consider very likely, that he'd have accompanied us had he not been on duty."

"Poor Willie," said Jack, "I can believe that. I've no doubt his heart was with you, but as he can't come to us, we must attempt to go to him; let us start at once."

On hearing this, the gleaming eyes of Osman Abdallah up in the corner, seemed to burn with even a redder fire, and Rose trembled from head to foot.

"Courage, dear," whispered Jack to her; "the ordeal will soon be over."

"Give me one of the little daggers," said she, hurriedly, "and promise me, moreover, that if you are bound to have recourse to your pistols, the fourth shot shall be for my heart."

"I promise, and I will perform," said

Jack, resolutely; "but now Rose, be firm. Dressed as a youth, I dare not be seen showing you too much attention; it would attract suspicion. Now, Bob and Evan, move on in front, but only strike up when it is necessary to distract attention from us, and then give as much noise and as little tune as ever you can."

"All right, sir," replied the two drummer-boys, in a breath, and away they went.

CHAPTER XXXVII.

ADVENTURES AND MISADVENTURES—IS THE WAY CLEAR?

IT certainly did require no ordinary degree of courage to go down that spiral staircase amongst the drunken horde who were keeping revelry in the well-shaped yard, and in all the rooms on the basement story of the round Afghan fort.

Jaggery is an unfermented drink, on which account it escapes the condemnation of the Koran, and those who are intoxicated thereby are considered inspired, not drunk.

As they crept down the circular stairs, they saw by the light of ruddy torches that gleamed everywhere below, that the Afghans were still holding high carnival.

Luckily, perhaps, they got amongst them ere they were perceived, for the sight of them descending that staircase might have instilled distrust and suspicion even into befuddled and intoxicated brains.

As it was, however, Rose first attracted the attention of the revellers by inadvertently stepping on the toes of one of the most irritable.

His response was a savage curse and a more savage blow, beneath which poor Rose went to the ground as though she had been shot.

In an instant she was on her feet again, and on Jack's turning round and asking her what was the matter, she answered that she had fallen; for she feared that, did she tell the truth, our hero's hot temper might draw them all into a scrape that there would be no getting out of.

Such might not, however, have been the case, since many of the Afghans were quarrelling and fighting amongst themselves.

Still, it was best to avoid a row with them if possible; and Rose was glad, by a falsehood, to avoid the occasion of one.

The next danger she encountered was from a strapping Afghan lass sportively almost knocking her turban off.

Had her long coils of yellow hair once escaped from their confines, it would have been all up with her and her companions, but she saved herself by quickly clapping both hands to her head, at which the practical joker laughed and claimed a kiss, which Rose gave with no little degree of loathing, though glad enough to keep the peace at any price.

"What little hands," exclaimed the sooty wench, with a laugh, as she next seized one of Rose's in her grasp; "and by Allah, what a tiny wrist for a warrior, too!"

She was about to push Rose's sleeve up above the boundary of the blacklead line, which would have been an even worse catastrophe than the hair coming down, but Jack, who saw her intention, whisked her up in his arms, swung her half round, and then kissing her once, twice, thrice, with apparent rapture, said—

"HE CHARGED WITH HEADLONG SPEED ON VERE AND DUNBAR."

"Tut, he is but a boy ; and if he's puny, he's brave, to make up for it. I am the lover for such a fine lass as you, and sorry am I that I've to return to the city on the instant."

This diversion gave Rose time to move on and to recover her composure ; but Jack was by her side in another twinkling and muttering—

" Bear up ; it'll be over soon."

It was not doomed to be over as quick as he thought, however, for at this moment a stalwart Afghan, not so intoxicated as the rest, pounced down on Bob and Evan, and lifting them on to a table just as he would have done a brace of young kittens, by the napes of their necks, he commanded them to strike up a tune.

Not a word of his lingo could they understand, but his conduct and gestures made his requirements more than guessable, and, of course, they dared not refuse to obey, the more so as others of the drunken crew took up the whim and the cry.

What a noise they made, what a travestie of drumming, and what a wild dance and hideous faces they made whilst so engaged !

That they were anything but savages would never have occurred to either the most barbaric or the most enlightened comprehension ; and Jack and Rose, had the perils round them been less, could have laughed most heartily at the entire performance.

Of course they had to await its close, for not until then could Bob and Evan rejoin them ; and how ardently they longed for it to be over may be imagined.

It was so much quicker than they had anticipated, owing to two tipsy and quarrelsome Afghans upsetting the table whereon they were performing in their mutual struggles, and a second later Bob and Evan limped from beneath it, and looked out for their friends.

Jack Vere made himself conspicuous for an instant, and the sharp Welsh eyes of Evan ap Morgan spotted him at once, almost.

" Now, I hope that we shall succeed," said Jack ; " come along all, boldly."

He went on a little too boldly, for hardly had the muttered words escaped his lips when he went headforemost, over a pair of expanded legs, on his nose.

He assumed the perpendicular almost as quickly as Rose had done a few minutes previously, but the Afghan drew his sword and barred the fugitives' outward path, and some more, equally pugnacious, hastened to follow his example.

Matters looked now desperate indeed, for Jack and his friends knew well enough that Afghans are just as ready to cut each other's throats as those of their foes.

Bitterly did he curse his stupidity, therefore, in not avoiding the fierce savage's legs, who was in truth a very Hercules of a fellow.

Rose's quick invention, however, happily came to the rescue.

She glanced hurriedly round, and perceiving that no one was looking at that moment in her direction, she tugged a tall Afghan whose back was towards her, right heartily by his long hair and when he swung himself round with a curse, she with a look of innocent horror pointed out to him Jack's threatener as the perpetrator of the insulting outrage, and with a cry like that of a wolf the fellow went right at him and dragged him with him to the ground.

" Now, Jack, push on," said she ; " and let them fight it out together."

Jack could hardly help laughing at her clever *ruse de guerre*, but he took good care to push on at the same time, and now there did seem to be a chance of their escaping from the fort, for they had got right into the narrow passage that led to the outer gate, which they perceived to be open, whilst the heavy portcullis was raised fully half way up.

What was their horror, therefore, to see, just as they thought themselves sure of getting out on to the plain without further molestation, a huge elephant with gay and embroidered trappings, mahout on head, and seated in its towering houdah no less a personage than Ackbar Khan ?

CHAPTER XXXVIII.

BOB'S RUSE—UP, OFF, AND AWAY—A CHASE.

ALL indeed seemed to be lost now. Death stared them in the face whichever way they turned, for to retreat was not to be thought of, and yet to go on seemed to be equally perilous, for besides the big elephant there were Afghans on camels, Afghans on dromedaries, and Afghans on fleet horses as well.

And now trumpets were blown and kettle-drums were beaten, and the huge elephant went down upon its knees and Ackbar Khan descended to the ground.

The fugitives noticed as he did so, that in lieu of his usual plumed cap of steel, his head was swathed in bloody bandages, and that his left arm was carried in a sling.

He seemed to reel, too, as he walked; so much so that two of his followers hastened to support him; and between them he stalked with a fierce and lowering visage straight for the entrance to the fort, wherein they themselves stood irresolute.

Meanwhile the tumult within was increasing instead of subsiding.

It became evident an instant later that the majority of those within were about to rush forth to meet their prince (soon no doubt to become their ameer or emperor), perhaps in the faint hope by the warmth of their welcome to avert his wrath.

"Comrades," whispered Jack Vere, hurriedly, to his companions, "we can't go forth or back, it is too late. We must shrink up against the wall. 'Tis our only hope."

There could be no doubt about that, and a precious faint hope it was at the best.

Still 'twas better than nothing, and drowning people catch at straws.

Up against the wall they squeezed themselves, therefore, with their backs thereto.

The fierce glare of the torches would be on them in another moment, yet for all that amidst so many heads they might escape the fierce tyrant's notice.

That moment would decide the awful question one way or the other.

Right and left he struck at the now cringing and salaaming slaves with the flat of his drawn scimitar, and one hapless wretch who did not get sufficiently quick out of the way, received the edge, in a manner that made his head part company with his shoulders in the twinkling of an eye.

Bitter were the oaths and maledictions that Ackbar Khan hurled at his guards for the neglect of their duty in admitting the rabble into the fort, and leaving the gates open and the portcullis raised.

He vowed that they should all be tortured to death; that he would make a fearful example of them, and so on; and the four crouching, shrinking fugitives shuddered lest he should suddenly demand what had become of the prisoners or take it into his head that they had escaped.

But no, this did not seem to strike him as possible, and onwards he passed with the crowd; and then a great many of his followers, who had come out with him from the city, dismounted and entered the fort in turn, until at last all seemed to have gone in who meant to do so, and consequently the best moment for the attempted escape had arrived.

"It's now or never," whispered Jack to his companions; "in another minute we may be missed from our prison chamber."

He took Rose's hand as he finished

speaking, and they crept forth from the fort.

Those who were without would not notice them, he hoped, or if they did, would at all events fail to see anything suspicious about them, and let them pass on their way unquestioned.

The bonfires had by now all died out, or dwindled down to heaps of glowing cinders ; and those who had danced, and howled, and made merry around them, had gone away.

If, therefore, the four could get past such members of the Ameer's staff as still sat on camel-back, or horse-back, without being challenged or stopped, they would stand a tolerable chance of reaching the cantonments in safety.

But was it possible to run the gauntlet of all these lynx-eyed Afghans, without attracting their attention and their suspicion ?

It might have been possible had not the alarm been given of their escape at the very instant that they were stealing forth from under the dark shadow of the fort.

Jack's heart died within him then, for he knew that the white raiment of himself and Rose, so conspicuous in the semi-darkness, must betray them, and that capture was next to certain.

" Let us make a dash for the elephant, and hide underneath his body. See, he is close by, and they will never think of looking for us there," suggested Evan.

It was a capital idea, and the terrified four hastened to act upon it.

A quick run, and they got underneath their strange shelter ere they were perceived.

But how long would it remain a shelter ? Certainly only whilst it continued motionless.

When it moved, they would have to clear away, or be trampled to death beneath its feet.

The noise and uproar within the fort were now something terrible, and looking towards the arched gateway, and the dark narrow passage that led into its interior, the fugitives saw Ackbar Khan, still supported by two of his guards, and followed by a crowd of seeming demons brandishing torches and divers weapons, come rushing forth.

" Rose," said Jack, clasping his girl-comrade around the waist, " I think I'd better do what you asked me as a last favour, now. I look upon our escape as absolutely hopeless."

" Oh, Jack, if you think so, for sweet pity's sake do," was the gentle and undaunted response. " Any fate rather than that of falling again into the hands of that fearful man. Press your pistol muzzle against the roof of my mouth, and pull the trigger. I will not flinch."

" Master Jack, don't, don't," moaned Bob Rogers ; " I've an idea. If we could only clamber on the back of the elephant over his tail, we might force that driver chap who's perched between his ears to urge him in whatever direction we liked."

" Bob, you've saved us," answered our hero, in the same low key ; " you and Evan climb up on each side by the trappings, and I'll give Rose a lift over his back."

Bob and Evan were as active as monkeys, and the gorgeous trappings, with which the huge elephant was adorned, were capital helps to climbing.

The elephant whisked round his trunk, and nearly caught hold of Evan with it ; but " a miss is as good as a mile," as the old proverb hath it, and when the mahout looked round in turn, it was to glance down the muzzle of a pistol that Bob Rogers had clapped almost against his ear, and to receive the assurance that he'd be shot dead if he didn't do exactly what he was told.

That mahout understood English, and he comprehended Bobby's expressive gesture quite as well.

Therefore he replied humbly—

" What shall I do, sahib ?"

His instructions came from Jack Vere, who in his eagerness and impatience had almost thrown Rose up on the elephant's broad back, and actually overtaken her by the time she had climbed into the houdah.

" Steer straight for the nearest gate of the cantonments," said he, " as hard as you can pelt, too. I know what speed an elephant is capable of, and if you don't keep him up to it, or try to play me false in any way, we will drag you into the houdah, and there hack you into kabobs, by Allah and the prophet we will!"

The threat was quite terrible enough, and the mahout thrust his sharp steel probe deep into the monster brute's tough skin and, guiding him in the way he should go by a tug of his loose, flabby, dexter ear, away they went.

And not a single instant too soon, for Ackbar Khan by the glare of a score of brandished torches had already espied them, and with one breath shouted to the mahout to bring back the elephant on peril of his life, and with the next yelled to such of his guards and followers as were mounted to recapture the runaways, even if they had to slay the elephant to effect it.

So that in the course of a minute or two, the fugitives had a score of Afghans, mounted on camels, horses, and dromedaries, spurring after them like mad.

Now an elephant is not a swift animal, say who will to the contrary, and Jack and his friends saw very clearly that they would be overtaken by the horsemen at all events in a very few minutes, and these were the best armed of all their foes.

At this juncture, and just as he had begun to despair again, our hero discovered, to his great joy, that the houdah in which he, and Rose, and Evan were seated contained a perfect armoury of weapons of every description.

There was an excellent double-barrelled carbine of English make, and with percussion locks, a brace of long steel-barrelled horse-pistols, with powder-horns and bullet-bags, and cap-boxes let into a dozen or so of little pockets, all of a row; whilst, fitted into an iron socket or bucket, at one end of the houdah, and sticking bolt upright therefrom like the mast of a ship, was one of the longest spears that our hero had ever cast eyes on.

"Bob," said Jack Vere, "you keep that beggar to his duty"—meaning the mahout—"and perhaps we'll pull through it yet."

"All right, sir," quoth Bob; I'll keep him at it, never fear. I'm so terribly frightened."

Jack couldn't help smiling at the characteristic retort, and then he said to Rose—

"You must help fight, comrade. I know you're a good shot."

"Right, Jack," replied Rose, blithely. "See, I can use the ledge of the houdah for a rest, and so steady my aim. You take the carbine and I'll use the pistols."

"I'll keep loading for both of you, then, as fast as you can fire," said Evan.

Bob had quite enough to do in seeing that the mahout didn't play any trick, and that he steered straight as a needle for the nearest cantonment gate.

Meanwhile, the elephant lumbered on at the rate of twelve miles an hour.

CHAPTER XXXIX.

"OH, HAVE YOU SEEN THE ELEPHANT?"

YES, at the pace of twelve miles an hour, whilst the savage Afghan horsemen were coming on at the rate of about fifteen, brandishing their swords and spears.

But suddenly Jack's carbine spat forth flame and smoke, and down went the two foremost pursuers on the plain.

"Hold your fire, Rose. They aren't within pistol range yet," said Jack, seeing that his girl comrade was about to follow his example. "Your time will come, never fear."

It seemed doubtful whether it would, though, for the Afghans, taking warning by the fall of their comrades, diverged to right and to left, urged their beautiful steeds to the fleetness of the wind, and then, first a solitary rider on one side, and, directly he was perceived, one from the other, would sweep to within range of the elephant, discharge his jezail not at the riders, but at the vaster bulk of the animal, and then, throwing his body behind the neck or off-flank of his horse, speed out of range, hidden all save a foot or, at most, a portion of a leg, from Jack's aim.

These were harassing tactics.

Jack fired thrice, and missed each time, whilst the Afghan bullets were plumping into the carcass of the elephant and causing him to sway and reel in a manner most prejudicial to a good aim.

At any moment, too, a ball might touch a vital part, and then down he would sink, and it would be as much all over with his riders as with him.

Added to this, the cantonments were still a good mile away.

Bang! went Jack's carbine.

At last another Afghan horseman bit the dust.

But almost at the same instant Bob Rogers uttered a cry of mingled rage and horror, and Jack, glancing round, saw that the mahout had suddenly slipped to the ground, and was about to plunge a knife that he had drawn from his girdle deep into the body of the elephant.

A gasp of horror escaped our hero, for doubtless the wretch was aiming his blow at the poor brute's heart.

But Bob Rogers, who guessed the same thing, was too quick for him, and, levelling his pistol, had the good fortune to put a quarter of an ounce of lead through the treacherous mahout's body instead.

Down he went on his back, with his great yellow eyes rolling in agony, and the next instant the elephant had inadvertently planted his off fore-foot on his upturned face.

Jack and Rose shuddered, and turned away horror-stricken from the awful and disgusting sight, whilst Bob Rogers exclaimed, in ear-piercing accents—

"Oh Master Jack, I'm so frightened but I shall have to make this beast get on," and slipping into the mahout's vacated seat, across the narrowest part of the elephant's neck, he first seized one of its ears, and tugged it in the direction in which it ought to go, and from which it had swerved on the dropping off of its driver pretty considerably, and then drawing his dagger, used its point with good effect.

"Bravo, Bobby," exclaimed Jack, who then blazed away again and again at the advancing, circling, and retreating horsemen.

And soon Rose had a chance in turn of paying a little delicate attention to the camel and the dromedary riders, with her brace of pistols.

But before very long, and just as the cantonment wall loomed distinct and apparently more than half a mile ahead of them, the elephant, who still obeyed Bob's guidance with perfect docility, received a shot in one of his fore-legs that crippled him, and diminished his speed very perceptibly.

The Afghans perceived it, and cheered. The horsemen approached their prey in narrowing circles, and the camel and the dromedary riders grinned, as they saw every chance, after all, of being in at the death.

"Never mind. Keep him at it, Bobby!" sang out Jack; "matters are black, but they have been blacker far. Hurrah, for old England! Here goes again!"

The "here goes again," applied doubtless to the almost simultaneous bang! bang! of the barrels of his carbines, which rendered two camels at once riderless.

"Now Evan, reload like lightning, Rose, blaze at 'em in turn. Bravo, comrade, you've dropped one and winged a second. Pass on your pistols to Evan. What, not reloaded the carbine yet? You must be quicker, my lad, if our bodies and souls are to continue to hang together. Never mind, I'll try and skewer one *ad interim.*"

And possessing himself of the long lance, Jack thrust at a camel-rider who was in the act of levelling a matchlock at Rose, and ran him right through.

By this time his carbine was again ready, but he could not afford to pay any attention to the camel men or the dromedary men this time, for the light-armed horsemen were too near.

Three bullets from the unerring matchlocks had plumped into the elephant's huge carcass at once, and he was reeling, and seemingly very much inclined to go to grass.

Jack avenged the poor brute on two of its persecutors, who dropped from their saddles never to rise more, but the rest were swooping nearer and nearer, and Jack couldn't help muttering to himself—

"Heaven, how is it that our people don't hear us, and come forth to our rescue? We shall yet be lost!"

But another second, and to his intense surprise, he heard Bobby singing joyfully—

"Oh, have you seen the elephant? the wonderful big elephant,
The little, big, tall, thin, fat, short, stout, elephant;
Who's called Ka-foo-see-lum!"

And at the same instant their pursuers seemed to haul off; and upon hurriedly glancing round to learn the reason of Bobby's sudden burst of music-hall minstrelsy, and the evident discomfiture of the Afghans, Jack perceived that they were hard against one of the cantonment gates, which presently brought the elephant up sharp.

"Hurrah!" roared our hero, now every whit as much elated as Bobby himself. "Halloa, there! Help, help! We are friends. Open and let us in. The Afghans are upon us!"

There was no response.

What could it mean?

The cantonments were all black and grim.

Not a watchfire to be seen.

Not the footstep of a sentry to be heard.

A deadly horror and despair sank down upon Jack's heart, and Bobby, muttering—

"Oh, how frightened I am!" probed the elephant madly forward.

The huge brute thereat uttered an awful trumpeting roar, rushed on, and smashing in the heavy gate as though it had been so much matchwood, fell with it, blocked up the orifice, and with a moan expired.

Happily, not one of our four friends was injured by the fall.

CHAPTER XL.

INTRODUCES MISTER BARNEY O'MURPHY, ESQUIRE.

JACK VERE was the first to alight from the fallen elephant, and his first act was to help Rose down, and then over the riven fragments of the smashed-up gate.

By that time Bob Rogers and Evan ap Morgan had also gained *terra firma*, and then all four looked around them with a terror that was blended with awe.

"The cantonments are deserted. The troops have marched!" was Jack's first exclamation.

"Oh Master Jack!" quoth Bob thereupon; "how lucky 'twas that the Afghans never guessed it, or they'd have followed us instead of galloping away."

"I hope they have galloped away past returning. If they only use their eyes, and their ears, and their wits, they'll soon discover there's nothing to be afraid of here."

This from Evan, and to it Jack replied—

"We dare not stop to hazard their

return, for the dead elephant would form but a puny obstacle in the way of their blood-horses. Besides, every assassin in Cabul will be here half-an-hour after the news reaches the city that the cantonments are deserted. The troops cannot have got very far across the plain, not so far but that we should be sure to overtake them even on foot before daybreak. We must attempt it, anyway."

"Look, sir, look yonder," exclaimed Bob Rogers, at this juncture. "There are some of our infantry still in the little garden in front of the general's house. I can see their black glazed shakoes and long great coats through the gloom, can't you, sir?"

"Yes," said Jack, "distinctly. What can they be doing there I wonder?"

"Let us go and see," answered Rose, pressing his arm. "At all events they are friends."

"Yes, dear, but they may not take us to be the same, clad as we are. We must apprise them of our approach in good plain English. I'm precious glad to see them, any way."

As he concluded, Jack shouldered the double-barrelled carbine which as well as all the other weapons they had found in the houdah, save the long lance, the fugitives had appropriated, and they all hurried towards the grim and silent soldiery.

"You must know the watchword of the night," said our hero presently, to Bob and Evan; "bellow it forth, so that there may be no danger of their shooting us."

The boys did as they were bidden, but elicited no answering countersign.

"It's very strange," ejaculated our hero; "they must certainly have heard you."

"Oh, dear; I'm in such a fright," said Bobby, "that I shall have to run forward to see what is the matter. I'm too great a coward to stand this anxiety any longer."

Away he dashed as he finished speaking, crying out the while—

"Don't shoot me, I'm not an Afghan, but Bobby Rogers the drummer. Why don't you say something?"

He was soon in front of the silent men, but after one glance, he stood with his arms akimbo, staring at them in a kind of idiotic manner.

He was still in the same position when his fellow-fugitives came up.

"They aren't soldiers then?" said Bobby. "They are only old shakoes and cloaks hung up. Old flint-lock muskets, too—I'm blest!"

"By George, so they are," quoth Jack. "Now what is the meaning of all this? In happier times it would have signified some absurd practical joke. But all joking has been out of fashion with our poor fellows for many a long week; and yet it has evidently been done for some reason or other. Bob or Evan, would you mind creeping cautiously round the house, and peeping in at all the windows, eh?"

"I'll go, Master Jack, although I'm so horribly frightened," said Bobby, at once.

"And I also, because I aren't frightened at all," echoed Evan ap Morgan.

No sooner said than done; and soon after they went they came back again.

"Oh, sir, said Bobby, "there is a big dragoon sitting in the drawing-room, talking to himself like mad, and drinking healths to the empty chairs."

"And he's got such a fire, and a large lamp on the table," added Evan.

Why, the man must be mad," said Jack. "Did he look mad, my lad?"

"Not a bit of it," said Evan; "but he looked very particularly comfortable."

"He must be warned of his danger," said Jack. "Can we get in to him, think you?"

"Nothing more easy, sir, with the French window opening right to the ground," answered Bob.

"Come on," then, retorted Jack; "and we will have a peep at this man."

Drawing Rose Trevor's arm once more within his own, and conducted by Bob and Evan, the little party made their way round to the back of General Elphinstone's pretty wooden bungalow, or one storied villa, and presently all four were looking through the unshuttered window at the single occupant of the chamber within.

In the general's cosy invalid-chair,

over the back of which hung his military cloak, sat, sure enough, a stalwart dragoon, with his brass helmet cocked considerably on one side, his stockinged feet on the fender, while his boots were placed inside, possibly to dry, his sword between his legs, and at the corner of the table, handy to his grasp, a couple of decanters, evidently containing port and sherry, accompanied by a couple of glasses and a brace of long horse-pistols.

"Well, an' here's to me last night ov comfort this side the grave," said he, pouring himself out another glass. "An' sure," he added parenthetically; "'twas meself as was intended by Nature to be a gintleman, and its sitting in me own drawering-room that I am at last, though bad cess to it, I've the tiniment on a precious short lease, I'm sadly afraid," and as he concluded, he tossed off the general's dry sherry, and smacked his lips over it.

At this moment, Jack Vere tapped gently at the window-frame with his knuckles.

The big dragoon looked up with an air of disappointment rather than terror.

"The deuce take them, and it's the bailiffs sure come to turn me out ov possession," growled he, and then he lifted a pistol up from the table, and levelled it at Jack.

"Hold hard!" shouted our hero; "we are friends. We've escaped from the Afghans."

"Eh, sure; then it's meself as is very glad to hear it," retorted the big dragoon, getting up and opening the window. "Will it please ye to step inside and have a warm and a drop of wine? I'm sure ye're kindly welcome if ye only will."

As all four fugitives were by this time well-nigh frozen, especially poor Bob and Evan, who, as it will be remembered, were clad in little more than black lead, the invitation was most readily accepted, and in they all went one after the other.

"And how did you manage to pass the sentries?" asked their host, curiously.

"By Jove! they didn't try very hard to prevent us," laughed Jack. "So that was your idea, was it? May I ask your reason for dressing up all the shrubs?"

"Faith, an' is me rason that yer want? Well, 'twas only a thrick to keep off the Afghans as long as I could, in order to have the chance of kaping up the appearance of a gintleman all the longer. But here, I'm forgetting all the rites of hospitality. Do yez sit down and do me the honour of taking wine wid me. It's rale port and sherry."

CHAPTER XLI.

MUSIC HATH CHARMS TO SOOTHE THE SAVAGE BREAST

JACK VERE immediately poured out a glass and handed it to Rose.

She was on the point of raising it to ner lips when the big dragoon seized it out of her hand, spilling its contents all over her dress.

"Thunder an' 'ouns, an' it's forgitting the ettiket that I am again!" said he. "Sure an' I'll ring for clane glasses, an' thin I'll go an' fetch 'em out ov the chinay closet; for ye must excuse the sarvints on account of their all having run away. Will ye just make yerselves at home, for faith, an' it's Mister Barney O'Murphy, Esquire, as is very glad to welcome yez at his bungle-ho, anyhow."

"My good fellow," said Jack, with emphasis, "believe me that this is no time for tomfoolery. The Afghans will kill us if we aren't very quickly out of this."

"An' won't the mane, cowardly spalpeens do it in any case?" retorted the Irish dragoon, in a tone of mild remonstrance. "An' be the same token, ain't it more feelosophical to wait an' be killed comfortably before a big fire an' in a aisy chair, or on a velvet couch, than to go thramping and sojering miles and miles across the snow, to have it done all the same?"

"No, no, don't say that; for while there's life there's hope," retorted Jack.

"Not in this case, me friend. Ain't the passes all snowed up, an' the Afghans an' the crows, an' the jackals, an' the vultures of the Khyber all a-waiting for our poor fellows? Ye don't git me from this comfortable fire anyhow. I was game to foight it out till the last man dropt be me side; but since it's come to running away, and straight into the jaws of death, faix! since thin, I've elected to stay here and ind me life like a gintleman, and I advise yez to do the same. So I'll fetch the clane glasses, and we'll have a song and, maybe, push back the table an' do a step or two."

"Listen to me, Murphy," said Jack, laying a hand on the dragoon's arm, "were we all men like you, we might, perhaps, fall in with your views; but this"—pulling Rose forward—"is a girl, and the daughter of a brave English officer who fell in his country's service; and you can guess what her fate would be if she fell into Afghan hands, the more especially as she is so very much coveted by that fiend Ackbar Khan."

"Blessed St. Pathrick! an' is it so?" exclaimed the Irish dragoon, bending on Rose a glance so keen that it seemed to be seeing through the blacklead, and making a guess at her proper complexion.

"Be Jabers! an' that alters the case intirely. A comely colleen, too, I can see that. A young Vanus that it 'ud be a privilege to shed one's life's blood for. Take a drink out of the decanter, me honey, an' rist assured that it's big Corporal Murphy as ud be torn to bits be wild elephants rather than a hair of yer bonny head should fall into the hands of the black Afghan devils."

"Now you are talking like a man, and what is more, a chivalrous and a noble one," said Jack. "A draught of wine and a mouthful of food, if it's to be had——"

"But, bad cess to it, there's not a scrap of vittals in the place," retorted the dragoon, interrupting our hero. "I meself had the good fortune to pick some snails off the shrubs when I was a-dressing thim up; but sorra a bit ov food, except thim and a half-starved mouse, has passed me lips the blessed day."

Rose, by Jack's advice, did take a good glass of the sherry, and then he made Bob and Evan do the same.

As for the decanter of port, our hero and the dragoon finished that between them in a very short time.

But hardly had the latter replaced it on the table than there was a rattling fire of pistols and matchlocks from without, and into the room leaped a whole crowd of Afghans, yelling and brandishing their weapons.

There were a score of them, at the least, and when once the besieged five had discharged their firearms in turn full in their faces, there was no time to reload, and they had to trust to cold steel to preserve their own lives and Rose's.

The young lady, however, was struck with a sudden and bright idea, and rushing across the room, she threw up the cover of the grand piano, and sitting herself down on the music stool, with her back to the combatants, she struck up a wild fantasia as hard as ever she could thump the keys.

It was a powerful instrument.

But the effect was more powerful still on the simple Afghans, who had never seen or heard such a thing before in their lives.

Whether it was a wild animal or some infernal machine containing gunpowder, and the noise it made the mechanism set to work to explode it, they didn't stop to ascertain, but with yells and shrieks of the most abject horror and terror combined, made a mad stamped of it, leaving Jack and his companions complete masters of the situation.*

"Let us out after them!" cried Rose, springing up from the music-stool. "Per-

---

* This incident may be thought improbable, but one almost identical with it really did occur on the departure of the British from Cabul.

haps their horses are tied up to the verandah posts or the garden rails, and we may be able to seize on them before their owners dare go near them."

Rose's idea was too good not to be acted upon, and it proved to be a kind of inspired one, for outside there were many horses piquetted, sure enough, and as the fugitives burst forth from the house they could see the Afghans creeping back to repossess themselves of their steeds.

They were too quick for them, and, hurriedly appropriating five of what, at a cursory glance, appeared to be the best, they flung themselves into the saddles, even Rose disdaining assistance, and set off with the speed of the wind.

All but Corporal Murphy, at least, and he was so long in overtaking them that Jack especially began to fear he had fallen a prey to the Afghans.

At last, however, he descried him coming after them on a big, powerful black horse, and waving his drawn sword.

"Have you had to cut your way through the rascals?" asked Jack.

"Not I. Sure an' I thought 'twas hardly sensible to lave the other horses tied up there for the raparees their owners, so I slashed all their bridles across an' then started them off in all consavable directions, yer honour."

"By Jove! that was a brilliant thought of yours, Murphy, since it may save us from immediate pursuit, and enable us to get clear away and overtake our people," replied Jack. "But what makes you call me 'yer honour' instead of friend?"

"Och! and it's because I'm a gintleman no longer, to be sure. I could call ye friend whilst me feet was under me own mahogany and I had the decanters of rale port and sherry before me; but now, bedad, I'm a simple trooper agin, an' all me drames av glory an' gentility have ended in smoke."

"Well, well, cheer up, Murphy! You may live to be a gentleman yet," laughed Jack.

*   *   *   *

All this while they were riding through the city of huts that formed—or, rather had formed—the British cantonments, for they were silent and deserted now."

Once or twice they thought they heard the sounds of pursuit, but were mistaken.

And at last they reached the gate of the cantonments, exactly opposite to the one by which they had entered—the gate which looked towards distant Jellalabad, the city of refuge which the retreating and half-starved British forces hoped they would be able to reach.

This gate was open, for the retreating force had not thought it worth while to close it behind them.

Through it the five fugitives rode, straining their eyes as they did so in the expectation of perhaps catching sight of the British rearguard, looming like a blacker shadow against the darkness of night.

But naught could they either see or hear of marching men, and so out in turn they rode into the darkness and mist, and urged their horses to a gallop.

For nearly half-an-hour had they ridden on, when a lurid and fearful glow in their rear caused them all involuntarily to pull up and look round.

What they saw was the entire mile of wooden huts and compounds that had formed the British cantonments in a blaze, and the conflagration was so vast and extensive, that the very firmament seemed to be aflame.

"The departure of the army has been discovered," said Jack. "Another hour and fifty thousand light-armed horsemen will be harassing its retreat!"

CHAPTER XLII.

ARE THEY PURSUED BY AFGHANS OR COSSACKS?

THERE was such a stillness in the snow-laden air that, though they were by this time so far away, the fugitives could distinctly hear the frantic yelling and hooting of the Afghan horde as they revelled in the pandemonium of fire they had created.

"JACK, RAISING HIMSELF, SAW A STRANGE PROCESSION."

" May they all be frizzled alive in it! May it be their purghatory, the deevils!" ejaculated Corporal Murphy. " May they be baked as maley as little pitaties, the raparees!"

But the fugitives were destined soon to hear sounds, ay, and to see sights as well, of a far more heartrending and horrible description, for they had not ridden on much further when little writhing, moaning heaps, dotted the whole plain, and as they came up to these, they resolved themselves into moaning and dying relics of mortality.

" So soon, so soon?" muttered Jack, as he noticed the scantily clad forms of the Hindoo camp-followers, and the dusky pallor of their faces, as with chattering teeth and quivering form they awaited death. " Oh, this is indeed horrible! Where will it end?"

What is loss to one is gain to another, however, and both Bob and Evan were glad to borrow from the dead such wrappings as were no longer of use to them, for they had begun to find black-lead a very inefficient protection against the intense cold.

" This retrait, sir, will be as bad as Napoleon's from Roosha," observed the corporal.

" At all events it will be shorter," replied Jack, " that's one blessing."

" In the sinse that our troubles will be over all the quicker, sir, ye mane?"

" Well, hardly, I trust, for I've still a hope that some of us will pull through."

" Thin it's plain, sir, that the last camp rumour never reached yez, that ten thousand Kohistanees are awaiting us on the banks of the Loghur river, and that four hundred thousand Ghilzies are in possession of the heights on either side of the Khyber Pass, and have sworn that not a European shall reach the other end. What does yer honour think ov that little bit of intelligence?"

" Why, that a hundred men to one is rather heavy odds against us, but still, Murphy, we are Britons, remember, and they are but Afghans," replied Jack.

" Pluckily said, sir, an' I won't growl any more," quoth the Irishman, heartily. " We are Britons, an' if we're fated to be licked, hang it, we'll give 'em a hard task, anyway."

At this moment Bobby Rogers, who had been looking round, exclaimed—

" Oh Master Jack, are those big birds in our rear? Look how they swoop and swirl, and how black they appear against the red glow of the conflagration."

Bob's words caused all to draw rein and look round again, and sure enough, the thousands of black flitting dots that Rogers had perceived, were difficult enough to make out, thrown forward as they were in relief by the red fire glow above.

But after a steady stare of a minute or so's duration, Jack said—

" They are Afghan horsemen."

" Ugh," grunted the Irish dragoon, " I wonder how many ov thim are Rooshan Cossacks in disguise? A precious lot I reckon, if rumour don't lie."

" There's generally some groundwork of truth in all rumours," said our hero, " and if there is in this one, it's a dastardly trick of the Russians, anyhow. But come, let us get on, and try and warn our people, or else directly the light of the conflagration fails, the foe will be swooping down on them."

They quickened their pace at this, riding very warily, however, so thick were now the bodies that covered the plain, and it seemed cruel and ungrateful to be thankful, though deep down in their hearts the fugitives undoubtedly were, that all of these that they had yet seen were Hindoo camp-followers, a feeble and effeminate race.

At last the five riders seemed to hear distant music in front of them, and that patch of denser darkness that we have before described as looming forth out of the lesser gloom of night, seemed to assume greater consistency and shape.

Soon the at first indistinct tune resolved itself into the well-known and spirit-stirring air of the " British Grenadiers," and almost at the same instant the black shadow loomed forth into marching men.

" We must not approach them headlong, or we may receive a volley for our carelessness," said Jack.

There was no time to say more, for at

this moment the fugitives heard a clear, manly voice, that seemed to be very familiar to Jack, suddenly shout—

"Rear rank, right about face. Prepare to resist cavalry. Present!"

And here followed the ominous click of musket locks.

"Hold!" sang out Jack, when he heard the command, hurriedly spurring in front of Rose Trevor. "We are friends—Europeans escaped from captivity."

"Recover arms!" was the responsive command. "How many are there of you?"

"Five, commanded by Ensign Vere, of the 44th," replied our hero.

"What! Jack Vere? Dashed if I aren't glad to see you—to hear you, I mean, for not a blessed thing can I make out but a dim shadow or two. Right about face again. Shoulder arms! — quick march! Here am I, Jack, in command of the rearguard; there's a position for a raw ensign. Shall be deucedly glad of your company to share the responsibility. Who have you with you?"

"Bob Rogers and Evan ap Morgan, the drummers, an Irish dragoon, and a lady, Willie," answered Jack, for he had recognised his fellow-ensign's voice.

"The dragoon will find his regiment in the van; let him ride on and join it. And the ladies and wounded officers are about a mile to the good. Take on your charge, Jack, and deliver her up, for the ladies have all to keep together. Hand over your horses to Brigadier Anquetil; they will be worth their weight in gold to help on the cannon; and then you three Kentish Buffs halt until we come up, for it will be no good retracing your steps."

"All right, old fellow. Consider all you desire done," replied our hero.

The five galloped along on the flanks of the marching columns as hard as they could, and very soon the camels that bore the ladies and the invalided were overtaken, and here Jack had to bid a sorrowful adieu to poor Rose.

"Stick to your horse as long as you can," he said, "for 'tis a good one, and a camel is not at all times to be depended on. I will see you as often as I can."

Rose's reply was rendered inaudible by sobs, for an inner something told her that they were about to part for ever.

And such, indeed, was only too likely to be the case.

A quick handshake with little Bob and Evan, and then a fonder and more lingering one with our hero—for they dared not kiss whilst so many were looking on—and she was gone, and then the Irish dragoon spurred off, shouting—

"Good-bye, an' good luck, yer honour! and may heaven be yer bed if ye're doomed niver to repose in anither feather one. But we'll give the raparees some hard knocks before we knuckle under, any way. Good-bye, yer honour!"

The lumbering of Major Anquetil's light field-guns now being distinctly audible, Jack, Bob, and Evan rode in the direction of the sound and delivered up their three horses for their use, upon which the Major observed, with tears in his eyes—

"Well, this is a godsend, for I'd have been bound to have left one of my bronze pets behind else, our cattle are so weak and knocked up."

Little did the speaker think at the time that cattle and horses alike would have to be killed and eaten to save the retreating army from absolute starvation ere another four and twenty hours had passed away.

CHAPTER XLIII.

"ALLAH AKBAR!"—THE CHARGE OF THE AFGHAN HORSE.

IT was bitterly cold standing still on that bleak, wind-swept plain until the rearguard came up.

And while they stood there, stamping their feet to keep a little warmth in them, the atmosphere seemed to grow more intensely and unbearably cold than ever.

In a minute or two it began to snow, and the great white flakes came pouring relentlessly down, as though intent on burying the retreating army under a snowy shroud.

At last a muffled and steady "tramp, tramp, tramp!" betokened the approach of the gallant Kentish Buffs, and very soon now Jack found himself by Dunbar's side.

"We are leaving Cabul in a very different way from that in which we approached it," said he to Jack. "We created a pretty considerable sensation there. Please Heaven, however, we'll return a second time, and then Azrael the Angel of Death shall bear us company, for we will take a bloody and a terrible vengeance for all the cruel and dastardly acts the treacherous Afghans, strong in their overwhelming numbers, have inflicted on us."

"Amen to that!" retorted our hero, bitterly.

And then, turning to Bob and Evan, he said—

"You must rejoin your fellow-drummers and fifers, my lads. It's once more strict military discipline, for we are no longer private adventurers."

Bob and Evan obeyed him without a word.

The little drummers and fifers were in the centre of the column, hemmed around by strong men, for they knew that ere long the Afghan horsemen would be down upon them.

And they came sooner than Jack had expected, for presently Willie Dunbar observed, anxiously—

"I hear a noise like a rushing wind, and the clink of steel and the thud of horses' hoofs seems to be mingled up with it. Can the foe be upon our track already?"

"Why, yes; didn't I tell you?" exclaimed Jack. "There are thousands of Afghan cavalry in hot pursuit. We saw them clearly as we came along by the glare of the burning huts."

"Ah! and so the rogues have fired the cantonments, have they? We saw a red glow in the sky, but thought it to be caused by some illumination within the city. We were too far off to see the fire itself. But can this be the foe, think you, that we hear?"

"I have no doubt of it," answered Jack.

There was no doubt a second later, for the terrible tekbin, or Mussulman battle-cry of "*Allah akbar!*" burst in a volume of shrill and devilish sound from out of the gloom.

Next, bright lance points, tossing manes, and fierce, rolling, bloodshot eyes seemed to mingle with the descending snowflakes.

And then the very earth trembled, as if with earthquake throes beneath the fierce onslaught of countless horses.

"Square against cavalry!" yelled Dunbar, at the top of his voice.

"Rally—close to centre—form company square!" echoed Jack, hoarsely.

"Come, my men, look lively! Close up—close up! A hedge of steel without one weak point," roared Dunbar, again. "Remember, the safety of all depends upon us this night. Steady and ready, men!"

A genuine British cheer was the response, as the Kentish Buffs closed up, shoulder to shoulder and three deep, to resist the attack of the Afghan cavalry.

As they did so the snowstorm passed temporarily away, and the moon shone out from between jagged and riven masses of clouds.

It threw the shadow of the Kentish Buffs, as they stood at bay, far out over the white plain, and revealed to them at an opportune moment the foe, as they came sweeping on, shouting like so many demons—

"*Allah akbar! Alhamba! Alhamba!* *Alijannah! Alijannah!*"†

A great red flag, surmounted by a golden crescent, floated high above all their silk-tasselled and feather-tufted spears, and the moonlight shone on their plumed caps of steel and shirts of ringed mail, making them look as though they were of frosted silver.

Their faces were the only dark objects about them.

It was a gallant sight—a sight that recalled the glory and the chivalry of the middle ages.

In the language of Scott, " 'twas worth ten years of peaceful life, one glance at their array," for though they were demons of lust and cruelty, these Afghans were a fine race—very tigers in strength and fury.

And their horses looked every whit as wild, with their thin, quivering nostrils and rage-flashing eyes, as they came surging down—a living avalanche—upon the British square.

Came down, however, happily to break and to recoil, as the mightiest wave of ocean breaks and recoils from the small rock, for like a rock in the midst of ocean stood the gallant Kentish Buffs, a living citadel of steel.

For a moment there was dire confusion in the brilliant Afghan line, for the swarthy sons of Mahomet had left some of their bravest and their best grovelling on the ground in their death agonies beneath the line of stubborn English steel.

But suddenly one among them, who seemed to be a head and shoulders taller than any of his compeers, rallied them with uplifted sword, and voice of thunder.

" On, on !" he shouted. " Do you

* Kill! kill!   † Paradise! paradise!

shrink from the fray? What fear ye? There's glory for all, but for those who fall, an entrance into paradise. On, on, then! Hack, and spare not!"

Encouraged by these fiery words, the fierce Afghans came on again like a whirlwind, nor did a withering volley with which they were greeted, when within half pistol range, deter them for a moment.

Up they swept, right to the flashing muzzles of the British muskets, and many a fierce lance-thrust replied to that of the British bayonet.

At that awful moment, when his gallant Buffs were falling thickly around him, and it was almost doubtful whether the swarthy followers of the prophet would not succeed in breaking the square asunder, Jack Vere recognised in the warrior who had rallied them, and urged them on to the second onset, Ackbar Khan.

The bloody bandages still swathed his head, and his left arm, though it certainly had the bridle round it, was pressed up close to his steel-ringed chest as though it were useless.

But grasped firmly in his right hand was a lance fully twelve feet in length, with which he was doing terrible execution,

Jack discharged a brace of pistols at the fiend in human shape, in rapid succession.

The first shot missed, but the second ball carried away the tip of his left ear, and glancing up, he recognised his assailant.

With a roar like that of a wild beast, he came tearing right down on the square again, and actually made an attempt to leap his horse over the triple line of soldiers who composed it, in order to get at his hated foe.

But, as his horse rose to the leap, it was bayonetted through the heart by an English soldier, and steed and rider went down with a crash outside the British line.

CHAPTER XLIV.

THE ESCAPE OF ACKBAR KHAN—THE GUNS TO THE RESCUE.

SECURE that fiend at all hazards. It is Ackbar Khan, the leader of the revolt!" sang out Jack ; and the gallant Kentish Buffs tried hard to do so, by the most effectual of all manners —a few hearty bayonet thrusts.

But the slippery Asiatic was too nimble for them, and extricating himself from his dying horse, was up and away with the agility of a fiend's imp and a mortal monkey rolled into one.

But mounted on another steed, he was soon leading on his barbarous followers again, this time flourishing a huge hilt-less sword, and shouting, in hoarse accents—

"On, on, children of the prophet. The road to heaven is through the midst of these English dogs."

And then once more the wild horde, with all their snorting horses and flashing spears, came surging down against the slender British square.

This time they seemed to shake it to its very centre, and Jack Vere and Willie Dunbar knew well enough that their little square of three hundred men, once broken, not only defeat but actual extermination awaited them.

Happily, at this juncture a louder and more authoritative voice spoke out than even the arch-fiend, Ackbar Khan's.

'Twas the thundering chorus of the six English nine pounders, which Major Anquetil had brought up to the support of the hardly-pressed Buffs.

The iron balls tore through the crowded ranks of the showy Afghan cavalry, making long and bloody lanes in their course.

They wavered, they recoiled, and then, whilst Ackbar Khan was making a frantic effort to rally them, in order to lead them to capture the guns, a second volley from the six field pieces rendered their confusion irretrievable, and, swayed by one instinct, away they tore in headlong flight.

Ackbar Khan, wounded, and evidently feeble though he was, for Jack noticed that he reeled in his saddle, disdained seemingly to follow their cowardly example, for he first spat and then shook his sword threateningly towards the foe, who had, for the time escaped him ; after which, wheeling his matchless charger round as on a pivot, he made after his glittering cavalry, taking no heed of the bullets and cannon balls that pinged and hummed round and about him, and evidently in his pride constraining the pace of his war-horse to the slowest possible walk.

"To give him his due, the fellow is as brave as a lion," said Jack Vere.

"More likely, in common with many Mussulman fatalists, he believes that he has been brought into the world for a special purpose, and that neither lead nor steel can deprive him of life until that purpose is accomplished," replied Dunbar. "But see, Anquetil has limbered up his guns again, so we must once more be moving."

And the necessary commands being given, the square resolved itself into troops, and renewed its weary march in open columns of sections.

The dead had to be left behind upon the snow, and there were no wounded, for the Afghan, when he once strikes or thrusts, kills.

Brain, heart, or throat, are his marks, and if he misses them, he misses altogether.

"Ah, and it was a deadly brush that we had with the niggers about that infernal bridge to-night, before we marched out," said Dunbar to Vere. "Our loss in officers was so heavy that if either of us survive this unfortunate retreat, I shouldn't wonder, Jack, if you found yourself in command of the regiment, with me for your major."

"Heaven forbid that we should owe our rapid promotion to any such awful fatality," replied our hero. "But who are already gone, Willie? Tell me who are already gone?"

"Well, Colonel Ross was speared through the heart, and Major Tomlinson had his head sliced off at a single slash. Captains Freeman and Faulkner were both shot dead, and Captain Hurn was bayonetted. So that the portion of the regiment which is in the van of the column is commanded by Lieutenant Gilbert, and here are we two, as you see, without anyone above us."

"And the men? How many bayonets can we still bring to the fight, Dunbar?"

"We marched out of cantonments six hundred fighting men. Ah, Jack, we were a thousand only a month ago, and we've lost more than twenty just now!"

"*C'est le malheur de guerre*, old fellow. Let the drums and fifes speak up; they will cheer the spirits of the men. The foe know where to find us, and so there is no longer any need of a grim and silent march. Let us laugh in Death's face whilst we may."

"Ha, ha, ha! and so we will. Have you any choice of a tune, Jack?"

"Yes, let them begin with 'The flag that braved a thousand years the battle and the breeze.' By Jove! it has done so, and, despite this single miserable reverse, the Union Jack of Old England shall yet do it again, and when next it flaunts through the passes and over the mountains into Afghanistan it will be better for the slaughterers of white women and children had they never been born."

"Ay!" responded Dunbar. "It is an easy matter for their millions to thrash our hundreds; but let them wait until they have our thousands to deal with, well-fed and well-clothed fellows, too. By George! they'll make these Afghans tremble."

So the young men continued to converse, the snow falling in great white flakes, and so fast that presently it was over their boots, and, by the time that the dawn loomed greyly through it, almost up to their knees.

*   *   *   *

Surely such a desolate, dreary dawn had never, never been seen before, save during, perhaps, the awful retreat of the grand army of Napoleon across Russia after the fatal burning of Moscow!

The little drummers and fifers could no longer play, their lips and fingers were so benumbed with the bitter, biting cold, and often it was hard work to prevent the more despairing and exhausted of the soldiers from staggering out of the ranks and laying themselves down in the snow to die.

Neither Jack nor Dunbar could gather the slightest notion of what was going on in front, owing to the denseness of the snowfall.

But they had a suspicion that what looked like a dense mist in their rear was, in fact, the foe following them doggedly and silently, like their doom.

Another hour, and the tired soldiers no longer sought to fall out of the ranks, but began actually to drop in them.

Some were trodden down into the snow and to death by their comrades before they were perceived, and others, endeavouring to rise again to their feet and failing, besought their companions to bayonet them rather than allow them to fall into the hands of the cruel and remorseless Afghans.

At last the command to halt was brought from the front, and with gasps of thankfulness the tired soldiers of the rearguard piled arms, and then threw themselves down upon the snow, seemingly content to lie there and die.

"This is bad," said Jack to his friend. "Unless this kind of stupor is combatted with and overcome, it will not require the Afghans to settle us."

"And they know it," rejoined Dunbar, still more gloomily. "There are thousands of them within gunshot of us. I can hear their fiendish laughter, now and then, borne towards us on the the breeze."

"Ah," sighed our hero, "I fancied I heard them too. The villains know what they are about. Another twenty-four hours, and not one of us will be strong enough to raise a hand to guard his life."

"Pray Heaven that we be through the Pass before that time comes, Jack!"

"Comrade, we shall enter the Pass, but never emerge from it, for it will be our slaughter-house and our sepulchre," replied Vere, despondingly.

And then each thoughtfully gazed at the silently descending snowflakes.

CHAPTER XLV.

STILL PURSUED—THE HORRORS OF THE RETREAT.

WHILST they thus stood despairing, Bob and Evan came up to them, carrying in their blue, half frostbitten hands some raw rice that had just been served out, a fist-full per man, and a few wild radishes they had dug out of the earth with their swords.

They pressed Jack and Dunbar to partake, but both sorrowfully declined.

"Eat it yourselves, my poor boys; Heaven knows you look as though you wanted it badly enough," replied Jack. "Our hearts are too full for us to feel hunger."

"Don't go fretting about Miss Rose, sir," answered Bob, "for they've killed a baggage pony, so that the invalids, the ladies and the children, shall not starve. They've got to eat it raw, poor things, but I daresay it tastes nice enough in times like these."

"Oh, Heaven! to think that our delicate English ladies are reduced to this," gasped Jack.

But now, the quarter of an hour's halt being over, the bugles sounded the "advance" again, for to remain longer on the snowy ground was never to rise more.

So the Kentish Buffs staggered to their feet and moved on afresh, the boys contriving to get some resemblance to a tune out of their drums and fifes, but which sounded at best like a hollow mockery, and then the ranks were seen suddenly to waver and break, and more than fifty men, rushing forth therefrom, commenced to struggle and fight like mad over and for something that lay stretched upon the plain.

"Fall in there, fall in!" roared Willie Dunbar, as loud as he could.

"This is open mutiny," echoed Jack Vere. "I will shoot with my own hand any man who is not in the ranks by the time that I have counted twelve."

A volley of hoarse and seemingly maniacal laughter was the retort to this threat, and the struggle still continued with greater desperation than ever.

It was terminated by a cry of "the foe! the foe!" and then, as upon hearing the on-rush of galloping horses and the wild battle-cry of the approaching Afghans the fierce contenders ceased their unnatural strife and returned to the ranks, the young officers noticed that the majority of them were greedily picking huge bones, and by what was still left upon the snow perceived that it was the skeleton and offal of the baggage pony that had caused the fierce struggle.

The foe must have been hovering very near to have beheld and taken such prompt advantage of this, but for all that they were not quite near enough to effect a complete surprise.

The rallying square was formed sufficiently quick enough to present an unpleasant porcupine-like appearance, as they came plunging in brilliant disorder out of the snow-storm, to disappear into it again at a sign from their leader Ackbar Khan, who drew rein for an instant to brandish his tasselled spear at the sullenly retreating British, and to yell after them—

"*Shookr jour vestie!* (Praise be to God), the wolf, the hyena, and the vulture will do our work for us. Ha! ha! you are doomed to perish, all! all!"

And as he concluded, he was lost in the snow shower again.

"I will owe fifty pounds to whoever shoots that fiend down the next time that he appears," said Jack, who, whilst he had been speaking, had fired twice at him and missed.

But those who heard him, only chuckled drearily, for of what value was fifty pounds to any of them now?

An ounce of meat would have been a much bigger prize.

"Ugh! isn't it horrible, knowing these wretches are so near as to be able to swoop down upon us without a second's warning, when we are least prepared for them?—and yet they are hidden from our view by this accursed snow!" growled Willie Dunbar.

"Yes," replied Jack; "for one can hardly tell what are snow-flakes and what are spear points; but, Willie, there are those in England, ay, and in India, too, who will terribly avenge us. Let that be our comfort, for we have no other."

The snow was now up to the knees of the marching troops.

From the front could sometimes be heard the roaring of the hungry camels and the bellowing of the starving artillery bullocks, and as the awful day wore on, many a time the ranks of the Kentish Buffs had to divide or surge aside, to avoid a dead or dying animal.

But the gaunt, hungry soldiers, dared no longer fall out to satisfy their hunger.

They now knew how close the Afghans were, and unity was strength.

They could hear the mocking laughter of their invisible foes, every time dead horses, camels, bullocks, or men became thicker in their line of march; alternating now with tents, litters, and heaps of abandoned baggage.

"Good God!" exclaimed Jack Vere, at last to his comrade, Willie Dunbar, "if this goes on much longer, the ladies and the children will have to tramp it on foot like the rest of us. There will be no help for it."

"Oh, don't say that, Jack. The shah's 6th Native Cavalry are in the van, and each trooper will take up a lady or a child in front of him."

"The children, perhaps, but I doubt if there is a horse in the army strong enough to bear anything heavier than its rider. Remember they are nearly famished, too."

"Ay, I remember," replied Dunbar, sadly.

"Ha!" exclaimed Jack, suddenly; "what is that writhing upon the snow to your right?"

"A young Hindoo girl. Some lady's attendant. We must save her," said Dunbar.

Not another word from either, but off they set at a run, sword in hand.

She was not a score of yards away on the right of the marching columns.

Her bare black arms and face, and the heavy masses of blue-black hair formed a marked contrast to the whiteness of the snow.

The two young officers had nearly reached her when a gigantic Afghan, mounted on a horse as white as the ground itself, wearing a flaming yellow headdress and a scarlet chogah or cloak that streamed from off his shoulders, came like a thunderbolt out of the mist and pinned her to the earth with his long spear.

One shriek and one quiver of her ebon limbs and she was still; whereupon plucking forth his lance, whose very tuft of white feathers twelve inches below the double-edged barb, was encrimsoned with her blood, he bore down on Vere and Dunbar.

The former sprang aside just in time to avoid the thrust, and at the same instant there was a sharp report, and a bullet through his right shoulder made the Afghan drop his formidable weapon, wheel round his charger and disappear into the snowstorm again.

It was Bob Rogers who had rushed out of the ranks and fired the opportune pistol-shot, and now all three used their utmost speed to regain their companions, fearful of a sudden rush and a cutting off at the hands of the Afghans.

CHAPTER XLVI.

DARKNESS AND DESPAIR.—THE MARCH OF THE SPECTRAL HOST.

ON and still on, weary hour after weary hour, with the same horrors repeated in everyone of them.

Every minute the two young officers who commanded the rearguard expected to see their men give up altogether in despair, and throwing themselves down in the deep snow, calmly await the approach of the Afghan foe.

But the love of life is inherent in all natures, and the worn-out, wearied men staggered and reeled on; the numbers who sank to the ground to be bayonetted and left behind, gradually increasing from four to five an hour to more than a dozen.

At length, and full soon, for the days were at their shortest, darkness came on, and then a halt was called, and it soon became known that nobody in all that force was competent to conduct the army aright until daylight came again.

Would daylight ever dawn for any of them?

Who could say?

Not one there.

How Jack Vere wished that he could go forward and obtain an interview with Rose, if only for a moment, to bid her an eternal adieu, in case he should have an opportunity of meeting her no more—an event only too, too probable under the circumstances.

But the wish was vain, for he dared not leave his men even for an instant.

He had to post his outlying and inlying pickets to guard against a surprise and consequent wholesale slaughter; and he had also, in turn with Willie Dunbar, to visit those posts during the night in order to ascertain that such sentries were neither asleep nor dead.

The Buffs piled their arms in sullen silence, and sank down beside them.

There was nothing to eat, nothing to light a fire with, nothing to preserve their lives until morning.

"Oh, I am so cold. I shall die if I don't get a warm!" sobbed Bobby Rogers.

"And so shall I; and indeed I wish I was dead now," echoed Evan ap Morgan.

"Here are two dead men," said Jack Vere, looking around; "they will want their cloaks no longer. Put them on, over your own, my poor lads. I'll help to turn them over.

The cloaks were obtained and Vere and Dunbar's swords slashed them to the necessary degree of shortness, and then they helped the boys on with them.

"Now I should be all right, but for my hands, and I believe they're frost-bitten," said Bobby Rogers.

Jack and Evan rubbed them in turn, but it seemed to do them no good.

"Stay, I'll make a fire," said Dunbar; "luckily I have the materials."

He scooped away the snow off the ground, and piled in a heap an old pistol-case, a brier-wood pipe, and a sandal-wood card-case that he found in his pockets. A fusee-box was the last contributed, after its contents had raised the necessary flame.

Over the bright little flame thus manufactured, and which burnt for nearly five minutes, the four warmed their hands and faces, and to a certain extent unfroze themselves, after which the two officers set about the performance of those military duties that were required of them.

When they returned from posting their cordon of sentries, absolutely bolstering each other up for mutual support, and scarcely able to avoid falling from weakness with even that, they were rejoiced to find the men in better spirits, and busily cutting up and devouring a pair of emaciated bullocks, that had been sent to the rear for their especial use and behoof by Major Anquetil, as they had become too weak to help on the guns, or even to bear the smallest burden.

The men were eating the meat raw, with the hunger and rapacity of wolves.

Now that there was plenty and to spare, they crowded round Jack and Dunbar begging them to try some, and declaring how excellent it was; whilst there were not wanting volunteers to carry a portion of the food to all the outposts and sentries.

To tell the truth, both the young officers partook of the strange repast as greedily as the rest, as did Bobby and Evan likewise, and as they ate hope arose afresh within them.

"Well, by this time to-morrow we shall know the worst, at all events," said Jack.

"Yes," answered Dunbar; "for this end of the Pass cannot be many miles distant now, and it is but seven miles through, whilst sixteen miles distant, on the other side, is Jellalabad, with the 9th Lancers and the Cornish Light Infantry within its walls.

"Quite so," responded our hero; "and we are victualled for another twenty-four hours."

Thus with brighter hopes, officers and men laid themselves down on the cold snow wrapped in their cloaks to endeavour to snatch a little sleep, though strange sights and sounds, continuing for hours together, were to prevent them from having any for a long time.

For after awhile, just as it had done on the previous night, the snow left off its steady downpour, and the moon condescended to gleam indistinctly and dimly through a gauzy rack of clouds that continued to scud across her pale face.

Scarcely had she done so, when Jack and his comrade, having both sharp ears, became aware that a large body of cavalry was approaching them, not from the direction of the enemy, but from that of the head of their own column.

"Halloa! That is very strange! What the deuce is up, I wonder?" exclaimed Dunbar.

"Well, I can't possibly conceive." answered Jack; "it is certainly most peculiar and unaccountable."

They were not left long in doubt, however, for within ten minutes from the time when the neigh of horses and jingling of cavalry accoutrements first attracted their attention, they saw, vaguely and indistinctly it is true, but yet plainly enough to be sure of their men, the beturbanned and silver-grey uniformed Native Cavalry of the shah defiling past them in glittering troops, and most assuredly going over to the enemy *en masse*.

"Who goes there? Halt!" cried Jack Vere, springing to his feet. "Evan, whip up that sleeping boy's bugle, and sound the 'turn out, double quick!' You can do it, I know. Bobby, wake up and beat the long roll. Stand to your arms! Quick, men!"

Both young officers gazed at the deserters.

"That leaves us barely two thousand fighting men," grunted Dunbar, in reply.

"Just so. But, by Heaven, we will give them our blessing to take with them, at all events," retorted Jack; and, observing that all his men were by this time under arms, half mad with rage and excitement, he, in a commanding voice, issued the order—

"Present! fire!"

A couple of hundred muskets rang out at once, tinting the snow around with a rosy flush.

But the men having only just opened their eyes, their hands and fingers being numbed, and the light most vague and uncertain, not a single horseman fell; and bursts of mocking laughter greeted them.

Ere, with their trembling hands and chattering teeth, they could handle and bite their cartridges, and reload and cap their muskets anew, the treacherous cavalry were out of range, and a few minutes later the Buffs could hear loud shouts of welcome and fraternisation, as they united their ranks with those of their insurgent countrymen.

"Well, open foes are better than false friends, and they might have deserted us at a more critical time," said Dunbar. "Let us turn round, and go to sleep for an hour, for it is quite probable they will return to attack us again."

"HE RAISED HIS RIFLE, AIMED AT THE TIGER, AND FIRED."

"No, no ; it is time for another outpost round !" was Jack's reply.

Dunbar would not let him go alone, and they again set forth together, taking the relief sentries with them, and bringing back those whose time had expired.

This over, and it took an hour, the young officers tried again to snatch a little slumber, knowing full well that they stood greatly in need of it, as doubtless the hardships and dangers of the morrow would even exceed those of the day that had passed.

It had begun to snow again, and heavily, so they drew the flaps of their cloaks over their heads and ears, and even their eyes, for nothing could be seen now, even if they kept the latter open, so dense and feathery was the downpour.

They soon found that there was much to be heard, however, and that fact again made sleep impossible.

They were strange sounds, and indistinct, yet continuous hour after hour.

"What can it be ? Oh, what can it be ?" asked brave little Bobby.

"Heaven alone knows !" responded Jack Vere. "Unseen perils are always the worst."

"God grant that 'tis not tens of thousands of those Afghan devils, pushing on and past us to barricade the passes to our troops," said Dunbar.

"Well, old fellow, we cannot be sure of anything ; listen to the challenges all along our line, challenges that never seem to be responded to.

"Hark !

"There's a musket shot. By Jove, they do not reply even to that. But I tell you what, Dunbar, our progress has been so slow, that every ruffian from Cabul has had time to overtake us and pass us on foot," replied Jack.

"And if but a tithe of them have done so, and have pushed past us on either flank, we shall have more than a hundred to one against us on the morrow," said Dunbar.

"Well, well, let the morrow take care of itself. We can die but once, and we will die hard, Dunbar. We will die precious hard, believe me, with our hands on our hilts, and our blades red with our foemen's blood. But, by Jove, old fellow, I feel sleepy at last, and there is still time, I think, for forty winks. Eh, what say you ?"

"I'm just about the same way of thinking, Jack. Let us take them."

"Done. Our next sleep may be sounder and longer. Who knows ?"

"Ay, who, indeed ? Good night, old fellow, good night."

And overcome at last by mingled drowsiness and fatigue, the two young British officers rolled themselves in their cloaks and were soon off as sound as tops—decidedly humming tops as well.

Evan and Bobby seeing this, lost no time in following the example, and did follow it, even to the snoring.

CHAPTER XLVII.

DEATH ON THE PALE HORSE—A SORRY AWAKENING.

ENGLISH JACK'S sleep was not a natural and refreshing one, but was a distorted and vision-haunted slumber, as perhaps was but natural under he circumstances.

The most fearful of all these nightmare phantasies was one in which he lay amongst a moving, heaving, boiling mass of human corruption, which filled an entire gorge, between towering precipices of black rock that seemed to rise into the very skies on either side.

And as he looked down the terrible and almost dark ravine, he seemed to see a skeleton form, the skull crowned by hissing and writhing snakes, mounted on a huge and snow-white horse, from whose eyes and nostrils issued lurid lightnings, riding directly towards the spot where he lay.

As he drew near, he perceived that the ghastly rider carried a human form before him, kept on the white horse's neck by an encircling bony arm, and as he was about to pass him by, the other hand pulled aside the shawl that covered the face, and revealed the countenance of Rose Trevor, pale and corpse-like.

"She is the bride of Death," said the terrible rider, with a rattle of his bony jaws and loose, chattering teeth.

The horse and horseman seemed to sweep over him like a cold sea-fog, and the action served to awaken him.

Dawn seemed to be just breaking, and a few drums and bugles here and there were sounding the "assembly" in a most ghostly and dreary manner.

Jack Vere sprang to his feet, the sweat of deadly terror still on his brow.

As he did so Willie Dunbar shrieked aloud in slumber.

Jack bent over and woke him up, though not without difficulty.

"Arouse you, old fellow," said he. "What are you dreaming about?"

"Oh God, Jack! Death on the pale horse, and he was carrying your Rose away with him across his saddle-bow," replied Dunbar, wildly.

It was Jack Vere's turn to tremble and turn pale now, and a deadly sickness seemed to fill his heart, as he learnt by Willie's confession that they both had been dreaming the same terrible and appalling dream — the same hideous nightmare.

"Don't say a word more about it, comrade," said he. "Now, my boy, play that bugle a little blither. Bob and Evan, have you never grasped your drumsticks before? By Jove! these men's repose is as sound as that of the seven sleepers."

The sleep of some was a good deal sounder, poor fellows, for 'twas the sleep of death.

"Oh Jack, this is dreadful, they are half of them stiffened corpses!" said Dunbar.

"This is indeed dreadful. Oh, if we had but a thousand bold, strong English here, we would yet beat the Afghan devils; but now, stir up all those who survive, or they will soon be stiffened corpses, too. Besides, the living deserve our pity more than the dead, who are at rest."

Slowly, and stiffly, and laboriously, those of the gallant Buffs who still lived raised themselves from the ground; snow men, with icicles for hair, and beard, and whiskers.

"Fall in, men, fall in! Shoulder arms! Quick march!" bellowed Jack.

He was listlessly obeyed by the majority, but a few staggered and fell again.

"Despatch us! Kill us! For God's sake shoot or bayonet us!" the poor Englishmen cried.

And in more than one instance the request was complied with.

"Company, forward, march! Muskets at the short trail if they are too heavy to be shouldered. Throw off your knapsacks, belts—everything that's useless," cried Jack again. "The snow is over, and the sun will soon cheer us. Courage, fellow countrymen, courage!"

On they limped, and staggered, and reeled at this, and soon they were passing poor Major Anquetil's light field-pieces, that he had been so proud of.

Now they lay unlimbered and dismounted in the snow, and spiked, so that they should be of no service to the Afghans, at all events.

The snowstorm had passed away, and the morning was clear and bright; but it was a dubious blessing this brightness, for it disclosed many horrors that before had been hidden.

Far as the eye could reach to the rear, and thickly on either side, the level and snow-covered plain was dotted with the dead bodies of human beings, horses, camels, dromedaries, and bullocks, in company with heaps of baggage, litters, drums, weapons, knapsacks, and other impediments to rapid flight; while flocks of broad-winged vultures were hovering over all, and with hoarse croaks settling upon the dead in every direction.

But the most ominous feature of the scene, was the narrow and awful pass that would conduct them either to freedom or to death, towards which galloped glittering squadrons of light-armed Afghan horsemen, intent on bloodshed and slaughter.

"Oh, the poor women and children!" was the exclamation of many and the thought of all, for the whole length of the straggling British column could now be seen, the thousands of camp followers having deserted it in the middle of the night, and throwing away everything, pushed on ahead, intent only on saving their own lives.

So that, the 6th Native Cavalry having gone over to the enemy, it now consisted of barely two thousand men, the dragoons being half of them without horses, and the artillery wholly without cannon, whilst there were twenty thousand hostile horsemen in front and in rear, and to right and to left of them, and Heaven alone knew how many thousand more waiting to dispute their passage through the pass.

There could be no doubt either that the Afghan cavalry in the plain were intent on immediate mischief, and the nature of such mischief they did not long leave our poor fellows in doubt of.

It was to capture and make prizes of our women and children.

They were surrounded and protected by the handful of dragoons and horse artillerymen, a slender guard indeed, of about three-score sabres at the most.

On these the Afghan hordes soon bore down from every direction at once, to be beaten off, and then to swirl down again, like swallows on the wing, hacking, hewing, and thrusting one moment, and off with the fleetness of the wind the next.

But this was tiring work for exhausted men, and famine-weakened horses, and soon the slender cordon began to be pierced, now here, now there, and anon in two or three places at a time ; and then shrieking women and sobbing girls and terrified children would be pulled from their steeds, or off their camels or dromedaries, and thrown like sacks of corn across the pommels of Afghan saddles, to be galloped away with, as fair and legitimate spoil, their captors laughing at their horror and discomfiture.

"Oh, this is horrible!—terrible!" exclaimed Jack. "Can we in no way assist them?"

"We should not be authorised to leave our posts, were our mothers or sisters amongst the unfortunates," replied Dunbar, biting his nether lip.

"But there is one amongst them dearer to me than mother or sister," groaned Jack Vere.

And then he added, with a shriek—

"Why, there she is, clasped in the arms of that Afghan, mounted on the snow-white charger. I know her beautiful form, her dress, as she lies so limply across his saddle. And that horseman is—yes, God of Heaven, he is indeed the merciless fiend, Ackbar Khan!"

"And his charger is the pale horse, whereon death was mounted in my dream!" replied Willie Dunbar.

CHAPTER XLVIII.

IN THE AWFUL PASS—THE INVULNERABLE FOES.

IT seemed as though Ackbar Khan had heard the heartrending exclamations of the two young men, for his eyes suddenly turned, and rested on them, as he cantered to the rear, and, propping Rose up in front of him, so that she should effectually shield him from hostile bullets, he galloped with an air of bravado, and with a burst of mocking laughter, close past the flank of the Kentish Buffs.

"It is her. Heavens, how pale she is! Like unto a corpse, and as unconscious as one, too!" gasped Jack Vere, as though he were choking. "Pray God she may perish in her swoon!"

Then, impelled by a sudden and irresistible impulse, he shouted out to his men—

"Fire! It matters not which you hit, both are better than neither. Fire!"

Some of the Buffs obeyed him, others could not bring themselves to do so.

Those who did, owing to trembling hands and benumbed fingers, sent their leaden messengers of vengeance and mercy wide enough of the mark, which the next instant was out of range.

"Nothing more can be done," groaned Jack; "God can both avenge and protect her better than we can. On, on, my men, for the end is surely at hand."

The crests of the huge mountains by now loomed threateningly and awfully before them.

The "Dark Pass" that they had to traverse was before them.

Another half hour and the head of the column would have entered it.

That is to say, if the Afghan cavalry permitted any of them to live to do so.

Unceasing were their charges, but the British infantry still presented a sufficiently formidable front to repel them, and to send them swinging back.

"There is the little girl we saved from the temple," shrieked Bob Rogers, presently. "Look, lying out on the plain beside the dying camel. Oh, I know her face so well."

"And I," echoed Evan; "oh, sir, do let us try to dart out and bring her in."

"Not to be thought of, my brave lads. It would be certain death," said Jack Vere.

At this instant, an Afghan dashing past on his black steed, thrust his long lance into the child's loose bundle of clothing, and raised it again with her hanging thereto.

The stout ashen staff, narrowing to the barb, bent with her weight for an instant, and then sprang straight again.

The Afghan laughed, but the child uttered no cry or shriek, and so he bore her out of sight, and as she vanished from view, poor Bobby uttered a groan.

"Poor little thing! how white she was!" wailed he.

Five minutes later, the head of the column had entered the gloomy pass, and it was now so short, that in another quarter of an hour the rear-guard had been engulphed by it also. Engulphed is the best word we can use, for it seemed to have swallowed them up.

"Could the entrance to hell itself be more forbidding and awful?" said Jack to his companion.

"More awful!" was immediately echoed from rock to cliff, and cliff to rock.

Though the day was by now two hours old, they had said good-bye to it directly they had entered the gorge.

The Afghan cavalry did not follow them into the pass.

They knew better.

Thousands of them dismounted, piqueted their horses, piled their arms, and camped at its mouth, hurling curses at the British rear-guard, but that was all.

Poor wretches, all had entered it, but not one had emerged on the other side.

"Things are not so bad as I had

feared," said Jack Vere, suddenly; "we are not followed, and the pass appears to be deserted by the foe."

"Appearances are sometimes very deceptive, sir," replied the old greywhiskered sergeant; "the silence and desolation alarms me. They indicate treachery and slaughter."

"How do you make that out, Baker?" asked Willie Dunbar.

"Why, you see, sir, if there weren't still worse characters above, we should see wolves, jackals, and hyenas slinking away to their dens at our approach, and whole swarms of vultures rising into the air, and as neither of these flesh-eaters are in front, you may rest assured that Afghan devils are."

"Happy then are those who have only themselves to think of," said Jack, sorrowfully. "I feel for you, Baker, because you are a married man."

"I was, sir, an hour or two ago; but the last that I saw of my poor Betty was her headless body, just as we were entering the gorge. The Afghans had hacked her almost to pieces, and I only want to live now to pay 'em out for it."

Scarcely had the sergeant ceased speaking, when shrieks, and screeches, and moans of terror, agony, and consternation arose from the head and the centre of the on-toiling column, and peering anxiously forward, Vere, Dunbar, and the rest of the Buffs, saw huge stones, and boulders, and rocks—some of the latter tons in weight—leaping and crashing down the precipices, and rebounding from the hills and hillocks at their base plump into the dense masses of soldiery and swooning, shrieking women and children.

At the same instant thousands—ay, seemingly tens of thousands—of wild and fanatical Afghans showed themselves on every ledge and angle of cliff, waving aloft swords and jezails, creases and matchlocks, crowbars and pickaxes, and joining in one chorus of—

"*Ulla, ul Allah hue*," so wild, unearthly, and altogether devilish in its triumph and vindictiveness, that it was hard to imagine it was not the banner-cry of legions of incarnate fiends.

"This is a death-trap, indeed," exclaimed Jack Vere, with blanched lips.

"And to go on or back is equally destructive," echoed Willie Dunbar.

"The worst of the whole is that the inhuman fiends are where we cannot possibly retaliate. We can't get at them; our muskets will not carry so far. Theirs will be a bloodless victory, and we shall be exterminated to the last man, and woman, and babe."

Crash, crash, crash! came down more stones, and boulders, and rocks, again accompanied by a perfect tempest of jezail balls, and even arrows.

The rear-guard of Buffs could see their comrades in the van, the dusky Sepoys of the 54th Native Infantry, and nearer still the helpless women and children, and wounded officers, dismounted dragoons and artillerymen, falling singly, or in half-dozens, dozens, or scores, before and beneath these down-crashing missiles.

The noise of the big rocks as they plunged down, crashing from peak to peak, was louder than thunder, and between the intervals—short enough, in all conscience—the wild cheers of the yellow and crimson turbaned mountain warriors, sounded wild and shrill as the never-ceasing rattle of their firearms.

The end had indeed come.

CHAPTER XLIX.

INDISCRIMINATE SLAUGHTER—ALL, ALL DESTROYED.

BUT there was no halting, for to stand still was worse than to go on, and to retreat all knew to be a hopeless task, with thousands and thousands of the *élite* of the Afghan cavalry encamped at the Cabul mouth of the pass, the other end of the trap.

So the survivors scrambled over the rocks and boulders, beneath which comrades, and wives, and little ones were crushed out of life and shape, to be stricken down in turn by similar cruel and mighty missiles.

Jack and his Buffs could see, as they gained the scene of death and indiscriminate slaughter, the Afghans, so high up amongst the ledges in the black cliffs that they looked no bigger than crows, loosening with pick and crowbar other huge masses of rock to crush and destroy them also.

"Shake hands, comrade," said Jack Vere to Willie Dunbar. "In another ten minutes all will be over. We have not a single chance of escape—no, not one."

"Good-bye, Jack, dear fellow," was the retort; "if I could fall hacking at some of those rascals' ugly mugs I should die a deal more contented. But what is to be, will be, I suppose."

Then Bob Rogers and Evan ap Morgan would shake hands with Jack in turn.

They were very pale, poor little fellows, and trembled from head to foot.

"I shall play my drum," said Bob; "I'm never in a funk then, or at least not in as bad a one. Evan, let us give them the long roll for the last time, shall we?"

The Welsh boy assented, and the next instant the two little brass side-drums, beaten with a nervous vigour that threatened to send the ebony sticks plunging through the sheepskins, awoke a hundred echoes in the dismal and awful gorge.

Then once more down came the huge fragments of rock, the torrent of jezail balls, the rain of matchlock bullets, the shower of arrows; and earthward were stricken Jack's poor Kentish Buffs, many crushed out of the most distant resemblance to humanity.

It was some comfort even then to find that Bobby, Evan, and his friend Dunbar were amongst the uninjured.

"On—on!" he shouted; "death may yet spare some of us!"

But noboby dared hope for such a mercy.

Even those whom rock and bullet spared, began now to fall, owing to their shoeless feet becoming frost-bitten, and refusing longer to support them.

Others stopped to scoop up in their blue hands snow or ice, wherewith to assuage their burning thirst, and directly they had swallowed it these seemed to go raving mad.

And still more there were, who, staggering out of the ranks to avoid some down-leaping mass of rock, disappeared bodily in the deep snowdrift that bordered each side of the narrow way, never to be extricated more.

And some sang in their delirium, and others were suddenly afflicted with snow-blindness, and screaming out that "All was dark to them," stumbled and fell, to be trodden under foot by the rear-rank men; whilst not a few yelled out—"*Aman, aman!*"* as if those demons perched up on the inaccessible precipices were at all likely to reply to such appeals except by mocking laughter.

"Whoever I hear disgrace us by such another shout as that, I will slay with my own hand," said our hero, flushing redly with passion. "Those who ere

---

* "Quarter, quarter!"

long will avenge us, my lads, will drive our cowardly butchers to shriek that word often enough. Let that thought content ye, men of Kent."

There was a faint attempt at a cheer at this, but it was a hollow mockery of one.

We will not dwell too long on this terrible, this awful, but true scene, which we have exaggerated naught, rather striving to hide than to set prominently forth some of its horrors.

Suffice it to say that the down-hurling of huge fragments of rock, and the continuous volleys of matchlock balls, never ceased during an onward march of four miles.

And that by then, of the two thousand and odd British soldiers of all arms that had entered that awful pass, only a hundred and fifty were alive and capable of staggering forward ; and of women and children not one.*

At this juncture the handful of survivors came within sight of the Jellalabad end of the gorge, and the faintest of all faint hopes arose within the breasts of some of them, that they would yet be able to reach it and gain the open country beyond.

Such hope, however, was the next instant crushed by perceiving a huge barricade of rocks, stones, and *débris*, rising to a height of, at least, a dozen feet, right across the pass ; with a green flag (the colour of the prophet) planted on its summit, and thousands of crimson and yellow turbaned heads, and gleaming jezail barrels o'ertopping it.

At this a great wail went up to the narrow strip of blue sky visible o'erhead, for every member of that haggard, bleeding band, knew that this was the end.

The defenders of the barricade raised a triumphant cheer when they saw them approaching, for they had begun to fear that they would never reach that point, and that there would not be a single Feringhee for them to slay.

On the other hand Jack Vere, Willie Dunbar and a few more, felt fiercely thankful that at last they looked upon foes whom there was some possibility of getting at, and even death did not now

seem half so fearful when it could be met sword in hand.

" My gallant Buffs," said English Jack Vere, " there are still three score of us left, and yonder are the murderers of white women and children. I need say no more. We've no chance of escape, but we have of vengeance, and, lads, I will conduct you to it."

" Company forward, quick march !" cried Willie Dunbar, springing to Jack's side in front. " Now then, you murdering rascals ahead there, clear out and make way for the men of Kent."

" Bob, Evan, you are the only two drummers left alive. Make your sticks fly, and beat the point-of-war. You'll never do it again, so do it well, my boys," roared Jack, again.

The poor lads caught some of his enthusiasm, the drums brattled out right merrily, the dispirited soldiers of the Bombay Infantry made way for the Kentish men to pass on, closing in resolutely on their rear, and cheering them faintly.

On, on, with no thought of wavering.

The Ghilzies, Kurrachees, and Afghans look over their terrible barricade in surprise, mingled with something like awe, at the way in which sixty men are advancing upon six thousand, posted behind almost impregnable works.

Then, rushing forward, they pour upon them a volley that reduces their number by one third at the very least ; but still they are not seen to recoil.

No, they rush right on and up.

" Close up, men," said Jack.

Some fall from weakness, others reel back dead before they are even touched by Afghan steel or lead ; but a score at the least reach the top of the barrier, take an Afghan life, and then yield their own up joyfully to a dozen wounds at the least from Afghan lead and Afghan steel.

Jack Vere does more, for he seizes upon the green flag, tears it away from its staff, thrusts it in his bosom, kills two brawny Ghilzies with point and edge of his regulation sword, and is then, and not till then, hurled back, bleeding and insensible.

A minute later, and Willie Dunbar shares his fate, and Bob and Evan have fallen before him.

* Our readers will find the above account true to the History of our Indian Empire.

So do all the rest in turn.

The mighty work of slaughter is consummated, and a vast and united roar of triumph ascends to the pitying heavens, as the last Feringhee invader of Afghanistan is seen to totter and go down.

" *Shookr poor Vestie!* " such is the united cry of thousands of Afghan throats, and it is reverberated from cliff to cliff, until it reaches the thousands of glittering horsemen that are encamped at the other end of the gorge, who at once despatch the fleetest mounted of their number to carry the news across the plains to Cabul.

Ah, speed quickly, and make the most of it, cowards, traitors, and assassins, for your glory will not last for long!

The avenger is on your track, and full soon shall the red-coated legions of Britain return through those passes, and recross those plains, to carry fire and sword into the very heart of your dominions, and to level your pride to the very dust.

Then shall the sturdy Britons, few in number but strong in valour, well led and well fed, point to their flaunting colours, the invincible Union Jack of old England, and say—

"There floats our flag, touch it who dare !"

And are Jack Vere and Willie Dunbar, Bobby Rogers and Evan ap Morgan all dead? the reader may be inclined to ask.

Well, not all of them, we can answer that much, and those amongst them who do live are destined to go through more daring and desperate perils and adventures than any that we have yet recorded.

CHAPTER L.

TWO SAVED AND TWO LOST—IS IT A DEN OF WILD BEASTS?

ABOUT six or eight hours after the cruel and vindictive Afghans, aided by their allies the Ghilzies and Kurrachees, had destroyed, as they thought, the army of General Elphinstone to the very last man, one of the victims raised himself feebly on an elbow above the still river of prostrate forms that filled up the bottom of the gorge, and looked about him.

It was Jack Vere.

The moon shone down brightly.

Its light illumined the upturned faces of the dead.

And approaching with lightning speed, Jack saw, or seemed to see, Death on the pale horse, just as he had seen him in his dream the night before.

On it came, the white charger's hoofs apparently striking phosphorescent fires from out the pallid faces of the dead, that he spurned in his flying course.

To Jack, the grim rider and flame-vomiting steed seemed to be upon him.

And then he noticed that, as when he had last seen him, he carried a human-like form across his saddle-bow, but this time it was not that of a slim and graceful girl, but a gigantic and hardy warrior clad in gleaming mail.

Jack recognised in the burden Ackbar Khan, his livid face disfigured by a ghastly gash, and a cross of blood slashed across his bare bronzed chest.

Then, as he and his fell captor vanished away over the now forsaken barricade that rose abruptly in his rear, a noise seemed to fill the awful pass like the murmuring of a troubled sea, and then in a single second Jack thought there rose up from the blood-tinted snow the British dead, women, children, all just as they had fallen.

They muttered the two words "vengeance! victory!" Then sank back again to their eternal rest.

We do not affirm that our hero saw all this, but we most positively state that he thought he did, and that he held that steadfast belief to the day of his death.

Our hero seemed to sink into an unconscious state after this, and when next he recovered the full use of his eyes and ears, he saw sights and heard sounds around, which convinced him that did he wish to save his life, he must look sharp about it.

The whole gorge, indeed, resounded to the growlings and snarlings of legions of wild beasts, and on straining his eyes he could see wolves, and hyenas, and jackals supping upon the dead in all directions.

With the greatest difficulty, Jack extricated himself from the dead bodies that lay across and atop of him.

He found himself rather shaky, but yet stronger than he had dared to hope.

But alone amongst the dead!

Life was his as yet; but could he possibly escape from the hideous horrors that surrounded him?

The intense cold had stopped the bleeding from Jack Vere's wounds, which, though numerous, were none of them very deep.

It had been a crushing blow from a blunt instrument on his head that for a time had deprived him of all strength and reason.

Undoubtedly it had saved his life.

Jack looked about and around again for an instant, undecided which way to go, and then it struck him that it would be cruel to go any way at all before he had, at all events, assured himself that Dunbar, Bob, and Evan were no more.

He knew that all four of them must have fallen close together, and sure enough he had not taken three steps in the direction of the barricade when he felt himself clutched by the leg.

"Oh, don't leave me, don't leave me, for the love of Heaven!" exclaimed a piteous voice.

No sooner did he hear it, than Jack knew it was Bobby's by the tone.

"Thank God, I have found one," he muttered, fervently, as he picked him up.

The poor boy was so feeble he could hardly stand, and so Jack plumped him down again, saying—

"You mustn't use your legs until it is necessary. Sit you there and I'll rejoin you in a minute, after I've had a good hunt for Evan and Mr. Dunbar."

"Oh Master Jack, I do hope you'll find them. I wish I could help you, sir."

"You mustn't try it, my little man. Just hoard up what strength you've got left."

Then Jack began his search, and, despite the near presence of the beasts of prey who were prowling about in all directions, he continued it until not a hope remained of his being able to find them.

In fact he had closely inspected the face of every Kentish Buff who lay at the base of the barricade, and all to no avail.

The moonlight shone clearly enough to convince him his friends were not amongst the dead.

But he was sure he had seen both of them fall, so how were they not there?

Had they escaped?

But this, to our hero, seemed almost absurdly impossible.

At all events it was no good to stay there looking for them any longer, with the chance of attracting the attention of a couple of hyenas or wolves at any moment.

So he returned to where Bobby was sitting on a big stone.

"They've got the start of us," said he; "they are not here; they have escaped."

"They would never have gone without us, Master Jack. Willingly, at least!" said Bob.

"I don't believe they would, my man, but they have gone, nevertheless. I've looked at the face of every one of our poor fellows, and I'm convinced they are not amongst them."

"Well then, Master Jack, do think of yourself, for look at the wild beasts all around," cried Bob.

"Just what I was thinking of, Bobby, so come along, old fellow, and we will be off."

"No, no, sir; I am far too feeble. I should only hamper your movements, and in the end sacrifice you. You mustn't think of me ; indeed, I can't put one foot to the ground."

"Then you must lean on me that side, for leave you here I won't, my dear boy."

Bobby still urged him to do so, but Jack was obdurate.

"We both go or we both stay, that I am resolved," said he, and so at last the drummer consented to accompany him.

It was slow progress, for both were very exhausted and weak, and Bob could only limp painfully. Again and again he still urged our hero to abandon him, but he would not.

Jack thought he saw a pathway winding up one side of the gorge, and at its summit the mouth of a cave.

This might afford them shelter for awhile, could they but reach it.

They therefore shaped their course right across the gorge of death, and at last had nearly reached the commencement of the upward-tending pathway, when their blood, or such little as was left of it, ran cold at seeing a huge tiger lying stretched out within a couple of yards of it, and already regarding them with his fierce, cruel eyes.

"Oh, Master Jack, he'll settle us both and eat us up as well," groaned Bobby.

"Well, there's no good going back, for he sees us and could overtake us, if so minded, in a couple of leaps. Therefore we'll just chance it and go on," said our hero.

And they did go on, and, to the agreeable astonishment of both, the tiger allowed them to pass unchallenged.

He seemed to make a feeble effort to rise, and then to sink down again.

The fact was he was already gorged to repletion.

The fugitives gave a gasp of relief, however, when they had left him in the rear, and then they shrank up as close as possible against the black side of the cliffs, so that the other animals who were prowling about the plain should not see them and give chase ; and in this manner the mouth of the cave was at last reached.

Happily, for poor Bob could not have dragged himself on another dozen steps.

They were about to enter, when they heard something moving about inside.

Horror of horrors ! was it then only the den of some wild beast ?

END OF VOLUME I.